YEARS

of pure reading pleasure

100 Reasons to Celebrate

We invite you to join us in celebrating
Mills & Boon's centenary. Gerald Mills and
Charles Boon founded Mills & Boon Limited
in 1908 and opened offices in London's Covent
Garden. Since then, Mills & Boon has become
a hallmark for romantic fiction, recognised
around the world.

We're proud of our 100 years of publishing
excellence, which wouldn't have been achieved
without the loyalty and enthusiasm of our
authors and readers.

Thank you!

Each month throughout the year there will
be something new and exciting to mark the
centenary, so watch for your favourite authors,
captivating new stories, special limited
edition collections…and more!

Available in March 2008
from Mills & Boon®
Superromance

Love and the Single Mum
by CJ Carmichael

Secrets in Texas
by Carrie Weaver

Everything but the Baby
by Kathleen O'Brien

It Takes Two
by Joanne Michael

It Takes Two

JOANNE MICHAEL

MILLS & BOON®

Pure reading pleasure

*All the characters in this book have no existence outside the
imagination of the author, and have no relation whatsoever to anyone
bearing the same name or names. They are not even distantly inspired
by any individual known or unknown to the author, and all the
incidents are pure invention.*

*First published in Great Britain 2008
by Harlequin Mills & Boon Limited,
Eton House, 18-24 Paradise Road, Richmond, Surrey TW9 1SR*

© Julia Bayly 2007

ISBN: 978 0 263 86151 8

38-0308

*Harlequin Mills & Boon policy is to use papers that are
natural, renewable and recyclable products and made from
wood grown in sustainable forests. The logging and
manufacturing processes conform to the legal environmental
regulations of the country of origin.*

*Printed and bound in Spain
by Litografia Rosés S.A., Barcelona*

Dear Reader,

There is something magical about the village of Tadoussac, Quebec. Maybe it's the bay that's ranked as one of the thirty most beautiful in the world. The town is on the North Shore where the Saguenay River fjord meets the St Lawrence River. That's certainly the draw for the resident pods of beluga, minke and even the occasional blue and fin whales who call the area home. Then again, it could be the miles of trails and paths crisscrossing the wooded hills, or the scores of artisans, musicians and gourmet chefs who contribute so much to the local flavour.

I fell under the spell the first time I rode the ferry across the Saguenay River. As if on cue, a small pod of brilliant white beluga appeared. Since then, I've been back several times and the beluga are always there to greet me.

I have tried to remain true to the village's unique character. There really is a marine interpretive centre and I encourage you to visit the Centre d'Interprétation des Mammifères Marins (the Marine Mammal Interpretive Centre) if you go. There, the staff with the Group for Research and Education on Marine Mammals is doing some excellent and important work. Check it out at www.gremm.org.

One of those people is Lucia DiIorio, a scientist researching the impacts of man-made sound on the beluga. Lucia's willingness to share information was of great help. Likewise was the rest of the staff and I hope they forgive the architectural licence I took.

But that's the thing about Tadoussac; it's full of welcoming people eager to share their special knowledge and talents. People like Bruno at Mer et Monde Ecotours who patiently guided me on my very first sea kayak excursion (www.mer-et-monde.qc.ca).

As for the allure of Tadoussac, don't just take my word for it. The folks at www.tourism@tadoussac.com are ready to help you plan your adventure, and whether you're into nature, whales, music, art, history, food or all of the above, get ready to make some wonderful memories. Oh, and be sure to say hi to the beluga for me.

Joanne Michael

For Lowell

CHAPTER ONE

NO ONE HAD SAID ANYTHING about needing reservations. If they had, Abby Miller knew she wouldn't be sitting here now, near the end of a long line of cars waiting for the few remaining slots on the Matane-Baie-Comeau ferry.

"Who'd have thought so many people wanted to get across the Saint Lawrence Seaway this time of year?" she said. In the back seat, Figgy pricked up her ears and made a low chuffing sound. "Go back to sleep, girl," Abby said. "There's no reason we should both be up at this ungodly hour." The small brown dog obligingly put her head back down on her front paws, sighed mightily and closed her eyes.

Abby glanced at her watch. Five-thirty. According to the brochure of ferry schedules open on the passenger seat next to her, the *Felipe* was due to depart the docks at six-ten. Abby had arrived at the terminal fifteen minutes earlier, thinking that would give her more than enough time to purchase a ticket and board the ferry for the two-hour crossing.

No such luck. She leaned back against the headrest and watched enviously as Québec Maritime terminal staff directed the rapidly dwindling line of cars in the *Passengers with Reservations Only* lane. The *Felipe* had a capacity of six hundred cars, and Abby had tried to count the vehicles as they drove into the cavernous opening. But so many had boarded before she arrived that she soon gave up, knowing it was an exercise in futility.

Next to the ferry brochure was her much read and well-creased road map, the route from her apartment in Andover, Massachusetts, to Tadoussac, Québec, highlighted in bright red. The helpful agent at AAA had assured Abby the drive would be a scenic one, albeit long, and had been telling the truth. Abby had made a right turn out of her driveway early the previous morning and had driven north in a straight line ever since. About halfway through the trip, late yesterday afternoon, she had left the interstate for the more rural highways of northern Maine. By evening, she had cleared Canadian customs and crossed the border into New Brunswick, Canada, picked up the Trans-Canada Highway and entered the province of Québec around midnight.

So near and yet so far, Abby thought, looking out her windshield at the choppy waters of the Saint Lawrence.

She sat up straighter as the last of the cars eased over the ramp between the dock and ferry. Abby could barely make out the ferry's darkened interior, but it looked like there could be enough room for all the cars in her lane. Her optimism, however, was premature.

Just as she was keying her ignition back on, she watched in horror as the terminal workers switched their attention to the scores of big rigs, panel trucks and large flatbeds that had been idling in the lane to her left.

When the last the of the trucks had been allowed on board, Abby saw the brake lights on the lead car in her lane flash. As if that were the signal, all the remaining cars roared to life and the line slowly inched forward. A terminal worker approached each car, handed the driver a slip of paper and then waved the vehicle on. The closer Abby got, the more convinced she became that she would have to make a reservation on the next available ferry— eight hours later or drive miles and hours out of her way to Québec City and the bridge.

She was now so close to the ferry, it blocked out the sky. She watched as the car in front of her—a late-model Saab with two mountain bikes lashed to the back bumper—was waved aboard. The attendant approached her car, the coveted white boarding slips in his hand. Rolling down the window, Abby offered him what she hoped was her most engaging smile, as if charm alone could magically create a space for her.

"Good morning," she said brightly to the young man, his Québec Maritime Windbreaker zipped to his chin, the hood pulled low over his eyes against the raw wind whipping off the Saint Lawrence. "Gosh, there are so many cars and I know I should have called ahead, but I really need to get across this morning and—" Abby knew she was babbling but couldn't help it.

The young man glanced in the car, saw Abby was the only passenger, mumbled something indecipherable, scribbled on the paper and handed it to her with one hand, pointing to the ferry with the other.

Abby accepted the slip with a genuine "thank you," clutching it in one hand even as she steered onto the ramp.

Once on the ferry, another Québec Maritime worker directed her to a spot behind the Saab and against the boat's port side hull. "We made it," she said exuberantly to Figgy, who was now sitting up and looking around, the noises of the ferry's interior—parking cars, slamming doors, metal clanging and the steady throb of the boat's engine—having wakened her.

Curious about the fate of the drivers behind her, Abby looked in her rearview mirror to see just how close she had come to being left behind. With the limited space behind her, it was obvious that, while she was not the last to board, not much of a cushion had remained. Her view was blocked as an older Jeep Wagoneer pulled up behind her, so close its grill filled the mirror.

"Okay," she said. "What say we get our stuff and head above decks?"

Thanks to her proximity to the inner hull, Abby had to squeeze out of the car. She then walked around to the passenger side, opened the door and began gathering her purse, some bottled water, the previous day's newspaper and Figgy's leash. Snapping the leash to the dog's collar, she stood and pulled gently for Figgy to follow her. Startled, she felt a tap on her shoulder.

A crew member was standing just behind her, saying something in French.

"Pardon?" she said.

The crewman, with obvious impatience, repeated himself, and Abby did her best to follow his rapid speech.

Dammit, she thought, *why didn't I pay better attention in high school French?*

She said, "I'm sorry, please slow down, I don't understand."

Glowering at her, the man pointed at Figgy and then jerked a thumb over his shoulder at a sign on the far wall. Looking past him, Abby felt her heart drop when she saw the illustration of a dog on a leash with a fat red line through it. She didn't have to be fluent in any language to know that symbol meant dogs were not welcome, allowed or wanted on the *Felipe's* upper decks.

"You mean I have to leave her here? In the car? What if something happens and I have to get to her?" Abby was horrified. Figgy had been her companion for the past five years, and there was no way she could leave her beloved pet alone in the dark musty hold.

Then she realized there was another option. "Never mind," she said to the crewman, not caring if he understood her or not. "I can ride down here. I can even take a nap."

She bent to put her things back in the car and again felt a tap on her shoulder.

The crewman had obviously been through this before with countless other passengers and their pets. Shaking his head, he pointed to another sign, this one with instructions in several different languages, including English. *Passengers are forbidden to stay with their cars.*

"Listen," she said, "I can't leave her down here. Can't you make an exception? Please?"

The crewman was looking at her impassively and Abby had the distinct feeling she'd have a better chance pleading her case to the nearby bulkhead.

She closed her eyes and took a deep, steadying breath. She knew she was being foolish, that Figgy would be fine down here for a couple of hours. But she couldn't get the image of some kind of maritime disaster out of her head. Abby knew she was tired; worn out from the stress of an all-night drive and then the uncertainty of getting on the damned ferry. All she wanted was to get up to the main deck, pay her fare, buy a large cup of coffee and find a sunny place to sit and enjoy the scenery for the next two hours.

She opened her mouth, unsure of what was going to come out, when a masculine voice to her right said, "Excuse me, I didn't mean to be eavesdropping, but can I help?"

Turning, she saw it was the driver of the Jeep Wagoneer. Given the tight quarters on the car deck, he had been unable to get past Abby's car since she and the ferry worker were blocking the narrow aisle.

"What?" she said.

The man smiled and, without a word to Abby,

turned to the crewman and spoke in French. Abby couldn't keep up, but she could have sworn she heard him say something about a doctor.

After a further exchange, during which the worker cast several questioning looks at Abby, the driver of the Wagoneer extended his hand for the crewman to shake. Smiling briefly, the man shook hands and looked at Abby again, then left.

Was that fear in his eyes? she wondered. No, she was just tired and seeing things.

"Okay," the driver said. "You're all set."

"What do you mean *all set?*"

"You and your dog. You can take him up with you."

"Her," Abby said, stunned at the change in fortune.

"What?"

"He's a her. That is, my dog, she's a female."

"Fine, you can take *her* up with you."

He turned to walk away and Abby called out to him. "Wait a minute! How did you—what did you, I don't understand. Dogs aren't allowed."

The man laughed. "I just told the guy I'm your doctor and you are under treatment for an emotional disorder. That's your therapy dog and I can't be responsible for what might happen if he separated you two."

"You told him *what?*" Abby asked, incredulous.

"Hey, it worked, didn't it?"

"And he believed you?"

He grinned. "Guys like that never want to hear more than they have to about *emotional* problems when it comes to women."

Abby got the feeling he was viewing the entire thing as one big joke. Whether it was on her, the ferry line or both, she couldn't tell. But she found herself smiling back at him. "I'm not sure if I should be insulted or grateful. But thanks."

"Don't mention it," he said, again moving off. "I always like to start my day by saving a damsel in distress." He stopped. "But listen, just in case. Try to keep a low profile up there, okay?"

"I will," Abby said, "And thanks again, I mean it."

THE SUN radiating off the brilliantly whitewashed outer hull of the *Felipe* was a deliciously warm counterbalance to the chilly morning air. Abby clasped her cup of coffee in one hand, breathed in its strong aroma and finally felt herself begin to relax. Figgy lay at her feet, tucked under the wooden bench on which Abby sat. The little dog was fast asleep, lulled by the ferry's steady vibration as it plowed through the waves toward the industrial city of Baie-Comeau on the far shore. Despite the clear weather, the cool temperatures meant most of the ship's other passengers were indoors, enjoying breakfast in one of the ferry's two restaurants or sitting in one of the lounges. As a result, Abby had the stern-side deck to herself.

They had been underway for more than thirty minutes and the hills around Matane had slipped from view below the southern horizon. With no land visible, it was easy for Abby to imagine they were in the middle of the Atlantic, not crossing one of North America's mightiest rivers.

More than one passenger had done a double take when Abby had stepped up to pay her fare, Figgy obediently at heel. But no one had said anything. She had been prepared for another go around with the ferry's personnel about the no-dogs-on-deck policy, but they must have figured that if she'd made it past the sentinels down below, there was an official reason for this particular canine to be with a passenger.

Her only regret was not getting her benefactor's name. But by the time she had gathered her things and convinced Figgy to jump out of the car, Mr. Wagoneer, as she had dubbed him, had vanished.

Taking another sip of coffee, she gazed out at the sparkling blue waters topped by a confusion of whitecaps. Breezy, yes, but not a strong enough wind to explain the water's turbulence. No, she figured the intense wave action had more to do with their proximity to the Gulf of Saint Lawrence, where the river met the Atlantic. It was an area of strong crosscurrents, which she suspected made for a tricky passage at the best of time for the ferry captains.

The sun was rising higher and the glare off the water made Abby squint. She was digging into her purse for her sunglasses when she heard the hatch next to her bench open and close and someone step out onto the deck.

"When I said to keep a low profile, I didn't mean you had to sit out here and freeze to death," a familiar masculine voice said.

Abby shaded her eyes against the sun and recognized Mr. Wagoneer smiling down at her.

"Mind if I share your bench?" he asked.

"No, not at all."

Stepping around her and turning the collar of his brown canvas coat up against the chill, he sat down on the bench, stretching his legs out until his booted feet almost touched the rail.

"So, I take it you had no trouble getting your small passenger on deck?"

"No," Abby said. "The hardest part was getting past the guy downstairs—and you did that for me."

He smiled, and held out a hand. "I'm Marc, by the way."

Abby shook his hand. "Abby. Abby Miller, it's very nice to meet you." How could she not have noticed down below just how handsome he was? Curly brown hair edged the navy-blue watch cap he was wearing and the corners of his clear-blue eyes crinkled with lines that come from a lifetime of laughing or working in the outdoors or both.

"And your friend?" Marc nodded toward the sleeping Figgy.

"That's Figgy Piggy," Abby said, laughing self-consciously.

"Figgy Piggy?" Marc's eyebrows rose.

At the mention of her name, Figgy got up, stretched, walked out from under the bench and sat staring at the man and woman.

"It's a long story," Abby explained.

"Well, it's a long crossing," Marc said. "Hey, are you hungry?" He leaned away from her and dug in the large outer pocket of his jacket. Pulling out a slightly crumpled white paper bag, he held it out to her. "I picked these up just before I got to the dock."

Abby peered inside to see a half-dozen glazed doughnuts. As the smell reached her nose, she suddenly remembered she hadn't eaten since the previous day's rushed supper on the road. She heard her stomach rumble and hoped Marc didn't catch it over the sound of the ferry's engines.

"Wow, thanks, yes, I'd love—Figgy! No!"

To Abby's horror, Figgy jumped up, put both front paws on Marc's chest and tried to stick her head into the bag.

"Whoa girl, down." Marc held the bag out of reach with his right hand and used his left to gently take Figgy's paws from his chest and push her back to the deck.

"I'm sorry," Abby said. "She's really such a good dog but she's a shameless beggar."

As if to prove the point, Figgy cocked her ears, put her head on Marc's lap and looked up at him with pleading brown eyes.

"She does have it down to a fine art," Marc said. "When's the last time you fed her?"

"This morning when we got to the dock. Figgy, come here." Abby tugged firmly on the dog's leash.

Instead of complying, the dog cast Abby a disdainful look, put her head back down on Marc's leg and drooled slightly.

"Okay, that's it—get over here," Abby ordered.

With great reluctance, Figgy began to back off, but Marc said, "Don't worry about it. I like dogs. And this one's a real character."

"No, I don't want her to bother you," Abby insisted.

"It's no bother. Besides, it's my own fault for

getting her here in the first place. Can I give her a little piece of doughnut?"

"Sure, and if you do, I guarantee you'll have a friend for life."

"In that case, here's one for you, too." Marc handed Abby a doughnut before he pulled a chunk off his own and handed it to Figgy, who downed the morsel in one gulp.

"One piece is enough for you, okay?" Marc said to the dog.

"Yes, now lie down," Abby commanded.

Looking from one to the other, Figgy lay down directly at Marc's feet, keeping a watchful eye for any crumbs.

Satisfied that Figgy was not contemplating another sneak attack on Marc's bag of doughnuts, Abby sat back and enjoyed the fresh pastry and hot coffee.

"Now I'm doubly in your debt," she said, licking the last of the glaze from her fingers. "Dog lover and provider of treats."

"All in a day's work," Marc said loftily.

"What a morning. First I wasn't sure if I was even going to make it onto the ferry and then the whole thing with Figgy—"

"No reservations?"

Abby shook her head. "I guess you didn't have any either. I mean, you were behind me."

"Nah, I don't bother. I can usually pretty well guess my odds and what time I should get in line. Even then, it's not worth breaking a sweat over. There's always another one, right?"

Abby laughed. "That's a healthy attitude."

"So, where are you headed?" Marc asked.

"Tadoussac. It's on the north shore, about ninety miles west of Baie-Comeau."

"Yeah, I know."

"Are you from Québec?"

Marc nodded. "Born and raised. What brings you to Tadoussac? On holiday?"

"No, work."

"No kidding? Doing what?"

Abby smiled and had to consciously force herself not to feel for the well-worn envelope inside her shirt pocket. She had read the letter so often it was now committed to memory:

Dear Dr. Miller, it is with great pleasure that the Woods Hole Oceanographic Institute informs you of the board's decision to fund for a period of one year your research into the effects of noise pollution and related human contact activities on the social behavior of beluga...

"Hey, you still with me?" Marc asked.

"Sorry," she said. "I was just thinking of how

lucky I am. I'm going to be a visiting scholar based at the research center for marine mammals. Do you know it?"

When Marc didn't answer right away, Abby added, "It's right in Tadoussac."

"I know where it is." Marc's tone had lost some of its earlier warmth. "So, what, you're a scientist or something?"

"Actually, yes." No doubt about it, his attitude toward her had cooled several degrees.

"Great," he said, "Just what we need."

"Excuse me?"

"Never mind," Marc said, standing. "I'd better get back inside. Enjoy the rest of the crossing."

Abby felt confused by his sudden leave taking. "Okay, I will. Thanks again for all your help and for being so nice to Figgy."

"Sure," he said, stepping over the dog. "See ya." And he was gone through the hatch.

A SCIENTIST, Marc thought in disgust, sitting behind the wheel of his Jeep as he watched Abby and her dog get into her car and wait with the rest of the passengers for the ferry to dock at Baie-Comeau. *It figures.* Would he have stepped in like that to plead her case to the ferry worker had he known? Her brake lights flashed as she keyed the car to life. He sighed. Probably. Wasn't often he'd seen a woman that pretty on the Matane to Baie-Comeau run. Check that, he'd *never* seen a woman that pretty on the ferry.

Up on deck, in the bright light of the morning, she'd looked even lovelier than she had in the ship's gloomy interior. Complete natural beauty, he had thought, without a bit of makeup on her. He'd gotten a good look at those eyes before she had pulled on her sunglasses and saw they were an attractive shade of hazel, a perfect match to the coppery brown hair that framed her face.

Oh well, Marc thought, as he followed her off the ship and into the terminal lot. *It had been worth a try.* He knew he must have appeared terribly rude when he had made his abrupt departure, but he'd been afraid he'd have said something he'd regret had he remained.

It was stupid and irrational; Marc knew that. The woman had nothing to do with the situation in which he now found himself. It wasn't her fault that several years ago some politician had listened to some scientist who had sounded the alarm about the state of the province's fish populations. With the help of some highly paid lobbyists, the government had crafted the laws and regulations that had put Marc's father and many of his friends out of the fishing business for good.

Those laws had come down as decrees from on

high, with no opportunity for the fishermen to plead their cases. No, Marc recalled bitterly, one day their businesses were solid and the next they were told the quotas for the following season had been slashed, with some species put off limits completely. It had devastated the North Shore fleet and, Marc was certain, contributed to the heart attack that had claimed his father not long after.

Where were those scientists now? Now that unemployment was at an all time high. Where were their studies, their results and reports? No doubt they were off saving some other species at the expense of jobs and families.

Looking at his watch, he saw that he had a half hour to kill before his delivery was due at the marine supply warehouse. Making a right out of the lot, he drove toward the twenty-four-hour Tim Hortons doughnut shop just up the road. Good a place as any to pick up on some local gossip. *It's a shame, though,* he thought as he again pictured Abby in his mind. *Too bad someone that good looking has to be a scientist.*

ABBY HAD ONCE READ that the route along Québec's North Shore between Baie-Comeau and Québec City was one of the prettiest in Canada. As her car crested a hill that offered a panoramic view of the Saint Lawrence Seaway, she could easily see why. To the south, the Seaway was a wide, brilliantly blue plane as far as the eye could see. Each small town or village through which she passed was more quaint, more charming, more picturesque than the previous one. The distant mountains to the north were covered in dense spruce and fir and the closer rolling vistas of farmland and rocky knolls were almost enough to push all thoughts of the mysterious Marc from her mind.

Almost.

After his hasty departure, Abby had remained on her bench, puzzling over his strange behavior until, like Figgy, she had succumbed to the ferry's steady rocking motion and fallen asleep. She had only awakened when the announcement—made first in French and then English—came over the loudspeakers that the ferry would dock at Baie-Comeau in fifteen minutes and all passengers should make their way to their vehicles.

Remembering the stares from her fellow shipmates when she appeared with Figgy, Abby hung back until most of the travelers had already gone below. She had not seen Marc inside, nor anywhere below as she wove her way between the hundreds of cars, trucks, campers, vans and motorcycles that twice daily turned the *Felipe* into a giant floating parking lot. Once in her own car, she had glanced back at the Wagoneer, but in the glare of the halogen lights couldn't tell if anyone was inside.

Since she had been among the last to board back in Matane, Abby had had to wait while hundreds of vehicles in front were directed off the ship. When her turn came, she eased the car along, giving a small wave to the crewman who had almost prevented Figgy from going up on deck. He returned her wave, but with a suspicious look. She'd been so intent on navigating her way out of the lot, she had not paid any attention to where Marc was heading. By the time she remembered to look in her rearview mirror for his Jeep, it was nowhere to be seen.

And as she cruised down the road to Tadoussac, she was too excited to obsess about the moody stranger.

Twelve months, she thought happily. Woods Hole had not only approved her research grant, but had left the door wide open for a three-year extension pending the results of that first year. She had the full use of the lab facilities at the center and visiting-researcher status at the Centre d'interpretation des mammifères marins. The grant was not a huge one, but it was more than enough to get started. The amount would fund the research and provide a modest living stipend. The

Woods Hole Oceanographic Institute had even arranged for a one-year lease on a small apartment in Tadoussac within walking distance of the research center.

It was near lunchtime when Abby pulled her car over to the shoulder on the steep rise above Tadoussac. "It's perfect," she whispered, looking out the windshield at the view before her. Figgy, who once again had fallen asleep on the back seat, opened her eyes and sat up.

The tiny village of Tadoussac hugged a flat piece of land nestled within a bay of the same name. To the west, north and east, the rocky cliffs of the Saguenay River Fjord stood out stark and gray against the blue sky. The river itself emptied into the bay at the base of the hill directly below where Abby now parked. There, the road ended and from this height, Abby could see a short line of cars waiting to board the small ferry that made the fifteen-minute crossing to the other side, where the road continued on to Québec City and points west. In the bay, tiny boats bobbed up and down and she could just make out people strolling along the beach. Abby took another long satisfied look, then checked for traffic and pulled back onto the highway.

"Let's find our new home," she said, as Figgy

stuck her head out the window and took her first good whiff of Tadoussac.

After taking the next exit off the highway, Abby drove slowly down the town's narrow streets, following the written directions that had been forwarded to her. To her delight, each turn brought her closer to the bay's waters. Finally, she pulled up to a modest green bungalow in a row of similarly styled houses, located across the road from the beach she had seen from atop the hill.

This must be it, she thought, looking at the name and number on the mailbox at the curb.

Abby rolled the car's windows partway down before stepping out onto the street and shutting the door behind her. "Wait here," she said to Figgy and walked up the stone pathway and the three steps to the front porch. Looking around a moment before ringing the bell, Abby saw rows of plant hangers suspended from the porch roof. Empty now, she imagined they would soon be full of flowers.

Pressing the buzzer, she heard the faint sound of chimes from within the house. Moments later, the door opened and Abby was looking into the warmest, greenest eyes she had ever seen.

"Mrs. Doucette?" Abby said.

"Françoise Doucette," the older woman said. "And you must be our Abby." It was a statement, not a question. "Come in. Welcome!"

The door opened wide and she ushered Abby inside.

"I've been looking forward to meeting you," Françoise said.

"And I, you," Abby said, studying the woman. Standing a good head taller than Abby, Françoise was much sturdier, but Abby could not discern an ounce of fat on the woman's body. Her gray hair was pulled back in a tight bun and the front of her shirt appeared to be dusted in flour.

"How was the drive?" Françoise asked.

"Long," Abby said. "I left Andover at six yesterday morning and drove pretty much straight through."

"Then you must be exhausted. I bet you'd like to see your apartment."

"That would be really nice." Now that she had actually reached her destination, weariness was taking a firm hold.

"Follow me," Françoise said, heading down a hallway to what appeared to be the back of the house. "Your place has its own walkway and entrance from the front yard, but this is quicker now that you're inside."

As Abby followed behind, Françoise said, "It's small, but it's private and furnished. The marine center's just down the road, you can walk there in five minutes. We don't have a lot of shops and such here in town, but there is a general store and I go into Baie-Sainte-Catherine every Monday if you need anything."

She pushed open the screen door leading out to a fenced-in backyard and held it for Abby.

"There's a washer and dryer in the basement of the house, and you're welcome to use them anytime, it's included in the rent." They crossed the yard to a small, separate building. "Well, here we are." Françoise dug in her pocket and pulled out a key. She unlocked the door and pushed it open, then stepped aside so Abby could walk in.

"This used to be the garage," Françoise explained, following her inside. "We converted it to living space about ten years ago."

Abby stepped into the middle of the single room and looked around. *Must have been a small car,* she thought. There was just enough room to accommodate a sofa against one wall, an end table on one side and coffee table in front. A well-worn braided rug covered most of the floor and a simple wooden writing desk sat against the wall across from the sofa. Immediately to the right of the front door was a compact kitchen—the stove, refrigerator and sink all apartment-size. Much to Abby's satisfaction, bookshelves lined most of the available wall space, but it was the windows that truly delighted her.

Rather than walling up the space where the garage door had been, the Doucettes had installed floor-to-ceiling windows. The room was bathed in warm, natural light and would be, Abby could tell, for most of the daylight hours.

"The bathroom's through that door in the corner and the bedroom is right up there," Françoise said.

Looking in the direction the older woman was pointing, Abby saw a narrow gangway-style ladder against the far wall that led up to a loft space above the living room.

"What do you think?" Françoise asked.

"I think it's ideal," Abby said.

"It's not very big."

"It's fine. Besides, I'll be spending most of my time at the marine center or in the field."

"Now, you mentioned in your letter having a dog?" Françoise asked.

"Yes, but you said you allowed pets." Abby felt herself tense.

"Not a problem," Françoise said and Abby relaxed. "The yard's fenced in and there's even a doghouse out there from the days we had our own dog."

"I can't tell you how much I appreciate that," Abby said. "I'll take it."

Françoise nodded. "All right, then. I'll leave you to unpack your things and get settled. I have to get back to work. You can drive your car right up the side of the house and park it there."

Abby followed the woman back outside.

"The front gate is never locked so you can come and go through there. And here are your keys."

Abby accepted the small ring of keys and was about to ask Françoise how she would like the rent schedule set when her attention was diverted by the enticing aroma of fresh bread.

Taking a deep breath, Abby said, "What is that amazing smell?"

Françoise laughed. "It's either sourdough rolls or honey-oatmeal bread. I have them both going."

"You have time to bake *and* work?" Abby asked.

"Baking *is* my work," Françoise said. "I supply the breakfast and tea breads for the Hôtel Tadoussac and sell to a few regular customers directly."

That explains the flour on her shirt, Abby thought. "The Hôtel Tadoussac, is that the big white building with the red roof I passed on the way in?"

"The very one," Françoise confirmed. "It's pretty quiet up there now—the tourist season's not in high gear yet. But by mid-June, things really pick up. Now, I'd better get back inside before anything burns. Will you be all set?"

"I'll be fine," Abby assured her. "I don't have

much to move in, but I want to get it done and have a look around. Thank you."

Abby stood at the gate and watched as Françoise went back into the house. The Tadoussac Bay was spread out directly in front of Abby, and the view caused her to catch her breath. The rocky arms of the hills surrounding the town wrapped themselves around the waters of the bay, creating a calm harbor. A sand beach hugged the shoreline in a white crescent dotted with rafts of driftwood and massive boulders. Sailboats, large pleasure craft and older, working boats were anchored close to shore, while farther out seabirds—gulls, terns and cormorants—wheeled and dove into the water in search of a meal. The view was prettier than anything she'd seen on a postcard and Abby knew that even in a year she would not grow tired of admiring it.

CHAPTER TWO

"THAT'S THE LAST OF IT," Abby said, seven trips to the car later. She kicked the screen door shut behind her, set the final box on the floor and flopped down on the couch. Figgy instantly hopped up beside her.

Abby stretched her legs out, leaned her head back and sighed in contentment. New job, new town, new apartment—she couldn't remember the last time she had been this excited—or this nervous. Turning her head to the right, she could see the blue of the Saint Lawrence beyond the bay. She made a mental promise to take Figgy for a walk down on the beach after supper.

Thinking of supper reminded Abby she hadn't eaten since the doughnut on the ferry that morning. Having neither the desire nor the energy to go looking for the town's general store, she decided to postpone her first grocery-shopping expedition and ask Françoise for a restaurant recommendation.

Standing, she looked down at Figgy and said, "How about you go scope out your new yard?"

The dog jumped off the couch and followed her outside. As Abby continued on to the back door of the main house, Figgy busied herself dashing about the lawn and sniffing at the rose bushes lining the fence.

Abby walked up the back steps and knocked on the door. Expecting Françoise, she was surprised when a young girl appeared on the other side of the screen.

"Um, is Françoise here?" Abby asked uncertainly.

"You mean Gran?" the girl said and, before Abby could answer, she continued on. "Are you the lady that's going to live in the garage? My name's Sylvie. I'm eight, well, eight and a half, really. Do you like boats? I like boats. My dad said he'd take me on a boat ride this weekend. Is that your dog?"

Figgy had trotted over to the bottom of the porch steps and was looking up at them.

"Sylvie! I thought I asked you to—oh, Miss Miller, I'm sorry. Is Sylvie bothering you?" Françoise came up behind the little girl, wiping her hands on a dish towel.

"No, not at all," Abby said hastily. "She was just introducing herself to me."

Sylvie opened the screen door all the way and stepped out to get a better look at Figgy.

"Do you like dogs?" Abby asked her.

Sylvie nodded.

"Would you like to play with her?"

The girl's eyes widened and she turned to look back at Françoise. "Gran? Can I? Please?"

"Have you finished your homework?" Françoise asked.

"Yeah, well, almost. I'll do the rest after supper, I promise. Please?"

Françoise laughed and threw up her hands. "All right, I guess an hour of playing outside won't hurt. But, then you finish your homework *before* supper. Okay?"

"Okay," Sylvie said happily, dashing back inside. "Be right back," she called over her shoulder.

Abby and Françoise looked at each other, bemused, and moments later, Sylvie reappeared holding a worn soccer ball. Tossing the ball out into the middle of the yard, she clapped in delight as Figgy bounded after it and all three of them laughed as the little dog tried unsuccessfully to get its mouth around it.

"Her name is Figgy," Abby said to Sylvie.

"That's a weird name," Sylvie said.

"Sylvie!" Françoise said firmly. "Remember what we talked about—not everything you think has to come out of your mouth."

"Sorry," Sylvie muttered.

"That's okay," Abby said, smiling. "I guess it is kind of a weird name."

"One hour," Françoise said in a warning tone as Sylvie jumped down the steps and started kicking the ball for Figgy to chase. The two women watched a moment, then Françoise motioned for Abby to come inside.

"We just got back from delivering up to the hotel." With a nod of her head, Françoise indicated that Abby should take a seat at the kitchen table. "Can I offer you a cup of tea and something to eat?"

"Oh, no. I don't want to bother you. I was just hoping you could tell me a good place in town to grab a bite."

"We have a lot of good places," Françoise said. "Problem is, none are open at this hour. It's too late for lunch and too early for supper."

"I see." Disappointed, Abby realized she'd have to shop after all. "Well, if you could tell me how to get to the grocery store—"

"I can," Françoise said. "But right now you are going to have a cup of tea and some of these muffins I made today."

"No, I can't," Abby protested, standing.

"You can and you will," Françoise insisted. "Please, sit down. Make an old woman happy," she added in mock severity.

Abby sat down while Françoise put the teakettle on the burner to heat, then took out cups, saucers, spoons, plates and forks from various cupboards and drawers and laid out two place settings. Then came a wooden box. When Françoise opened the lid, Abby discovered a generous selection of tea bags. Finally, Françoise set down a basket holding a half-dozen muffins and several scones wrapped in a white cloth.

"Help yourself,' she said, indicating the basket.

Abby reached out and carefully selected one of the muffins. "Mmm…still warm."

"I always bake a few extra," Françoise said. "Come by any afternoon at this time and join me."

Right, Abby thought. *If I make a habit out of this, someone's liable to mistake me for a beluga.*

Out loud she said, "Is your granddaughter visiting?"

"Sylvie?" Françoise said. "No, she lives here in Tadoussac. I'm watching her while her father's away."

"She's adorable."

"She's that," Françoise agreed. "But give her the opportunity and she'll talk your ear off—in French and in English!"

"Is her mother away also?" Abby said, realizing a bit too late that her question sounded like snooping. When Françoise's eyes clouded, Abby instantly regretted asking.

"I'm sorry, that's none of my business. I'm not normally so nosy."

Françoise waved a hand at her. "No, it's all right. Sylvie's mother died three years ago in Toronto. That's when my son moved back here with my granddaughter."

"I'm so sorry," Abby said, unsure of what else to say. The silence hung heavy in the room as both women listened to the happy squeals of the little girl and Figgy's excited barking.

Casting about for something to say, Abby finally asked, "When does school let out up here?"

"Let out?" Françoise asked, shutting off the stove's burner and bringing the kettle to the table. She set it down atop a trivet and then took the seat opposite Abby.

"For the summer. When does her summer vacation start?"

"Oh, I see. At the end of June but Sylvie's been having problems with her reading and writing, so my son might have to enroll her in a summer program. Three hours every morning." Françoise poured hot water into Abby's cup.

"Thank you," Abby said, taking the cup and selecting a tea bag from the box. "What does your son do?"

Before Françoise could answer, they both heard a car door slam. The older woman grinned. "That would be him now. I swear, he can smell my blueberry muffins from a mile away."

Having just polished off one herself, Abby wasn't sure about being able to smell the muffins from that far off, but she'd certainly consider walking a mile for one.

Footsteps sounded up the walk and the front door opened and shut.

"Mom?" a deep male voice said.

"In the kitchen." Françoise called out.

"I couldn't get your organic twelve-grain flour, so I got double the whole grain. And they said they won't have any more fresh honey until this fall, so I picked up what they had left…" The voice came to a stop as its owner stepped into the kitchen and stared at Abby. Recognizing the man from the ferry, she returned his look of surprise.

"Marc, this is Abby," Françoise said. "She's the one renting the apartment for the year. Abby, this is my son Marc—Sylvie's father."

"We've met," Abby and Marc said in unison. Françoise looked confused.

"Met, but where?"

Before either could answer, the screen door slammed and Sylvie was in the room, running at her father, who scooped her into a hug.

"Hello *mon petit chou*," he said.

"I'm not a cabbage," Sylvie said with all the dignity befitting her eight years. "That's Abby, I mean, Miss Miller." She wriggled out of Marc's embrace. "She has a dog! And her name is Figgy and she likes to chase soccer balls. Want to come watch us, Dad?"

Marc laughed and ruffled his daughter's hair. "Not right now. I need to talk to your grandmother for a bit."

"And you, young lady, have some homework to finish, remember?" Françoise chided.

Outnumbered, Sylvie looked from her father to Françoise and back again. "Okay." Then she looked at Abby and brightened. "Miss Miller, can I play with Figgy again tomorrow?"

"You can play with Figgy every day if you want to," Abby said, then quickly added, "If it's okay with your father and grandmother."

"Can I, Dad, Gran? Please?" Sylvie's blue eyes were huge and round—and much like her father's.

"We'll talk about it later," Marc said.

"That's what grownups always say," Sylvie complained.

"That's because we are grownups," Marc said. "Now, homework. Scoot!" He gave her a light tap on her behind with his hand.

"So, how was she today," Marc asked softly, after Sylvie had left.

Before Françoise could answer, Abby rose to her feet. Not wanting to impose on personal family business, she thanked Françoise for the muffin and excused herself, saying she still had a ton of unpacking to do.

"Nice seeing you again," Marc said mildly, as Abby brushed past him.

"Yes, you, too," she said quickly and hastened out.

MARC CLAIMED the chair just vacated by Abby and helped himself to a cranberry scone from the basket.

"At least use a napkin," Françoise admonished him as Marc put the scone, minus a huge bite, directly on the table.

"Sorry," he said through his mouthful.

"Here." Françoise handed him a small plate and began clearing off the dirty dishes from the table.

"Thanks," Marc said, finishing the scone in three more bites and reaching for a muffin.

"How do you know our tenant? She's only been in town a few hours." Françoise's back was to him as she rinsed the dishes in the sink.

"We met on the ferry this morning." Marc recounted the episode with Abby and the ferry worker and their subsequent conversation on deck. He left out his own abrupt departure.

When Françoise returned to the table and sat back down, Marc waited until she finished making her own cup of tea before asking again about Sylvie's day.

"She said she had a good day when I picked her up," Françoise said. "But Madame Simard wanted to speak to me."

"Sylvie's teacher? What did she say?"

"That Sylvie's a bright, energetic, kindhearted girl who is showing no signs of improvement in either her reading or her writing."

"Dammit," Marc muttered. "How much longer will she be like this? It's been three years."

"How much longer are you going to blame yourself?" Françoise asked softly.

"Who says I am?" Marc shot back, then softened his tone. "Sorry, Mom, it's just been a rough couple of days."

Make that a rough couple of years, he thought ruefully. Was his mother right? Was he blaming himself for Thérèse's death? Why would he? He wasn't the one behind the wheel of the SUV that crossed the centerline, hitting Thérèse's compact head-on and demolishing it. No, if anyone was to blame, it was the teenagers in the SUV, pumped up on Lord-knows-what, out celebrating the first day of summer vacation.

So why do I feel so guilty? he wondered.

Because she hadn't wanted to take the damn car in the first place, but I talked her into it, Marc reminded himself. He'd wanted her to drive that day instead of taking the bus so she could drop the Toyota off for an oil change, sparing him the trip.

One fateful decision that had changed his life forever.

Françoise was saying something. "I'm sorry, Mom, what was that?"

"I said Madame Simard wants to talk to you about Sylvie."

"Right, okay, I can go tomorrow."

Françoise looked at him a moment. "How did things go in Rimouski?"

Marc laughed bitterly. "Struck out," he said. "The marina's not hiring any new boatmen this year. McDonnell told me he can't even honor half of the rehires from the winter layoffs."

"And Matane?"

"*O* for two," Marc said. "I went to talk to Bruce Charbonneau—his company's the one doing all the construction work on the road up to Blanc Sablon, but the Tremblay boys have that whole market sewn up."

"You mean the Tremblays got the entire contract for ferrying supplies from Godbout to Blanc Sablon?" Françoise said.

"Yeah, it's all in who you know—right?"

The Tremblays were one of the North Shores' oldest, largest and most influential families, with a fleet of sleek, late-model cargo boats. Most supplies ferried up and down the shore made the trip on Tremblay craft.

"Where does that leave you, now?" Françoise asked.

Marc shrugged. "Back to the plan of chartering day trips for tourists for the summer," he said with little enthusiasm.

"It's honest work."

"I suppose. Maybe it was a mistake. Moving back here. At least in Toronto I had a job."

"Yes, but that's all you had," Françoise reminded him. "A job that kept you away from your daughter. No, you're both better off here, for the time being anyway, with family."

"Yeah, and speaking of that," Marc said, "I was thinking on the drive down of renting the house out for the summer. We could sure use the money."

Marc and Sylvie were living in a house on one of the knolls overlooking the bay. He and Thérèse had lived there for two years before the lure of higher wages led them to Toronto. The view from the porch alone would make it an easy place to rent to one of the summer families.

"Where would you stay?" Françoise asked.

"I was thinking about the boat," Marc ventured.

"The boat! That's no place for Sylvie to live," Françoise said.

"I know. Maybe she could have my old room?" Marc let the question hang in the air. "I mean, it would only be for the summer and you said yourself she's a real help in the kitchen—"

"Stop it," Françoise said. "You don't have to convince me of the joys of having my grand-daughter staying with me. I love having her here."

"Thanks, Mom. I mean it." Marc stood and pushed his chair back beneath the table. "Now, I think I'll go check on how our princess is doing."

MARC FOUND SYLVIE lying facedown on the living-room sofa, drawing on a pad of paper. So intent was she on her work, she had not heard him come into the room. It gave Marc a chance to watch his daughter a moment and, as it always did at the sight of the freckle-faced youngster, his heart swelled with love.

In those horrible days and weeks immediately following Thérèse's death, Marc knew it was Sylvie alone who had kept him going. Dealing with her endless questions and simple needs had given him a reason to get up every morning. Otherwise, he very well could have curled up and died himself.

But Sylvie was his joy and had been from the moment she was born. Watching her now, he remembered what Thérèse had said the night Sylvie came into the world.

She's the best parts of both of us. How right his wife had been.

"Whatcha working on, *ma fille?*" Marc asked.

Sylvie jumped a bit. "Dad, you're not supposed to sneak up on people," she scolded. "It's not nice." She swiveled her legs around so her father could sit next to her.

"You're right. I stand corrected. Now, what have we here." He looked at the drawing Sylvie had been working on and was easily able to identify it as a portrait in pencil of Figgy. He shook his head in admiration. The drawing was on the simplistic side, but it was also quite realistic.

"This is very good," Marc said.

"Thanks. I'm going to give it to Miss Miller."

"That's very thoughtful of you." Marc put his arm around the girl and held her close a moment. "You had a good time playing with that dog, didn't you?"

"I sure did!" Sylvie said.

"How would you like it if you were here every day to play with her?"

Sylvie's brow wrinkled. "But I am here every day, Dad, while you work."

"Yes, yes you are. But how would you like to live here for the summer?"

"Really? Live with Gran? All three of us?"

"Well, that would be a bit much to ask of Gran," Marc said. "How about we try it just you girls for the time being?"

"Where will you live?" Sylvie asked.

"On the boat. Just for the summer season."

"Why can't we live in our house?" Sylvie asked.

"I was thinking, our house is so nice and we're so lucky to have Gran's house to stay at and the boat, well it's kind of selfish. So maybe we could let some other people use our house for the summer. What do you think of that?" Marc held his breath.

Sylvie was giving the matter ample thought. "I guess it's okay," she said slowly. "But they have to pay us lots of money!"

Marc stared at his daughter a moment, then burst out laughing. *Never underestimate the ability of a child to get right to the heart of the matter.* He gave her another hug.

"Now, is your homework done?" Marc said.

"I guess…"

"You don't sound convinced. Why don't you let me see it?"

Looking like she'd rather do anything but that, Sylvie reached down to the floor and picked up a spelling workbook and handed it to him. "This is what we were doing today," she said and went back to her drawing of Figgy.

Marc opened the workbook to the most recent assignment.

"You left half the answers blank," he said gently.

Sylvie shrugged and kept her eyes on the drawing.

"Sylvie?"

She slowly set the pencil down and looked at him. "I was supposed to finish it tonight."

"Finish?"

Sylvie nodded, looking down at her hands. "Madame Simard made us work in groups today. We were supposed to read the questions and answer them. But, I—I couldn't and the other kids laughed and—"

Whatever else she was going to say was lost as Sylvie broke into tears. Quickly, Marc slid closer to her and put an arm around his daughter's shoulders.

"Shhhh," he said softly. "It's okay."

Sylvie gave a mighty sniff and pulled away. "I *hate* it when the other kids laugh at me," she said, wiping her nose with her sleeve.

"No one likes to be laughed at, *ma fille.*" Marc pulled his arm back. "What did Madame Simard say?"

"Nothing," Sylvie said sullenly. "She didn't hear them. She just told me to finish my book at home. But Dad," she looked up at Marc, "I think she wants to talk to you."

Marc nodded. "Uh-huh, she does. Your grandmother told me."

"She thinks I'm stupid, doesn't she?" Sylvie's voice trembled a bit.

Marc felt his jaw tighten. "Did Madame Simard say that?"

Sylvie shrugged.

"Sylvie, did Madame Simard say you were stupid?"

"She thinks I need a special teacher and two girls in class said only stupid people go to the special teacher." Sylvie gave a loud sniff. "I'm sorry I'm stupid, Dad."

"Oh, Sylvie." He hugged her to him and stroked her hair. "You're not stupid. You just have your own way of learning things and you know what?"

"What?" Her voice was muffled against his chest.

"That makes you more interesting than any of the other girls in that school."

She looked up at him. "Really?"

"Really," Marc said. "Now, why don't you go see if Gran wants to go have supper? I think I'm going to take my two favorite ladies out tonight. We'll work on your homework before you go to bed. And, Sylvie," he added before she could hop down and scamper off, "I love you."

"I love you, too, Dad," she said.

After Sylvie left, Marc again picked up the drawing. It really was remarkable how well she had captured the likeness of the little dog.

"DAD, LOOK." Sylvie was tugging at Marc's sleeve and pointing. He glanced over to see Abby shutting the gate behind her and walking toward them.

"Oh, hello," she said.

"We're going to get hamburgers," Sylvie said. "Want to come?"

"Sylvie, I'm sure Miss Miller has other plans," Marc said in a cautionary tone.

"Other plans?" Françoise repeated. "The poor thing just got here, she hasn't had time to make any plans. I'll bet you're on your way to find a restaurant."

"Actually, yes," Abby said.

"Then why don't you come with us?" Françoise suggested.

"No, I don't want to impose," Abby said. "If you'll just point me in the direction of a place that's open, that would be great."

Françoise shook her head. "The only spot open right now is Pierrette's and that's where we're going. Please join us, we'd welcome your company. Wouldn't we, Marc?" She looked pointedly at her son.

"Sure, why not?" Marc said.

"All right," Abby agreed, "but under one condition."

"What's that?" Françoise asked.

"That you all start calling me Abby."

"Deal," Sylvie said. "Can we go now? I'm starving!"

"Okay, *ma fille*," Marc agreed. "Remember to hold your grandmother's hand when we cross the road."

Abby looked up and down the street and raised an eyebrow at Marc.

"I know, it looks deserted now," he said to Abby as Sylvie and Françoise walked ahead of them. "But, once the tourist season cranks up, it's going to be pretty busy. I want Sylvie to get in the habit now of never crossing unless there's an adult with her."

"Good idea." Abby fell into step next to him. "Listen, I really hope I'm not imposing, crashing your dinner like this."

Marc shook his head. "Don't worry about it."

"I have to say, you were the last person I expected to see today, much less at my landlady's house."

"Yeah, about that," Marc stopped and put a hand on Abby's arm, holding her in place. "I think I owe you an apology, I was kind of rude back there on the ferry this morning, rushing off like that."

"Were you?" Abby asked mildly. "I hadn't noticed."

"Right," Marc said. "I just wanted you to know it had nothing to do with you."

"Well, isn't that a relief." Marc could hear the sarcasm in her voice. "It's just, oh, never mind." He started to walk down the street.

"No, wait," Abby said. "I'm sorry, now I'm the one being rude. What were you going to say?"

"Well, when you told me you're a scientist, it just kind of hit me the wrong way and I wanted to beat it out of there before I said something really stupid."

Abby looked skeptical. "Because I'm a scientist? You're kidding, right? What does my being a scientist have to do with anything?"

Marc sighed. "It's complicated. I'm not sure I can explain it."

"Give it a try," Abby said. "Remember, I'm a scientist, I'm pretty clever."

Her tone might be teasing, but Marc knew his words had rankled. "Okay, look out there and tell me what you see."

"Out where?"

"There, in the bay."

Abby was quiet a moment. "I see boats, some people kayaking, a couple of buoys—that's about it."

"And farther out? In the Saint Lawrence?"

"Not much. Maybe…"She squinted into the distance. "Is that a container ship way out there?"

Marc nodded, "Time was, you'd have looked out there and seen a dozen, maybe two dozen trawlers and fishing boats anchored in that bay. The rest of the fleet would be farther out, heading for home."

He turned to look directly at her. "There were more than sixteen hundred licensed fishermen along the North Shore in the early nineteen-nineties—on the north shore alone. Must have been another four thousand going up to Gaspé and the Magdalen Islands. That meant almost three thousand boats going after snow crab, cod, eel, redfish, shrimp and lobster and almost five thousand processing jobs back on shore. Now look at it. It's deserted out there."

"What happened?" Abby asked.

"Scientists happened. Scientists and their studies and reports and quotas." Marc fairly spat the last word out. "Used to be a man could make a good living, support his family from the water. Not anymore. Got to be the size of the permitted catches didn't even pay the costs of going out. So, over the years, the fishing industry pretty much died."

"You can't seriously be blaming the researchers for that? They don't set the policies or make the laws."

"You're right, they don't," Marc agreed. "But they sure as hell have a lot of influence over the people in Ottawa who do. All I know is, every time someone shows up to do another damned study, we see a whole new batch of regulations telling us what we can and can't do."

Abby tried to reason with him. "But those regulations are necessary to preserve the species," she said. "Overfishing, pollution, destruction of habitat—those are the real reasons drastic actions had to be taken."

Marc could feel the familiar anger rising in him, but he knew he had to speak. "I understand about all that. In fact, if anyone took the time to ask them, they'd find out most fishermen do, too.

They know more about these waters than any college kid ever will. What they don't understand is why, when they're not the ones to blame for the problems, they're the ones paying for them."

"Meaning?"

"Ever see a Russian factory ship?" Marc asked, and Abby shook her head. "Giant monster of a ship. One of those babies will haul in more fish in a week than the old Tadoussac fleet took in a season. As for the pollution and habitat destruction, take a look at your own government. But I guess it's just easier to go after the little guys."

"There's a lot more to it than all that," Abby said.

"You're right. Because now this generation of fishermen and sailors have their own regs to deal with. Those boats out there? Most of them are charters for Saguenay River tours or whale watching. But thanks to a bunch of scientists, they're about to be regulated out of business."

"How so?" Abby asked.

"Our season's a short one up here. The nine hundred of us living in Tadoussac have four months—June to October—to make enough money to last the year. But the rules for the guys running the boat tours have made it damn hard for them. Only so many are allowed per square hectare, and they can only get so close to a whale. That sort of thing."

"So what's your answer?"

"Leave us alone to take care of our river and bay," Marc said, more loudly than he'd intended. Up ahead, Sylvie and Françoise stopped and turned around.

Marc took a deep breath, well aware he had no right to wage this verbal attack against Abby. "I'm sorry. I guess I'm just tired of people who don't even live here telling us how to run our lives."

"I can see that."

"Da-ad!" Sylvie called. "Hurry up!"

"We're coming," he said, and started walking with Abby. "Look, I know you have a job to do and I respect that, but if you can stand it, here's a piece of free advice."

Abby smiled. "I'm all ears."

"While you're here, take some time to get to know the people. Who knows? You might learn something."

ABBY DIDN'T KNOW how to react to Marc's attack on her profession. Fortunately, she was spared having to say anything thanks to Sylvie. Overjoyed to have an audience, the little girl kept up a constant stream of chatter during the rest of the ten-minute walk to the restaurant.

As Sylvie pointed out the various homes and

businesses and where different side streets led, Abby mulled over Marc's words. In her undergraduate work in marine biology and doctoral program in bioacoustics, she had come across numerous accounts of the decline of the Saint Lawrence fisheries, but she had to admit that Marc's was the first version she had heard from the fishermen's perspective.

Should she respond to his accusations? It was probably better to remain silent. She probably wouldn't be seeing him much this summer anyway.

Sylvie announced they had reached Pierrette's and led the way up the stairs.

Marc held the door for the women and Sylvie made a beeline for a table in the corner. "Can I get some *poutine*, Dad?" she asked before the adults had a chance to take their seats.

"How about we get a large order and share?" Marc said, sitting down next to his daughter. "You want to get in on this?" he asked Abby, who was seated opposite him.

"Sure, okay. What's *poutine?*"

"What's *poutine?*" Sylvie repeated in astonishment. "*Everyone* knows what *poutine* is!"

"Sylvie!" Marc and Françoise said in unison.

Sylvie picked up a menu and held it in front of her face. "I know, I know. Think it but don't say it."

"*Poutine* is a kind of French fries," Marc said, a grin tugging at the corners of his mouth.

"I thought French fries were *pommes frites,*" Abby said.

"In Québec, *poutine* is our own special kind of fries," Marc told her.

Abby shrugged. "Sounds good to me."

She opened her own menu and sent up a silent prayer of thanks that it was printed in French and English. A waitress appeared and it was obvious to Abby she knew the Doucettes.

"I'll have the Caesar salad with grilled chicken and a cup of French onion soup, please," Abby said, when the woman, who introduced herself as Claudine, turned to her, pen poised over her order pad.

"To drink?" Claudine asked.

"Iced tea?"

"That sounds really good," Françoise said when it was her turn. "I'll have the same, please."

"*Et tu?*" Claudine said to Sylvie.

"Can I have a hamburger and chocolate milkshake, please?" the little girl said, looking at Marc.

"That'll be a hamburger and a glass of white milk," Marc amended. "I'll have the roast chicken, please, and a cup of coffee."

"*Bon.*" Claudine said and left, returning minutes later with their drinks.

Abby took a sip of her iced tea and looked around. Aside from their small party, the only other diners were a couple of teenagers in a booth and three young men sharing a pitcher of beer at a table by the window.

"Quiet place," she said.

"Sure, right now it is," Marc agreed. "But like everything else in this town, try getting in after the end of June."

"What do people do here during the winter?" Abby asked.

Marc grinned. "Wait for spring."

Claudine reappeared and set a steaming plate down in the middle of the table.

Abby had never seen anything quite like it. "Did we order this?"

"That's the *poutine,*" Sylvie said happily, stabbing at the middle of the plate with her fork.

"Sylvie," Marc said in a warning tone, "wait your turn, *ma fille.*"

"Sorry, Dad." She withdrew the fork and looked at Abby.

"I thought you said *poutine* was French fries," Abby said.

"The French fries are under the gravy," Marc explained.

"And those little white—nuggets?" Abby knew she sounded skeptical.

"Cheese curds," Françoise said.

Marc reached for her plate. "I guess you could call this a true Québecois delicacy."

"Really." Abby watched Marc scoop out a large portion of golden fries smothered in the brown gravy and ripe cheese curds onto her plate and set it down in front of her. "Funny, when I thought of Québecois delicacies, I pictured croissants, crepes and soufflés," Abby said, looking suspiciously at the mound of *poutine*.

"Common mistake." Marc passed a serving of the *poutine* to his mother and took Sylvie's plate.

"We have all those things, of course," Françoise said. "But *poutine*, it's one of our own creations."

Abby poked her fork tentatively at the gooey mass on her plate, unsure of when she had ever seen anything that looked so unappetizing. Not wanting to appear rude, she took a small bite. Her eyes widened and she smiled.

"It's delicious," she said, taking another, larger, forkful.

"Another convert," Marc said triumphantly as Claudine brought the rest of the meal.

The remainder of the evening passed with the small talk of people getting to know each other. Abby deliberately avoided the touchy subject of her impending research, and Marc didn't refer to it, either.

When the checks came, Marc snatched up Abby's as well, before she could take it.

"No, I insist," he said when she started to protest. "Your first meal out in Tadoussac is on me."

"All right," Abby said with a smile. "Thank you. But the next one's on me."

"Fair enough."

IT WAS FULL DARK when the foursome walked out of the restaurant and the period streetlights lining the town's main street were glowing in the light mist drifting in off the bay.

"I want to thank you again for supper," Abby said to Marc as they made their way toward the Doucette home.

"My pleasure." Marc knew he had to explain his earlier intensity, though he wasn't about to apologize. "And look, I didn't mean to offend you about the fishing regulations and all. It's just, well, it's something I feel pretty strongly about."

"No kidding," Abby said. "And I hope you understand that I feel pretty strongly about what I do. And I'm certainly not here to put anyone out of work."

Marc nodded. *They never are,* he thought to himself.

CHAPTER THREE

THE FOG from the night before was just burning off when Abby shut the gate behind her the next morning. She looked back over the fence and saw Figgy contentedly chewing on a bone next to the apartment door. Confident the small dog would be fine until lunch, Abby turned, hitched her bag up onto her shoulder and walked down the road in the direction of the marine center.

The facility itself was housed in a large, three-story building on the banks of the Saguenay River. A sloping driveway led down to the structure through a parking lot and past a spacious dry dock.

During the five minutes it took for Abby to walk from her apartment to the center, she didn't pass a single person on the sidewalk. Off to her left, she could see some activity around a few of the boats tied to the town dock, but that was it. Farther out, past the bay, the mist still hung over the Saint Lawrence.

Glancing at her watch, Abby saw she was twenty minutes early for her introductory appointment with the center's director, so she forced herself to walk around the building for ten minutes before entering the double glass doors to the main lobby and visitors' center.

A pretty young woman at the front desk smiled at her. "May I help you?"

Abby walked over to the desk, reading the name tag on the woman's vest. "Yes, thank you, Marie. I have an eight-thirty appointment with Dr. Bouchard."

"Of course," Marie said, picking up the handset on her desk phone. "May I have your name, please?"

"Abby Miller. Dr. Abby Miller."

While Marie spoke softly into the phone, Abby looked around the lobby. The entire interior—walls, ceiling, carpeting—was blue. To the left of Marie's desk was a gift shop, its shelves crammed with stuffed plush whales, whale books, CDs of whale songs, posters of sea life, and the usual coffee mugs, glasses, T-shirts, hats, tote bags and key chains all with the whale theme.

"Dr. Miller?" Abby turned at the deep baritone voice to see a smiling, bearded man she judged to be in his late thirties.

"Dr. Bouchard?"

"I'm very pleased to meet you," Peter Bouchard extended a hand. "Welcome, and please, call me Pete. We're a pretty informal bunch around here, as you'll quickly see."

"Thank you." Abby shook the director's hand. "It's great to finally be here."

"Everyone is looking forward to meeting you. Most of the researches are out for the week, taking some last days off before the summer season begins. But they'll start trickling back in by the weekend. If you'd like, I can show you around."

"I'd love it," Abby said. "If we have time for it now."

Pete shook his head. "Now's the perfect time. Besides, I'm very proud of this place and welcome the opportunity to show it off."

Abby laughed, already liking the man who would supervise her research for the next twelve months. "Then by all means, lead on."

"This is our public area." Pete indicated the lobby and gift shop. "You've already met Marie?"

"Not formally," Abby said, shaking the woman's hand. "Hello."

"Marie is our director of volunteers," Pete told her.

"Do you have many volunteers here?" Abby asked.

"We have a volunteer staff of around thirty," Marie said. "They do everything from run the gift shop to give museum tours."

"In addition to Marie's volunteer army, we have ten full-time researchers working out of here with another half-dozen lab assistants," Pete told Abby. "Plus a full maintenance crew and a small secretarial staff."

Pete directed Abby into a darkened room to the left of the entryway.

"This is our museum," Pete said, as they walked down the hallway. "Keep in mind, we've still got two weeks before we officially open to the public, so things look a little rough right now. It's taken longer than we planned to change our exhibit for the year."

Both sides of the hall were pocketed with enclosed display cases depicting the life cycle of the Saguenay whales. In the museum itself, the first thing Abby saw was a massive skeleton of a fin whale hung from the ceiling, keeping a silent watch on a large-scale model of the Saguenay River Fjord, Tadoussac Bay and the surrounding area.

Along the walls, display cases hung open with an array of smaller marine models, and literature and photographs lay scattered around the floor.

"See what I mean." Pete touched the corner of

a drop cloth with the toe of his shoe. "But we'll have it ready to go by the time the tourists get here," he said confidently. "Now, right through here...." He led Abby through a door on the far side of the room marked Employees Only.

"The labs are all on the second floor," Pete said as they walked up a flight of stairs that opened into a long hallway, doors on either side.

They stopped at the second door and Pete rapped softly on the jamb.

"Chris, you in here?"

"Yo, boss, right here." A young man in a garish Hawaiian shirt and khaki shorts, his long blond hair tied back in a ponytail, bounced up from behind a stack of boxes, clipboard in hand.

"Chris Gervais, meet Dr. Abby Miller. Abby, this is Chris. You'll want to be very, very nice to him. He oversees the assignment of all laboratory space here and he is only too aware of the power he holds."

Chris shook Abby's hand. "Don't believe a word he says. I can't be swayed by sweet talk. Now, cash bribes, that's another matter entirely."

Abby laughed. "Happy to meet you, Chris. We'll have to talk about those bribes."

"Too late," Chris said with a grin. "Got your assignment right here. Your area's acoustic imprints, right?"

"That's right," Abby said.

"Okay, so I've set you up near the auditory lab. Your application didn't say anything about needing office space, but we have a couple of available rooms on the third floor. They don't have the best views in the place, but it would be all yours."

"Might not be a bad idea to take one," Pete said. "Just to give yourself a quiet place where you can go and shut the door. Plus, you could have your phone in there."

Abby nodded. "If there's space available, sure, that sounds great."

"Okay, then," Chris said. "Let's go back to my office and we'll get you squared away."

"Why don't you go on ahead with Chris," Pete suggested. "I'll wait for you in my office."

Back in Chris's office, Abby stood while he rummaged in a desk drawer for a moment, finally rising with a cry of triumph. "Aha! Here we go. Put out your hand."

Abby did as he instructed and he gave her four keys. "This one's to the front door, to the lab, to the audio lab and this one's to your office. I have all the duplicates in case you lose or forget one. See me for any lab supplies you need. We should have pretty much everything you could want in stock, but I have my own system for keeping track of it. It's convoluted, but it works. And since I'm the only one who understands it, it assures a bit of job security."

Abby laughed and, after getting directions, walked upstairs to the administrative level. Counting down the doorways, she stopped outside Pete's office. Peeking around the partially open door, she saw the director behind his desk, phone at his ear. He signaled for her to enter.

The director had what must have been the best view in the place. The windows of the corner office looked over the bay on one side and the Saguenay River on the other. As Pete spoke on the phone, Abby watched the ferry coming across the river.

"Okay," Pete said, hanging up the phone. "What do you think so far?"

"I think it's wonderful." Abby meant it.

"Good, very good. I have to tell you, we're all pretty excited about your research. It shows some real promise for long-term interest. The more we can learn about the effects of man-made noise pollution on beluga, the better we can help formulate policies to protect them."

"That's my goal," Abby agreed.

Pete leaned back, kicked his feet onto his desk and laced his hands behind his head. "I have to say, we were all pretty impressed with your credentials. University of Massachusetts doesn't exactly give graduate degrees away."

Abby blushed slightly. "Thank you."

"So, when did the sea first capture you?"

Abby laughed. "I can't really say. To be honest, I can't remember a time when I wasn't involved in something to do with marine sciences. I grew up in the little town of Wellfleet, on Cape Cod. My parents were both teaching scholars with the Cape Cod National Seashore Park. Mom's an anthropologist studying the indigenous people's uses of beached pilot whales, and dad's made the study of the physiology behind pilot whale beachings his life's work. Some of my earliest memories are of going out on the boat with them on research trips. When I was old enough, they hired me as their assistant and boat worker."

"I've read their papers—groundbreaking stuff," Pete said. "And you? Do you hope to follow in their footsteps?"

"You mean the groundbreaking part?" Abby smiled. "Well, that's every scientist's dream, isn't it? No, I'm here to add what I can to the general body of knowledge."

Abby knew her answer sounded rehearsed. Probably because it was. Growing up as the daughter of Drs. Norman and Lowell Miller had been both a blessing and a curse throughout her life. The shadow her parents cast was a huge one and Abby desperately hoped her own research in Tadoussac would finally enable her to step out of it.

In college and later in graduate school, every time she had met a new professor or scholar, the initial introductions were inevitably followed by comments about knowing the Millers and their work. Intellectually, Abby knew these people were not comparing her to her parents. Still, even now, she was plagued with the uneasy notion that she never quite measured up to her parents.

Belatedly, she realized Pete had said something.

"I'm sorry, could you repeat that?" she asked, feeling a bit foolish.

"I said, we welcome that." Pete leaned across the desk. "The data you collect this year on the effects of noise pollution—especially from watercraft—will be an invaluable tool to help us recommend regulations controlling the whale-watching industry. There's still so much we don't know about the extent the boats impact the whales' social behavior, breeding, calving, feeding and other life processes."

"And that's where I come in," Abby said.

"Right you are."

"How many permit-holding whale-watching boats are there around here?" Abby asked.

"A little more than fifty."

"Sounds like I'll have plenty of opportunity to study the effects of sound on the beluga."

"Anxious to get started?"

"Very," Abby assured him.

"Okay, then." Pete nodded. Abby had the feeling he was holding something back.

"Is there anything else I should know?" she asked.

Pete sighed and picked up a piece of paper off his desk. "In your acceptance letter, it was mentioned that you'd have regular, scheduled use of a boat."

"That's right. I need it to set my sensing equipment in the bay and up the Fjord and then make regular checks on them. In fact, I can't do much else until those are in."

"I see." Pete cleared his throat and looked Abby in the eye. "Well, I'm afraid that might be a problem."

"What kind of problem?"

"Normally, we operate two research vessels—"

"I know, the *Mistral* and the *Caprice*. Either one sounds perfect for what I need," Abby assured him.

"I'm sure they are," Pete said. "Trouble is, the *Mistral* went into dry dock two days ago and I just found out she won't be seaworthy for at least two months, maybe the whole season."

This was not good news.

"The thing is," Pete continued, "the schedules were already set and had to be redone for the one vessel with priority time going to our senior researchers."

Abby was getting a very bad feeling.

"Unfortunately," Pete said, "we couldn't fit you in."

Abby closed her eyes and took a deep breath. No boat meant no soundings. No soundings meant no data collection and no data meant no research analysis. The disappointment was palpable and she felt near tears.

"I do have an alternative," Pete said hastily.

"Really?" Abby's spirits lifted slightly.

"There are a limited number of charter boats available in Tadoussac. If you could find one, I'm sure the center could certify it and then you could use part of your grant to pay for it."

Abby thought that possibility over. "Do you have a charter you could recommend?" she asked.

Pete shook his head. "We're not allowed to," he said. "We get funding from the government and all of our business has to be based on bids. I can, however, give you a list of boats and their captains." He pulled a sheet of paper from a desk drawer and handed it to Abby.

It was a very short list, Abby thought, scanning it.

"Well, I'm glad I accepted the office," she said, standing. "Now I know how I'll spend my first day—calling boat captains."

THREE HOURS LATER, Abby hung up the phone in her new office, folded her arms on her desk and laid her head down on them.

There had been ten boats, and none of the captains were at the contact number listed next to each name. Abby had spent the morning tracking down the captains and had been referred to, among other places, a marina office, a café, a garage and a warehouse. When she'd finally reached them, one by one, they had said they were too busy or already booked for the entire summer, or else quoted a price that far exceeded the limits of her budget. It was not an auspicious beginning to her summer.

Raising her head, she looked at the clock mounted on the wall and saw it was close to noon. *Might as well break for lunch,* she thought.

Thinking she'd see if Pete or Chris would like to join her, she walked past the director's office, but saw the door was shut. Hearing the sound of several voices coming from within, she continued on without knocking. Downstairs in Chris's office, she saw the lab director was on the phone and decided to leave him undisturbed, as well.

For lack of anything better to do, she decided to walk down to the wharf across from the building and look around. At the foot of the center's dock, she saw the gleaming blue and red hull of the research vessel *Caprice* bobbing gently up and down. Abby watched enviously as a team of workers loaded equipment and supplies on board.

Continuing down the path to the docks, she considered her options. Find a boat and find it fast, or revamp her entire project. At the moment, the former seemed impossible, and the latter unacceptable.

MARC LOVED spending time doing routine maintenance on his boat. He found the work immensely satisfying. The engines of the *Percé* ran superbly, thanks to his regular attentions. He'd just spent the morning draining and replacing the oil and had come up to deck for some fresh air when he spotted a familiar form walking down the dock.

"Well, ahoy there," he called to Abby. He saw her looking around. "Up here."

Turning, she spotted Marc on the deck and watched him climb down the ship's ladder and hop onto the wharf next to her.

"How's your first day going?" Marc said, wiping his oily hands on a rag.

"I'm not sure."

"What's wrong?"

"Nothing, really," she said. "Well, nothing I can't figure out."

"Can I help?"

"Not unless you can get the owner of this boat to let me use it for the summer."

Marc looked at her a moment. "I thought the center had boats for the scientists to use."

"So did I," Abby said, sounding bitter. She told Marc about the loss of the *Mistral*.

"So, what you're saying is, without a boat, you can't do what you came here to do?" Marc asked.

"That's right," Abby said.

"And your research? What happens to it?"

"I honestly don't know. My grant is good for one year, and I may be able to get an extension. But it's more than that. I've worked too long and too hard to get here. And now, to think it might all have been for nothing…."

Marc heard her voice catch and swore he saw tears in the corners of her eyes. "I might be able to help you out."

She looked skeptical. "Really? How?"

"Were you serious about talking to the owner of this boat?" He jerked his thumb over his shoulder.

"Yes, yes, I was," Abby said eagerly. "Do you

know him? Do you know how I could get a hold of him?"

Marc nodded.

"Today?"

"Right now, if you want."

"Yes, please."

She sounded so excited, Marc couldn't tease her any longer. "Okay then. Allow me to introduce myself—Marc Doucette, captain, owner and first, second and third mate of the *Percé*."

"You! You own a boat—*this* boat?" Abby appeared flabbergasted.

"I do, or rather, she owns me," Marc explained. "That's kind of how it goes with boats."

"And you do charters?"

"Not normally. I'd rather haul freight to remote construction sites. Pays a helluva lot better than charters, but those pickings are pretty slim these days. And I've already told you the shape of the fishing industry around here. Want to come aboard and take a look?"

"Sure, I'd love to," Abby said.

"Okay, take hold of the ladder rung and then pull yourself up, like this." Marc grabbed a rung and swung himself up from the dock and onto the ladder. He quickly scrambled up, threw one leg over the rail and turned to give Abby a hand.

"Impressive," he said after she scooted unaided

up the ladder and over the rail to stand next to him. "Welcome aboard the *Percé.*"

"What does *Percé* mean?" Abby asked, looking around.

"I named her after *rocher Percé,*" Marc explained. "One of my favorite spots in Québec. It's this massive stone on the tip of Gaspé Peninsula with a huge natural arch in it. *Rocher Percé* literally translates to 'pierced rock.' If you get a chance, you ought to go check it out sometime."

"I might just do that," Abby said, "but right now, I'm more interested in *Percé* the boat."

"Forty-four feet from aft to bow, with a twelve-and-a-half foot beam," Marc said, unable to keep the tinge of pride from his voice. "She sleeps eight, has a full galley, head and plenty of storage space." He pointed above them. "The bridge is completely enclosed and accessible from deck or inside. She's outfitted with twin diesels and has all the latest GPS and navigational equipment." Marc pounded the rail with his fist. "She could use a coat of paint, but she's solid through and through."

"I wonder why you weren't on the list of available charters they gave me," Abby said.

"Probably because up until last night, I had no intention of doing charter work, so I hadn't put the word out yet. I've been working as a mechanic for some of the other captains. But that work's slowing down and my other plans kind of fell through."

"Can I take a look around?" Abby asked.

"Be my guest." Marc led her through the hatch to the lower decks. A narrow stairway ended in the galley, its appliances gleaming. Marc congratulated himself on keeping everything clean and in order. He knew how important first impressions were to closing a deal. He pointed down a hallway. "At the end there's the master bedroom and three smaller cabins. Two on the stern side and one on port, next to the head."

Abby walked down the hall and peeked into the boat's small bathroom. Next, she opened one of the cabin doors and peered inside. "Would I be able to use one of these bedrooms as lab space?"

Marc nodded. "Sure. In fact, you could pretty much move things around to suit your needs. Only place that's off limits is the master bedroom."

Abby raised an eyebrow.

"Home sweet home," Marc replied to her unasked question. "I'm bunking here for the summer. But that's not a problem," he added hastily. "Actually, it's a good deal, because whatever gear and equipment you bring on board won't be left unattended at night."

"I thought you had a place in town," Abby said, rejoining him in the galley.

"I do. But summer rentals are a premium around here, so I decided to let it out for the season. It's good money."

"Will Sylvie live here, too?"

"No, she's going to stay at my mother's."

"Figgy will like that," Abby said. "Now, you understand I need a boat for the entire summer, every day or at least on call."

Marc nodded. "Sure."

"That means no other charters once I bring my stuff on board."

"I understand. I can live with that." He could tell Abby was warming to the idea of having a boat for her exclusive use.

"Of course, I have some rules of my own," he said.

"Oh?"

"Once you're on board, keep in mind I'm the captain and what I say goes. If I think the conditions or situations warrant it, your plans may have to change. I won't put us or this boat in danger. Can you live with that?"

"I think so," Abby said. "I have to ask you, though—"

"Yeah?"

"Well, you know I'm here to do research and

you've already made your feelings on that score pretty clear. Agreeing to let me charter your boat is a huge favor. Why would you want to do that?"

Marc shrugged. "Simple economics. You need a boat and I have a boat. You have the funding to pay for it and I need the money. Besides—" he grinned "—what's that old saying? Keep your friends close and your enemies closer?"

Abby smiled back at him, and he was suddenly struck by how beautiful she was.

"True," she said "but are you sure you want to strike a deal with the devil?"

"As long as the devil's paying, you bet."

"I can definitely pay." Abby quoted him the price budgeted in the grant.

The amount was fair, Marc thought, though probably less than what he could make from day or weekend trips. Still, it would be a steady, guaranteed income. "Dr. Miller," he said, offering her his hand to shake on the deal, "you got yourself a boat."

CHAPTER FOUR

BACK ON TRACK! Everything was back on track and Abby couldn't have been happier. She felt like skipping down the dock but managed to resist the temptation. She could not, however, keep the grin off her face.

After leaving Marc, she retraced her steps to the marine building, anxious to get started on her work. She didn't want to waste any time in getting Peter's approval of the *Percé* as a designated research vessel.

Pushing open the center's glass doors, she spotted the director walking into the darkened interior of the museum. He looked over his shoulder at the sound of his name being called out.

"Well, don't you just look like the whale who swallowed the krill?" Peter teased. "If you don't mind the marine analogy."

"I don't mind one bit," Abby said happily.

"Anyone who goes from looking as down in the

mouth as you did this morning to having her feet barely touch the ground either just won the lotto or found a research boat."

Abby laughed. "The latter."

"Hey, way to hustle." Peter headed through the swinging doors into the museum, Abby following. "What's the boat? Marie told me she saw you on your way out to lunch and you'd struck out with the list I gave you." The director pulled a pad and pen from his shirt pocket.

"The *Percé*," Abby said. "Do you know it?

The director looked up, his expression serious. "The *Percé*? Is that Doucette's boat?"

"Yes, yes it is. Marc Doucette." Abby felt a sense of unease. "Is that a problem?"

He didn't answer immediately. "No, no, I don't think so," Peter said slowly. "It's just kind of a surprise, that's all."

"You mean because his boat wasn't on the list you gave me?" Abby asked. "He told me that was because he'd only just decided to take on charters."

Peter nodded. "That and, well, let's just say Marc Doucette has a certain, how shall I put this? A certain *reputation* around here."

"What sort of reputation?"

"Well, not to put too fine a point on it, he's not exactly a huge fan of our work."

"Oh, you don't need to tell me that." Abby

quickly recapped the conversation she and Marc had shared on the walk to the restaurant the previous evening.

"Yeah, that sounds like Doucette," Peter said. "Then there was the incident last summer."

"What happened?" Abby asked.

Peter sighed. "Look, I don't want to dash your hopes, not when you've done so well in fixing the problem we left you with. But you'd better keep on your toes around Marc Doucette."

That sounded like a warning. "Why, is he dangerous?" Abby asked.

"No, at least I don't think so."

"But what about last summer?" Abby insisted.

"There was a group of science students from Université Laval in a Zodiac out in the bay…here on a field trip," Peter began. "Now, keep in mind no one saw anything specific, but when the students came back, they reported to the RCMP they thought a boat was deliberately harassing a pod of beluga. Turns out it was the *Percé*."

Abby wasn't sure what to make of the tale. "What happened?"

"Nothing," Peter said. "It was the students' word against Doucette's so the charge was never proven. If it had been, I'd be telling you to look for another boat."

Abby tried to reconcile the man who had

helped her with Figgy on the ferry with someone who would recklessly endanger whales.

"Then there's all his talk about what's happened to the fishing fleet. It's no secret he blames people like you and me for that. You heard that for yourself."

Abby thought a moment before speaking. "Do you think it's a mistake for me to charter his boat?"

Peter shook his head. "You said he made the offer?"

Abby nodded.

"Then I think you'll be fine. Just be careful what you say around him. He's a local boy and could cause trouble for you or the center if he wanted to."

"I'm renting an apartment from his mother, you know."

"Françoise? Hell of a nice lady. Not to mention one mean baker." He frowned. "Hey, stop looking so droopy. There shouldn't be a problem with either Marc or the *Percé*. I'll see about certifying the boat for research myself. Drop by my office on your way out today and pick up the forms Marc needs to sign."

Abby felt her spirits lifting. "What kind of forms?"

"Typical government paperwork. Insurance

guarantees, maintenance records, legal documentation, that kind of thing. Nothing Doucette's
never seen before."

"Thank you." That sounded straightforward
enough, Abby thought with relief. "How are
things going for your summer opening?"

"Getting there," Peter said, indicating the
display case. "We're just updating the materials to
make them interactive. The kids are going to love
it."

Abby peered closer at the cases and saw large,
colored buttons below each one. "What do these
do?" she asked.

"When they're up and running, they're going
to put the whole tidal flow into real time, accel-
erated time and slow motion."

"How does it work?" Abby had always loved
interactive displays and wondered how this one
would be set up.

Peter laughed. "Hey, I'm a marine biologist, not
a computer nerd. I can tell you how the real thing
works out there," he jerked his thumb in the direction of the fjord out the window above their heads,
"but I'll leave the techno-speak to the experts."

The director was being pleasant, but Abby
could tell he wanted to get back to his work. She
excused herself and with a slight wave headed
toward the stairway. Once in her new office, she

began making notes of all the equipment and supplies she would need before she could start her field work on the *Percé*.

The other offices were empty, so Abby had the third floor to herself. For a time, the only sounds were the muted street noise coming in through her open window and the scratching of her pen on paper. But try as she might, Abby could not keep her mind on the equipments lists and sound sampling schedules in front of her. An image of Marc Doucette kept intruding. Marc with his intense eyes, unruly hair, sun-creased face and boyish smile. Not to mention, the hard muscular body beneath his jeans and white T-shirt.

"Oh for heaven's sake!" she said. "Come on, girl, keep it together." How long had it been? Abby thought to herself. She knew the answer well enough. It had been six years since her last serious relationship. Up until her arrival in Tadoussac, she would have said that was not nearly long enough.

Now here was Marc Doucette, a knight in blue jeans coming to her rescue with his boat. *Business,* Abby told herself. *This relationship must remain strictly business.* She had one year only to prove to the oversight board at Woods Hole that her project was worthy of future funds. Not to mention to her brilliant parents and the world at large her worth as a researcher in her own right. No, she was not about to waste another summer on a man. No matter how good he looked in Levi's.

CHAPTER FIVE

ABBY WOULD HAVE LIKED to talk to Chris before leaving for the day, but the ponytailed lab supervisor was nowhere to be seen. Instead, she scrawled a note and pinned it to the board on his office door, asking if he would have time to meet with her the following day to organize the sensoring gear she planned to use aboard the *Percé*.

Waving good night to Marie, she walked out the front doors and headed up the street to her apartment. The instant she pushed open the gate leading to the backyard, she was tackled by a brown, furry streak.

"Figgy! Down, girl, easy..." The dog obediently sat on her haunches and grinned up at Abby.

"Miss M—Abby!" Sylvie called from the back porch. "Guess what? I taught Figgy a trick. Want to see? I can show you right now. Can I?"

Abby laughed, and set her purse and briefcase on the ground next to the door leading to her apartment. She figured the little girl had gotten the dog to sit and stay for a cookie or chase and retrieve a ball. "Sure, show me what you've got."

"Okay!" Sylvie said with real enthusiasm. "Figgy, c'mere." Figgy whirled around and trotted over to Sylvie. Together, girl and dog walked over to a makeshift teeter-totter in the corner of the yard.

"Are you watching?" Sylvie called back over her shoulder.

"I'm watching," Abby said, curious to see what was about to happen.

Sylvie gave a hand signal and Figgy promptly sat down, then Sylvie walked around the teeter-totter until she stood opposite the dog. When she gave a second hand signal, Figgy sprang up, ran to the end of the teeter-totter that was resting on the ground, stepped on it and walked up the plank until her own weight caused the other end to lower. The little dog then walked down the other side, hopped off the plank and sat down facing Sylvie.

"Good girl!" Sylvie said. "What do you think? Pretty cool, huh?"

Abby was speechless. It was beyond cool.

"Sylvie," she said. "How on earth did you teach Figgy to do that? In one day?"

Sylvie shrugged. "I just did," she said, scratching the dog's ears. "It was fun."

MARC HAD WATCHED the entire demonstration from the kitchen window. It was obvious to him from Abby's reaction to the trick that this was the first time the little dog had walked a balance beam. Had Sylvie really taught the dog to do that in a day? And if she could do that, why could she not gain that confidence when it came to her reading and writing skills?

"Impressive, isn't it?"

Marc turned at the sound of his mother's voice.

"I'll say. How long's she been working with that dog?"

"Ever since she got home this afternoon," Françoise told him. "Marc, I've never seen anything like it. It's as if she's talking to that dog and the dog understands every word she's saying."

Marc snorted.

"I'm telling you, it was amazing," Françoise insisted. "The way she just kept at it, and so patient."

"Too bad she doesn't approach her schoolwork the same way." Marc watched Sylvie lead the dog through the routine once again. He turned back to his mother. "You say she did this all on her own?"

Françoise nodded.

A familiar feeling of helplessness came over Marc. It was like his daughter's exceptional drawing abilities. They seemed to spring from some deep reservoir of talent, but one that didn't extend to reading and writing. Was it all a matter of confidence?

"You're meeting with Madame Simard tomorrow, aren't you?" his mother asked.

"Hmm?" Marc was still watching his daughter.

"Madame Simard, Sylvie's teacher? You're meeting with her tomorrow, remember?"

"Oh yeah, that's right, I am."

"I wonder what she'd make of this," Françoise said.

He would find out tomorrow, Marc thought.

"SYLVIE, you're a miracle worker!" Abby said, after the girl led Figgy through her teeter-totter routine a third time. "And you," she said to the small dog, "you're just full of surprises, aren't you?" Figgy wagged her tail in agreement, then rolled over to have her belly rubbed.

Kneeling down to comply with the dog's wishes, Sylvie said, "Can I teach her more tricks tomorrow?"

Abby laughed. "Sure. What did you have in mind?"

Sylvie shrugged. "Don't know. Dad has some old tires somewhere. Maybe Figgy can jump through them."

"Just remember she's a little dog," Abby said, bending to retrieve her purse and case. "Now, if you'll excuse us, I want to take Figgy for a walk along the beach before supper."

"Can I come, too?" Sylvie asked, eyes bright.

"I think you've had enough time with Abby's dog for one day, *ma fille*."

Abby and Sylvie both turned to see Marc standing on the porch.

"Abby would probably like some time alone with her dog," he said.

"Aw, Dad," Sylvie protested.

"And I bet you have homework, don't you?"

Sylvie grimaced. "Yeah, I guess so," she mumbled.

"Thanks for being such a good playmate for Figgy, Sylvie," Abby said to soften the girl's disappointment. "It makes things a lot easier for me to know someone is looking out for her."

"I had a good time." Sylvie patted Figgy on the head. "Bye, Figgy. See you tomorrow."

Abby watched her disappear into the house.

"I'll be there in a moment, *ma fille*," Marc called, then walked down the steps to stand next to Abby. "Are you sure she's not being a bother?"

Abby laughed. "Quite the opposite."

"Okay, but if she gets to be too much, let me know. I guess I don't have to tell you she's already in love with Figgy."

"I think it's mutual," Abby said.

"How'd it go at the center?" Marc asked. "Any problems when you mentioned the *Percé?*"

Abby shook her head. "No, but I do have these forms for you to fill out and sign." She dug in her briefcase and pulled out a large manila envelope and handed it to Marc.

He took it and stuck it under his arm. "I'll take a look at them tonight and give them to you first thing in the morning. Is that okay?"

"That should be fine. Peter—Dr. Bouchard—led me to believe the faster he gets them back, the quicker you get paid."

"Pete Bouchard, huh?" Marc grinned. "And how is his lordship these days?"

"Oh, you two know each other?" Abby said neutrally.

Marc nodded. "Yeah, Pete and I go way back. He was a senior at Tadoussac High School when I first made the varsity soccer team."

"I never pegged you as a jock." An image of a younger Marc Doucette running up and down the soccer field flashed through Abby's mind.

Marc laughed. "I wasn't. But there's not much to do in Tadoussac, and out of town games gave us the chance to meet pretty girls."

"That's something I never considered," Abby said wryly.

"And Pete was cool with using the *Percé?*" Marc was serious now.

"He was glad I'd found a boat so quickly," she said carefully.

"That doesn't answer my question."

Abby wasn't quite sure how much she should tell Marc. "Well…" she started awkwardly.

"Okay, spit it out. If we're going to be spending a lot of time together, I need to know the score."

"You're right," Abby said. "Pete mentioned something about college kids seeing you harass a pod of whales and the RCMP getting involved. Not that anything was ever proven, but he said I should be careful.…" She heard her own voice trailing away as Marc's eyes turned hard as flint.

"Go on," he said evenly.

"He suggested I should be careful because you could cause trouble for the center," Abby finished hastily.

Marc barked a humorless laugh. "*I* could cause trouble for *them?* That's rich." He shook his head. "I can't believe that whole stupid story hasn't died. You want to know what happened? Why nothing was ever proven?"

Abby nodded.

"I was out in the bay, just coming in with some cargo from Rivière-du-Loup when these kids in a Zodiac came screaming between my boat and this group of whales. They started cutting circles around the whales, herding them into a tighter and tighter bunch. I thought for sure they were going to hit one. Anyway, I got on my horn and yelled for them to knock it off, that I had their registration number from the boat and was going to turn them in. Well, the little shits beat me back to the dock, and by the time I got there, they had told the RCMP it was the *Percé* that'd been harassing the whales and that *they* had forced *me* to back off." Marc kicked at a loose rock near his boot. It was obvious that even a year later, the event still chaffed at him.

"Why didn't you tell all this to the authorities? To Pete and the RCMP?" Abby asked.

"What the hell good would it have done?" Marc said gruffly. "I'm a Tadoussac fisherman with a reputation for stirring up trouble when it comes to government regulations on the water. The kids in the Zodiac were science students from Laval. Be honest now, if you'd been there, who would you believe?"

When Abby hesitated before replying, Marc nodded. "Uh-huh, that's what I thought."

Abby was sure she'd seen a flash of hurt in his eyes.

He turned to walk back to the house, pausing on the top step. "I've got to be somewhere early tomorrow morning, so I'll leave these for you with my mom." He held up the envelope. Then he was gone behind the slam of the screen door.

MARC TOSSED THE ENVELOPE of forms onto the small table below the wall phone then slumped down on one of the kitchen chairs. Françoise had gone to deliver some gift baskets of bread and muffins and Sylvie was in her room. The house was silent. Marc let out a long breath and rubbed his temples with his fingers.

He'd figured the story about the kids in the Zodiac would get passed along to Abby at some point this summer. Marc just hadn't thought Pete would set a land-speed record doing it. "The jerk," Marc muttered, recalling the righteous indignation Bouchard had shown on the docks as he stood with the RCMP when Marc had jumped down from the *Percé*. The marine center's director had believed everything his precious little science students had told him.

The two men's mutual dislike stemmed all the way back to high school.

Though Pete was older, he'd lacked Marc's natural athleticism, a fact that rankled Pete to no end back in high school. It hadn't helped when halfway through the season, the soccer coach had made Marc a starting center, a move that had pushed Pete back to second string.

After Pete had graduated and left Tadoussac to attend college, Marc had lost track of him and was somewhat surprised when he showed up in Tadoussac several years ago to take the helm of the marine center. The son of a North Shore fisherman himself, Pete had become a rabid conservationist and strong proponent of regulations that Marc saw as detrimental to anyone who made a living on the water.

Since the Zodiac incident, Marc had kept his distance from the center and its staff. He glanced over at the envelope. *Am I ready to take on a job that will put me in direct contact with Pete Bouchard and the rest of the bunch down at the interpretive center?*

The answer came almost immediately as he sat in his mother's silent kitchen, the sun's fading rays dancing across the far wall. He needed the steady income the charter would provide. He had no choice but to say yes.

ABBY LOVED this time of day. The setting sun was casting the world in warm hues of red and orange. Out in the bay, pleasure boats bobbed gently in the still waters. She had let Figgy off his leash when they had reached the beach and now she looked for her. She spotted the dog romping in the surf about a hundred feet farther up the shore.

Abby grimaced as Figgy came trotting back. "You're going to smell wonderful tonight."

Figgy shook herself and sprayed Abby with salt water.

"Thanks," she said.

Abby knew she should have been concentrating on what needed to be done the next day to get her study going, but her thoughts kept drifting back to Marc and what a puzzle he presented.

On the one hand, if Pete was to be believed, Marc Doucette was a potential threat to the very marine mammals Abby had spent years studying. On the other hand, if not for Marc, those studies would be on indefinite hold. He had to have known that when he made the offer to charter the *Percé*. By his own admission, Marc had a healthy disdain for the kind of science Abby conducted, yet his contribution was going to be invaluable to the body of scientific knowledge surrounding the beluga. She shook her head. The man was, if nothing else, complicated.

Glancing at her watch, she saw it was getting late and realized she was hungry. Whistling for Figgy, who was growling at a large piece of sea kelp at the water's edge, she turned to head back to her apartment. By the time she had gotten back to the stairs leading up from the beach, she had reached a conclusion: A professional relationship with Marc Doucette, puzzling though he was, would not pose any real problem to her work. In the end, she told herself, that's all that mattered.

CHAPTER SIX

"I FORGOT TO TELL YOU, Suzanne Daigle called for you yesterday after you left," Françoise said as Marc helped himself to a third maple-pecan scone the next morning.

"Oh?" What on earth could the town's director of tourism want with him? "How's she doing?"

"Fine," Françoise said. "The baby's due in two months."

Marc laughed. "Just at the height of the tourist season. Suzanne always did have the best timing."

"Be nice," Françoise scolded. "She's about to make you a second cousin. Or is it first cousin, once removed? I never can keep those things straight." She shook her head. "Anyway, she wasn't calling to talk babies," Françoise carried the coffee pot to the table and refilled Marc's mug with the steaming black brew.

"Thanks," Marc said. "So, what did she want?"

Putting the pot back on the counter, Françoise picked up her own mug and sat down at the table.

"Suzanne got a call at the tourism center from a family in Hull looking for a place for the summer. I'd told her you had decided to rent the house out and she was wondering if it was still available."

Marc nodded. "Yeah, wow, that would be something if I could get that nailed down this week. Did she leave a number?"

"No," Françoise said, "but the people are supposed to call Suzanne back later this week."

"Okay, I'll drop by her office on the way to Sylvie's school and ask her to have them call me directly," Marc said. "If I'm not around, can I leave your number as a backup?"

"Sure. What do you want me to tell them if they call here?"

"Well, you know the house as well as I do, so let them know what's there. It's available anytime for as long as they'd like."

"What are you asking for rent?"

Marc considered a moment then rattled off a figure.

Françoise nodded. "That's about the going rate."

"Speaking of *going,* that's what I'd better do." Marc rose and carried his empty mug to the sink. "I'm going to walk Sylvie to school and talk to Madame Simard before classes begin."

"Sylvie's here?" Françoise said. "Where?"

Marc laughed. "Where do you think? She

spotted Abby's dog in the yard and that's as far as she got."

"Send her in to say good morning to her grandmother before you leave."

"Will do." Marc headed toward the back door. "And Mom?"

"Yes?"

"If this rental works out today, I'm thinking Sylvie will move in here over the weekend?"

"That's fine," Françoise said. "I'm looking forward to it."

"How was Figgy this morning?" Marc asked fifteen minutes later as father and daughter were walking up the street toward the school.

"Good," Sylvie said. "I sure wish I could stay with her all day."

"I know, *ma fille,* but school's important, too."

"I guess," Sylvie mumbled and then looked up at him. "Are you going to talk to Madame Simard today?"

"Mm-hmm."

Sylvie's eyes went round. "Am I in trouble?"

"Trouble, why would you think that?" Marc asked.

"Why else would you talk to my teacher?"

Marc thought a moment. It had been a long time since he'd been a kid in school, but he did remember the unholy terror that had filled him anytime his parents had gone to meet with his teachers, whether he had done anything wrong or not. "You're not in trouble, *ma fille*," he reassured his daughter. "Madame Simard just wants to talk about your studies and maybe how we can make it more fun for you."

"Oh." Sylvie didn't sound convinced.

They walked on in silence until they came to the Tadoussac tourism center. Marc instructed Sylvie to wait by the front door while he went inside. When he spoke with Suzanne, she agreed to pass along the information when the interested family called later in the week. After thanking her, Marc collected Sylvie and they continued on to school.

The closer they got to the four-story brick building, the slower Sylvie walked. By the time they were standing across the street from the school, she was visibly dragging her feet.

Hunkering down until he was eye level with his daughter, Marc said softly, "Sylvie, don't you like school?"

Not looking at him, she scuffed her right shoe along the sidewalk.

"Sylvie…" Marc tilted her chin up with his hand.

"I dunno," she said. "I guess."

"Don't you like coming here?"

She shrugged. "I guess."

"Is it Madame Simard?" Marc asked.

"No, she's okay."

"Is it the other kids?"

Another shrug. Marc felt his jaw tighten in frustration. His little girl was intelligent, of that he had no doubt. But what was preventing her from doing well at school? It was as if a door inside her had slammed shut the night Thérèse was killed. More and more the intense love he felt for his daughter was mingling with the emotions of helplessness and despair. Somehow, he was failing her.

"All right, *ma fille*." He stood up and took her hand before stepping into the street. "Let's go."

"WHAT CAN I TELL YOU? Sylvie has shown no marked improvement since you enrolled her here two years ago."

Through the open window, Marc could hear the sounds of youngsters laughing and yelling as they enjoyed their final moments of freedom before the day's lessons began.

Madame Simard, seated behind her desk, picked up a file folder and flipped it open. "Her homework and class projects are always turned in on time, but show no creativity and no indication of processing the materials."

"No creativity?" Marc found that hard to believe. "Madame Simard, have you looked at her drawings?"

The teacher nodded. "Oh yes, and they are quite good. But Sylvie spends way too much time at such things. I've told her time and time again, drawing is for art class."

"But, it's how she expresses herself," Marc said.

"Mr. Doucette," Madame Simard said impatiently, "art and expression are not helping Sylvie learn to read and write, and that's what we're here to talk about, aren't we?"

"Of course," Marc said. "Please, go on."

"As I said, there are other children who have had some trouble last year but are making great strides now. It's just Sylvie who is lagging behind."

Marc didn't miss the message in Beatrice Simard's words. Sylvie's failure to improve was no fault of the school's. He sighed. Why was it some teachers were such martinets?

"What do you suggest?" he asked, shifting as he felt his left buttock falling asleep in the cramped chair Madame Simard had offered him.

"Monsieur Doucette, we may have to consider the very real possibility that Sylvie will not be able to remain with her classmates this fall."

"I'm not sure I follow you," Marc said.

The teacher glanced down at the file folder. "I'm talking about Sylvie not advancing to the next grade."

"You mean hold her back a year?" Marc said.

The woman nodded, tapping the folder for effect. "The trouble is, it's not so much Sylvie *can't* do the work, it's that she *won't* do it."

"And you think holding her back will change that?" Marc asked.

Madame Simard did not answer right away. "Her mother died suddenly three years ago, is that correct?"

"Yes, a car accident in Toronto," Marc said. "Do you think that has something to do with this?"

"Sometimes when children experience such a sudden loss, it triggers latent learning disabilities and cognitive problems," Madame Simard said.

"Learning disabilities and cognitive problems?" Marc repeated.

Madame Simard nodded. "Imagine a lightbulb with a damaged filament. It may work fine until something suddenly hits it, then it simply goes out."

"Are you saying my daughter's brain is *damaged?*" Marc felt himself losing his temper.

"I'm suggesting her ability to learn may have

been affected, but without the proper tests, it's impossible to say." She shrugged. "But given her performance—or should I say lack of performance—in school, what other explanation could there be?"

Marc couldn't believe what he was hearing. Standing so suddenly his chair fell back to the floor with a crash, he leaned both his hands on Madame Simard's desk and glared at her.

"I think there might be any number of explanations," he said, struggling to keep from shouting.

"Monsieur Doucette, please understand, I'm not blaming you."

"No, maybe not," Marc said. "But I'm ready to blame you."

"Me?" Beatrice Simard's eyes flew wide. "Why on earth—"

"Because you are a teacher! And my daughter is your student. She's not damaged, she's not stupid. She's a little girl who needs to learn how to express herself in front of other people and *that's* your job, not forcing her to repeat a grade."

"I'm well aware of my job, Monsieur Doucette," Madame Simard said huffily.

Marc took a step back from the desk. "Good, so tell me how I can help you do your job better."

"I honestly don't know," the teacher said. "If you are determined to have Sylvie advance with her class, I will keep trying to get her up to the next level. But I warn you, if she's not improved by the time the fall term starts, the matter will be out of my hands."

"Meaning?" Marc said.

"Meaning the school board takes a dim view of passing students to the next grade who have not earned the appropriate marks. I'm asking you again to seriously consider another option—like repeating the year—for your daughter."

Marc jammed his hands into his pants pockets. As condescending as the teacher was, Marc knew she was right. What point was there in advancing Sylvie to the next grade if she couldn't do the work? But holding her back? How would she feel when her friends moved on ahead of her? No, there had to be a better way.

"I appreciate your input, madame," Marc said, "but for now, Sylvie is staying right where she is. When does the next report card come out?"

The teacher glanced at a calendar on the side of her desk. "At the end of June."

"Okay, then. Let's give Sylvie the next month and see how she's doing. If things haven't changed, then you and I can talk about her repeating a grade. Agreed?"

"That's fine, but I warn you, Monsieur Doucette, for Sylvie's sake, start considering it now. For her to show enough improvement to advance to the next grade at the start of fall term will take nothing short of a miracle."

"Then I guess I'd better start praying," Marc said.

FRANÇOISE WAS PULLING a pan of strawberry muffins from the oven when she heard a light tap on the back door. After setting the hot tray down on the nearest—and only—clear space on the counter, she dusted her hands on her apron and walked to the back of the house. Peering out the door's window, she saw Abby standing on the porch, looking as if she was heading off to work with briefcase in hand and a backpack slung over her shoulder.

"Abby, good morning," Françoise said with real pleasure, opening the door and ushering Abby inside. "How was your night?"

"Wonderful," Abby said. "I slept like a log. And the view from the loft! What a great sight to wake up to."

Françoise chuckled. "I'm glad you like it. Frankly, I was worried all that sun so early in the morning would keep you awake."

"Not a problem for me." Abby followed the older woman into the kitchen. "I'm an early riser from way back and… Omigod." She halted in the doorway.

Françoise spun around, alarmed at the sudden change in Abby's voice. "My dear, are you all right? What's wrong?"

"No, I'm fine, but what's all—all *this?*" Abby pointed into the kitchen

"All what?" Confused, Françoise followed Abby's gaze. Then understanding dawned on her and she laughed. "That?" she said. "Why, that's just the morning baking."

"Unbelievable. I bet this is what heaven is going to look like—and smell like."

Every available square inch of surface area in the kitchen was covered with some kind of baked good. Loaves of bread lined the counters next to the sink; the kitchen table was buried beneath trays of muffins, scones and individual squares of coffee cake. A folding table had been set up near the stove and was sagging under the weight of cookies and bear claws.

"Have you had your breakfast?" Françoise asked.

"No, not yet. But I did finally make it to the store last night, so I've got cereal." Abby was still staring at the goodies.

"Cereal," Françoise scoffed. "That's no break-fast. Here." She took Abby firmly by the arm and led her to the kitchen table. Pulling a chair out, Françoise motioned for the younger woman to sit down.

"Try one of these," she said, placing a plate down with a dark-colored muffin on it. "Something new I just started doing. They're *morning glory muffins,* and they've got molasses, ginger, carrot and zucchini in them."

Abby picked up one of the moist muffins and took a bite. "It's delicious."

"Thank you." Françoise raised her eyebrows. "I hope the people at the Hôtel Tadoussac agree."

"Why wouldn't they?"

"They can be a pretty particular lot up there," Françoise said.

"Summer people?" Abby asked, taking a sip of the coffee Françoise had placed before her and eyeing the platter of muffins.

"For the most part," Françoise said. "And for Lord's sake, don't be shy. Help yourself to another muffin or two." She pushed the plate toward Abby.

"Well, maybe just one more," Abby said, taking a muffin. "For the road."

"How do you know about summer people?" Françoise asked.

Abby laughed and almost choked on the muffin. "Sorry," she said, composing herself. "I grew up with them—or should I say I grew up *working* for them—on Cape Cod."

Françoise nodded. "So you know what they can be like."

"All too well," Abby said. "We learned from an early age to keep our distance. On the Cape in the summer, there were definitely two kinds of people—the ones from away and us locals."

"Tadoussac's pretty much the same," Françoise told her. "I was born here and never really left, and there are still homes up on the hill I've never set foot in."

"I'll bet those are the fanciest homes in town, too," Abby suggested.

"They are."

"Yeah, same with us. Million-dollar homes that get lived in a month or so every year. The rest of the time—empty."

"Doesn't seem right, does it?" Françoise said.

"That's for sure," Abby agreed.

The two women sat in companionable silence for a moment and Françoise was struck with how much she already liked Abby Miller. *Nice girl,* she thought to herself. *Polite, smart and easy to get along with.* But Françoise was sensing something else, too. In spite of her quick smile and infectious laugh, Abby seemed just a little sad. *She hides it well,* Françoise thought, sipping her coffee and regarding Abby over the rim of the mug, *but it's there*.

Out loud she said, "Do you miss it? Cape Cod?"

Abby didn't answer right away. "Yes and no," she finally said. "I mean, it's always going to be home, no matter where I happen to be living. But, well, when I did leave, it was time."

"How long ago was that?" Françoise asked.

"Let's see, I guess it's been five, no, six years since I've lived on the Cape full-time."

"What took you away? School?" Françoise instantly regretted her question when she caught the flash of sorrow in Abby's eyes. "Oh, I'm sorry! Marc is always saying what a busybody I've become…"

Abby held up her hand. "No, it's fine, really." She sat back and sighed, looking out the kitchen window to the bay beyond and fiddling with the handle of her coffee mug. "Have you ever noticed how it only takes one bad memory to erase all the good ones?"

Françoise was unsure how to answer that. Abby was behaving like a woman with something to get off her chest and Françoise decided to give her a moment of quiet to collect those thoughts and decide if she wanted to share them.

"Six years," Abby said softly. "It didn't seem

like such a long time until I said it out loud like that. It's funny, but growing up I never imagined living anywhere but Welfleet. That's my hometown—it's near the tip of the Cape. But, now, well, I can't imagine going back other than to visit my folks."

"Your parents are still there, then?"

"Yes, that's about the only connection I have there, these days," Abby said. "And you know what? Even they don't know the real reason I left."

Françoise bit her lip and considered. Never one for idle girl talk, she had little experience with the very real problems faced by other adult women. Marc was her only child; her cherished son. Over the past thirty-two years she had seen him through feverish nights, skinned knees, schoolboy crushes, marriage, fatherhood and, most recently, the loss of his wife and becoming a single parent. She could read her son and his moods like a book. Her own husband, Lionel—Marc's father, God rest him—had been the same way. Neither one of her men was able to keep anything secret from her, and both were forthright in sharing their emotions. She had no idea how to best coax whatever was troubling Abby out of the young woman.

Well, Françoise thought, *the direct approach has always worked with Lionel and Marc.*

"Sounds to me like there's a story in there waiting to come out."

"Oh, it's a story all right," Abby said.

"I have a reputation for being a pretty good listener," Françoise confessed, leaning forward slightly. "If there's something you'd like to talk about...." Then she held her breath, waiting to see if Abby would confide in her or simply stand, excuse herself and walk out.

FOR A BRIEF MOMENT, Abby felt tempted to leave. But there was something about this warm, cozy kitchen full of good smells that held her in her seat. How strange to feel she could tell Françoise the story she had never, ever told in its entirety.

"His name was Nathan Herrington," Abby heard herself saying, looking down at her hands. "His family had been coming to Welfleet every summer for something like four generations."

She glanced up and met Françoise's eye. "Growing up, we locals all knew to stay away from the summer people. I'm sure they said the same thing about us townies. I'm sure they felt we were good enough to work for them, but heaven forbid any of their precious darlings get involved with us."

"But you and this Nathan got involved?" Françoise asked softly.

Abby nodded. "That's putting in mildly. I'd just graduated and was working at the town marina that summer before starting grad school. We literally bumped into each other one afternoon when he was docking his sailboat."

The memory was still clear. In her mind Abby could see the Welfleet town marina, sailboats and pleasure crafts of all kind bobbing gently at their moorings. It had been one of those gorgeous early June days on the Cape and Abby had logged enough free time to take her beloved Boston Whaler on a cruise up the shore.

Coming back into the marina, she had been annoyed but not too surprised when a stylish sloop had cut her off, edging her out of her berth.

"Stupid jerk," she'd muttered, maneuvering around the sloop and easing her own craft into a less desirable slip at the far end of the dock. Abby was well aware of the marina's unwritten pecking order. When it came to the paying summer customers, the hired help had always given way, regardless of the situation. It was just one of the reasons Abby had preferred to steer clear of the affluent vacationers who flocked to Welfleet to escape the summer heat of Boston, Providence and New York.

Securing the final line to the dock, Abby had picked up her small day pack and headed toward the marina. She had been digging in the pack for her car keys and hadn't see the tanned young man in front of her. Crashing into him, she had nearly tumbled them both into the harbor.

"Oh!" Abby had exclaimed, fighting to regain her balance. "I'm so sorry."

"Why don't you watch where you're going?" the man had said, grabbing a post on the dock with one hand and Abby's arm with the other to steady them both. "Hey," he'd said, squinting at her with dazzling blue eyes. "You're the chick that nearly ran into my boat just now. Figures. You walk about as well as you navigate."

"Excuse me?" Stepping back, Abby had pulled her arm out of his grasp. "Unless someone has rewritten maritime law since this morning, I had the right of way back there." She'd jabbed her thumb over her right shoulder for emphasis. "You should be more careful. The way you handled that sloop, you could have hurt someone." Abby had felt her anger building. It had only been June, but already her work at the marina had brought her into contact with more of the spoiled, idle rich than she'd cared to count. Nothing was ever good enough for them, from the way she washed and prepped their boats to the location of the gas pumps at the maintenance docks.

The young man had crossed his arms over his chest and given her a cocky grin. "You're cute."

"What?" Abby had said.

"I've seen you around the marina." He'd tilted his head. "You can't steer a boat worth a damn, but you're cute."

"Hey, Nate," his companion had called from the sloop's deck. "Are we going to Salty's or not?"

"Be with you in a sec," Nate had yelled, not taking his eyes from Abby.

"Well, hurry it up, it's daiquiri night, two for one before five." Abby had noticed that two tall, slender, blond women had joined the man on deck.

"So how about it, you want to tag along and have a drink with me?" Nate had asked.

Still smarting from his jibe about her sailing skills and his patronizing tone, Abby had glared at him.

"I may get paid to work here and take care of your boats, but that sure as hell doesn't mean I have to party with you." She had turned to stalk off.

"Whoa, hold up there," Nate had said, grabbing her elbow.

Abby had looked at his hand. "Let go of my arm," she'd said through clenched teeth.

"Only if you tell me your name and have dinner with me," Nate had said playfully.

Lord, he was insufferable! Abby had thought. He was also undeniably handsome in white shorts and a blue polo shirt, his bare feet stuffed into a pair of leather sandals that probably cost more than Abby spent in a week on groceries.

She'd glanced over Nate's shoulder and had seen the trio on his sloop watching the exchange with interest. Suddenly, it had become very important that she not lose her cool in front of them. She'd taken a deep, calming breath and had tried to smile. "I'll meet you halfway," she'd said. "I'm Abby, Abby Miller."

"There, that wasn't so hard, was it?" Nate had let go of her arm only to take her by the right hand and shake it. "I'm Nathan Herrington, but my buds all call me Nate."

"Well, fine," Abby had said. "Nice to meet you. Now, if you'll excuse me…"

"What about dinner?" He'd refused to give way.

"No, I can't, but thanks anyway," Abby had said.

"Got something better to do?"

Abby could tell right off that Nate had been denied little in his privileged life. "You don't take no for an answer, do you?"

"Nope," Nate had said. "C'mon, it's just dinner with some friends up at Salty's."

Abby had hesitated. She'd never been to Salty's. Few locals could afford a place where appetizers cost around twelve dollars and entrées started at twenty-five. The trendy restaurant had been open for a year and Abby had yet to do more than turn around once in the parking lot.

Nate had taken her silence for agreement. "Alrighty, then, it's a date. You need a ride or do you want to meet us there?"

"I'll meet you there," Abby had said hastily, thinking if her rather strong second thoughts won out, she could simply drive straight home.

"Cool. See you soon." Nate had turned to join his three friends, who were then standing several yards up the dock.

"Dude!" his buddy had said, giving Nate a high five.

They had walked off talking—probably about her, Abby had thought. She had waited until they'd disappeared into the parking area before trudging up the ramp herself to the employees' lot.

In the end, Abby had gone to Salty's. Nate had been right, she really had nothing better to do. Besides, who was she to pass up a free, over-priced meal?

She'd been surprised to find herself actually having a good time in Nate's company. His friends had even showed polite interest in her and life on the Cape after Labor Day. But she'd not escaped the vague feeling they were watching her as they would a trained chimpanzee—as an object of entertainment.

Regardless, she and Nate had started seeing a lot of each other over the summer. He was funny and charming, and had an easy way with money, making it easy for Abby to ignore the warnings of her own friends.

"Don't worry," she'd told them gaily. "I know what I'm doing." After a while, as Abby found herself spending more time with Nate and his friends, her own group had stopped calling.

Nate's social life introduced a whole new world to Abby. Dinner at a different trendy Cape restaurant almost every night; professionally catered clambakes on the beach on the weekends; endless meandering drives along the shore in Nate's late-model BMW sport coupe convertible.

Abby had begun to believe she'd been foolish buying into the local prejudices against the summer residents. Sure, they kept to their own cliques, but why not? After all, they were from the same Boston neighborhoods or had gone to the same prep schools and universities. These were families who'd shared friendships for generations. Summers on the Cape were their time to play. It was understandable. Somehow, Abby had ended up feeling very lucky to have been admitted into their world.

Nate's father had developed some sort of computer software for medical imaging used by dozens of big-city hospitals. His mother was on the board of several major philanthropic groups. They both spent much of the workweek in Boston, coming to the twenty-two-room ocean-side mansion only for weekends. During the week, Nate had the place to himself and had quite a reputation for the lavish parties he threw.

Abby had grown up with her share of respon-sibility in keeping the house neat and in order, and it had seemed only natural to pitch in and help clean up after Nate's bashes. It hadn't even bothered her that he always found somewhere else to be when it came to the dirty work.

It had been a magical, wondrous summer and Abby had given herself over to Nate—body and soul—and believed every word he'd whispered into her ears…right up until the traditional end-of-season bonfire. Abby had taken special pains with her appearance that night, knowing Nate was leaving the next morning for Boston and his studies at Harvard. But, she had consoled herself, Boston was only a two-hour drive and they could see each other on weekends and holidays. She was looking forward to spending time with him and his family in their house on Beacon Hill. He'd hinted as much for several weeks.

When Abby arrived at the beach, she'd spotted him right away, lounging carelessly against the fender of his convertible. Abby had ridden her bicycle and had just finished locking it to a lamppost, when she'd turned around to wave. But her hand just sort of floated limply as she'd watched the love of her life take a beautiful blonde into his arms and kiss her passionately. Her throat dry, her heart pounding, Abby had watched as Nate and the blonde finally came up for air. Nate gave her a playful swat on the behind before opening the car door for her. The woman had slid into the passenger seat while Nate got behind the wheel. The car revved to life and pulled away from the curb, driving right past a shocked and immobile Abby. For a second, she'd swore their eyes had met, but Nate hadn't acknowledge her.

That was the last time she ever saw Nate Herrington. Later, she'd found out the blonde was his fiancée who had spent the summer touring Europe and had returned that day.

She'd been hurt and humiliated beyond words. All summer she'd hung on him while he squired her about the Cape with his friends, who must have known of his engagement. The only thing worse than the certain knowledge of how they must have been laughing at her was the deep shame she felt in facing her own friends, whom she had abandoned in favor of Nate. And she felt cheap, used and cheated. The next day, after pulling herself out of bed—her pillow still damp from her tears—Abby had made a promise to throw herself into the safe, albeit lonely, world of research.

ABBY MANAGED to pull herself back into the present.

"Wow," she said, with a shaky laugh. "Just look at me. Give me a muffin and I'll tell all."

At some point during Abby's story, Françoise had slid her hand across the table and taken Abby's. Now she gave Abby's hand a squeeze. "What did your parents say?" she asked.

"I never told them," Abby said. "They were at sea most of that summer on a research grant. I was leaving for grad school a few days after they got home and, well, I just couldn't face letting them know how stupid I'd been." She bit her lip.

Another hand squeeze, then Françoise released her grip. "Following your heart is never stupid," she said. "What's stupid is being untrue to your heart, and it sounds like that's just what that Nathan did."

"Maybe so," Abby said slowly, but she remained unconvinced. "Anyway, it was all a very long time ago." She glanced at the clock. "I'd better get a move on if I want to get anything done today."

Françoise stood up from the table. "I'd best get going, too. The hotel wants that second delivery on time."

"Second delivery?"

Françoise nodded. "I've already taken one delivery over for six o'clock. I think a baker's day is the only one that starts earlier than a fisherman's. Now, you take another muffin or two and then drop by later today to see what I have for you."

"Thank you," Abby said, choosing another muffin and making a mental promise to save it for later.

"Oh, and Marc left some papers for you. I think they're on the table by the back door." Françoise started loading bread, muffins, cookies, scones and cakes into boxes.

"I see it," Abby said, glancing down the hallway. She felt herself fumbling for the right words. "And Françoise, thank you. You are a very good listener. Even though that happened years ago, well, it felt good to tell someone about it."

Françoise watched Abby pick up the envelope Marc had left and shut the back door behind her.

There goes a girl who's been alone for too long, Françoise thought to herself. *I wonder if that son of mine is smart enough to see that.*

FIGGY WAS WAITING on the other side of the door when Abby got to her apartment a few minutes later. The dog shot out the minute Abby opened the door. Abby decided she'd conduct a little experiment and walked over to the teeter-totter. Figgy trotted over and stood next to her.

Looking around to make sure she was alone, Abby made a hand signal that mimicked the one used by Sylvie the previous afternoon.

Figgy wagged her tail and looked up at her.

"Okay, up!" Abby repeated.

Figgy barked in reply.

Abby repeated the signal, then grabbed the dog by her collar and tried to encourage her onto the ramp. Figgy dug all four feet into the ground and refused to budge.

Releasing her hold, Abby tried walking up the ramp herself to see if Figgy would follow her. Figgy watched a moment, then trotted off to sniff the base of a tree.

"Wretched little beast," Abby said in an affectionate tone, walking back to her apartment and leaving Figgy with the yard to herself.

Abby thought about her conversation with

Françoise and how easy it had been to confide in her. The whole sorry mess of her summer affair with Nate could still make Abby blush in shame. But somehow, telling it to the older woman had helped ease six years' worth of pain.

Abby shook her head and gave a rueful laugh as she collected the materials she would need for work that day. "Maybe coming to Tadoussac is going to help more than the whales."

CHAPTER SEVEN

WALKING DOWN THE STREET toward the center, Abby looked over at the bay and the town dock. She felt her heart give a flutter of anticipation when she spotted the *Percé* bobbing gently at anchor. The thought of actually getting out on the water and moving her research from the planning to implementing stage made her quicken her step. Marc had said he would not be at the boat until later that morning, and Abby wanted everything ready so they could begin loading equipment as soon as possible.

She was deeply involved in studying a chart of Tadoussac Bay's underwater topography an hour later when she heard a tap on her office door.

"You needed to see me?"

Chris, clipboard in hand, stood in the doorway. His hair was still tied back in a ponytail, but a tie-dyed pullover had replaced his Hawaiian-print shirt.

"Chris, good morning," Abby greeted him. "Thanks for coming by."

"I got your note," he said, stepping into the office. "Is now a good time to start putting together your gear?"

"Fantastic." Abby shoved her chair back and stood up. "I've got my list somewhere here…" She pawed through the paper on the desk. "Here we are," she said, and handed it to Chris.

As they walked down the hall toward the stairs, Chris looked over the list and mumbled to himself. "Yeah, we've got everything you need here. Plus a package that arrived from Woods Hole the day before yesterday addressed to you."

He held the door to the stairway for her and followed her down to the second floor. Fishing a key ring out of his pocket, he unlocked the door to a large supply room at the corner of the lab. He grinned. "Kind of like going into the best toy store in the world, isn't it?"

"I'll say." Abby peered into the windowless room. The walls were lined with shelves that held state-of-the-art marine electronics.

"The acoustic stuff is on those shelves over there." Chris pointed to the opposite wall. "Everything is tagged and numbered. When you take something, bring me the tag. That way I can keep track of who has what. Do you need me for anything else?"

Abby looked around a moment. "No, I should

be all set. Can I go ahead and take the gear to the boat as soon as I've selected it?"

"Sure," Chris said. "Who'd you get for a charter?"

"Marc Doucette and the *Percé*," Abby waited to see his reaction.

Chris seemed surprised. "Marc Doucette? No kidding? Wow, I guess you're in for an interesting summer."

"So I've been told." Abby wondered if the entire staff would have similar comments to make on her summer charter.

THE FIELD OF bioacoustics was, by nature, a highly technical one. Fortunately, Abby was not going to need a mountain of gear for her project. But what equipment she did need to successfully listen in on the underwater world of the Saint Lawrence beluga was specialized. Consulting her list, she quickly made her selections from the shelves, wrapped them and placed the items in a large cardboard box she had found behind the door.

"That should get me started," she muttered. Collecting the tags, she put the box on a rolling cart she had found in the main lab and wheeled it to Chris's office.

Chris looked up when he heard the cart lumber past. "Having fun?"

"A ball," Abby said, handing him the tags.

"Thanks. Sometime today I'm going to enter all this into the computer and then you'll need to sign the form agreeing that you've taken everything on the list."

"Okay," Abby said. "I'm going to be in and out all day."

"Yeah, that's why we give you guys mailboxes." Chris pointed to a bank of post office-like boxes set into the wall opposite his office. "Yours is number three-three-five."

"Great. Can I keep this cart and use it to take this gear right to the *Percé?*"

"Sure, just make sure it finds its way back home again," Chris said.

"Will do." Abby gave the cart a push toward the bank of service elevators.

MARC WAS ON THE DECK of the *Percé* sorting through cans of motor oil when a motion up the dock caught his eye. It was Abby, trying to force a wheeled cart up a small wooden step. Every time she got the front wheels on top of the step, she had to reposition her grip to shove the rest of the cart up. But whenever she changed the grip, the cart rolled back down the step. Marc couldn't hear her, but judging by the set of her shoulders, he imagined whatever she might be saying wasn't exactly ladylike.

Sliding down the ladder to the dock, he walked up to her and grabbed the cart. "May I be of service?"

"Marc! Thank goodness." Abby sounded exasperated. "You'd think someone with a doctorate in marine science engineering could handle a cart!"

"No, you're better off leaving this kind of delicate operation to the manual-labor guy," Marc teased.

"Ha, ha," Abby said. "Just pull, okay?"

"You're the boss lady." Marc gave the cart a solid tug.

"Careful!" Abby said, pushing from behind.

"What is all this?" Marc asked as they were wheeling the cart toward the boat.

"Acoustic testing equipment," she told him.

"Does it play in stereo?"

"Funny. Very funny." They came to a halt next to the boat's hull. Taking her hands from the cart, Abby pulled the band that had been holding her hair in a loose ponytail, and shook her head, letting the coppery mass hang around her face before gathering it back up with the band. Marc felt his chest constrict in an odd way at the sight.

"So, how do we get this stuff up to the deck?" Abby said. "Any bright ideas?"

"I suppose one of us tossing it and the other catching it is out of the question?" Marc teased.

"Good guess," Abby said dryly.

"Then I guess I'll just have to carry it." Marc took hold of the box and hefted it onto one shoulder.

"Careful!" Abby called as he climbed one-handed up the ladder.

"I've got it. Don't worry."

Once they were both aboard, Marc took the box down to the port side cabin.

Abby surveyed the room. "Going to be a tight fit."

"Here," Marc said, easing past her. "What if we lose the bed?"

"Can you do that?" Abby asked.

"Sure. Is there a wrench on the galley table?"

Abby went to see and returned a moment later with a wrench.

"Thanks," he said. Working quickly, he dismantled the twin bed. "There's a small cabin aft. We can put it in there for now."

With the bed out of the cabin, Abby had all the room she needed. A small table sat against one wall and shelves lined another.

"You want another table in here?" Marc asked.

"That would be great."

"There used to be a small table in this cabin," Marc said, pointing to the mounting hardware still in the floor. "It's up at my house. I've got to take a drive up later on. Why don't you come with me and see if it's something you can use."

"Okay, thanks," Abby said. "That's it for now."

Marc glanced around. "I guess that's right, I didn't see a kitchen sink in there anywhere."

Abby laughed. "No, that's coming next week. Actually, I've got my personal computer and gear to bring in and set up. Then I have to calibrate all this." She indicated the equipment they had just unloaded.

Marc looked at his watch as they made their way back to the upper deck. "We've worked straight through lunch. It's not much, but I have a couple of sandwiches and sodas in the galley fridge. We could grab a quick bite and then go after that table."

"As long as now's a good time for you," Abby said.

"Good a time as any." Marc disappeared down the hatchway leading to the galley. He returned a few minutes later balancing several sandwiches, a bag of potato chips and two cans of soda.

"Today's specials are chicken salad or chicken salad," he announced, holding up the cellophane-wrapped sandwiches for Abby to inspect.

"Tough choice. I guess I'll go with the chicken salad."

"Madame has excellent taste." He popped the lid from a can of soda and passed it to her, then opened the bag of chips and sat down on a hatch cover, patting the space next to him.

They ate their lunch in a companionable silence for several moments.

"Anxious to get started?" Marc asked.

"Started?" Abby reached for a handful of chips.

Marc nodded toward the hatch. "Are you anxious to put all that stuff in the water?"

"Oh, yes," Abby said. "I've been planning this for so long, it's hard to believe the project's actually going to get off the ground."

Just twenty-four hours ago she had been in utter despair watching other scientists' equipment being loaded onto the *Caprice*. Now she had a boat all to herself. No jockeying for research time. No adhering to another researcher's schedule. From Abby's perspective, the loss of the center's second vessel had worked to her advantage.

"Today's Friday," Marc said, interrupting her thoughts, "and I'm going to be busy moving Sylvie into my mom's house tomorrow and Sunday. How does starting bright and early Monday morning sound?"

Abby considered a moment. "That works. I can use the weekend to re-calibrate my computers and go over the charts."

"Charts?" Marc asked.

She nodded. "Yeah, I've spent the past six months compiling everything I could find on the underwater topography of the Saguenay and the bay. Then I compared that with known swimming and migratory patterns of beluga. That's how I'll know where to set my sensors."

"Uh-huh," Marc said neutrally.

"'Uh-huh,' *what?*" Abby asked.

"You plan on relying only on those charts?"

"Of course. How else can I determine the sites?"

"Well, you could try talking to some locals. They're pretty familiar with the whales and with the terrain here and… What's so funny?"

Abby shook her head. "Marc, no offense, but these charts are composites using the latest satellite imagery combined with computerized models. I think I can rely on their accuracy."

"State of the art, huh?" A small smile twitched at the corners of Marc's mouth.

"To say the least," Abby assured him.

"Okay, then, it's your party, we'll do it your way," Marc said, standing. "You finished?"

"Sure." Abby crumpled the cellophane wrapper and tossed it into the waste can Marc kept on deck. "Ready when you are."

MARC'S WAGONEER was parked at the curb in front of his mother's house. "Give me a moment?" Abby said, walking to the gate.

"Take your time," Marc said, lounging against the driver's door.

Abby unlatched the gate and spotted Figgy gnawing on her bone in the shade of a tree. Satisfied her little friend was fine, she quickly stepped out of the yard and re-latched the gate.

Marc drove along Tadoussac's main street toward the eastern side of the town. Taking a sharp right turn, he navigated a series of switchbacks leading up to the bluff overlooking the bay. Another turn down a narrow road that dead-ended a quarter mile later, and Marc pulled into a long driveway.

"You live here?" Abby climbed out of the car.

"I'm renting the place out for the summer," Marc said, digging some keys from his pocket. "In fact, I got a message that a family from Hull is taking it later this month. C'mon, I'll give you the VIP tour."

Abby was so intent on checking out the house and its surroundings that she stumbled on the first step leading up to the wraparound porch.

Marc caught her arm and steadied her. "Careful."

"Thanks," Abby mumbled, trying to ignore the pleasant tingle Marc's strong grip had sent up her arm.

While Marc pulled open the screen door, Abby surveyed the back of the house. Tall, windblown spruce and fir bordered the yard, completely hiding the house from the road. A shed or garage stood a distance from the house and what must have been a garden patch was turning to weeds between the two. Walking along the porch, Abby caught her breath as she rounded the corner. The lawn continued on another several hundred feet to the edge of the cliffs. Beyond were Tadoussac Bay and the Saint Lawrence Seaway. Though the village was visible below, the house was otherwise isolated.

Hearing Marc unlock the front door, she quickly retraced her steps. A place like this would go for a cool million, easy, in the Boston area.

Abby followed Marc inside and looked around curiously at the place he called home.

An airy living room with large picture windows looking out over the same view Abby had just seen from the porch. A massive fieldstone fireplace dominated one wall and hooked rugs covered the mellow hardwood flooring.

"My dad and I built that fireplace," Marc said, when he noticed Abby admiring it. "We spent an entire summer tromping over pastures and through the woods looking for rocks."

"It was worth it," Abby said, walking over and running her hands along the smooth stone. She closed her eyes and imagined curling up on the couch; fire blazing, all cozy and warm as a winter storm raged outside…

Sensing Marc move out of the room, she suddenly realized the memories the place must hold for him. After all, he had lived here with his wife. Sylvie must have been conceived here, Abby thought suddenly and felt her cheeks heat.

"You okay?" Marc asked, stepping back into the living room and looking at her closely.

"Fine, why?" Abby hoped he couldn't read minds.

"I don't know. Thought I'd lost you there for a moment and you look kind of flushed, that's all."

"Too much sun and wind, I guess," Abby said. *Get it together, girl!*

Marc shrugged. "Whatever. The table I was talking about is in the kitchen."

Abby followed him down the hallway, admiring the teakwood banister on the stairway leading to the second floor. Two swinging doors led to the kitchen, where Abby, the daughter of two gourmands, gasped.

"You like?" Marc said, with a smile.

"I feel like I just stepped into a photograph from *Gourmet* magazine," Abby told him.

Marble counters lined the perimeter of the room, beginning and ending at a huge gas stove with a double oven. An island in the middle of the room was covered with a well-oiled butcher block over which hung a rack laden with an assortment of copper skillets, pots and pans. Glass-fronted cupboards held sturdy-looking crockery and dishes. Windows looked out over the bay, and a breakfast table was set against the far wall with a smaller folding table nearby.

Marc pointed. "Will that work for you?"

Abby walked over to the small rectangular table. In her mind, she saw it covered with her computer, printer, charts and graphs. She nodded. "Yep, I can definitely use it."

She looked back at him. "So, who's the chef?" she asked.

Marc smiled. "You may find this hard to believe, but I am."

"You!" Abby said.

"A man of many talents," he assured her. "C'mon, we have time for a quick look at the rest of the house, then I have to get back to my mom's."

A second door led from the kitchen into a formal dining room with its own fireplace, albeit smaller than the one in the living room. Upstairs, four doors led off the hallway. Marc opened the first one on the left, then stood aside so Abby could peek in at the most decadent-looking bathroom she had ever seen.

A claw-foot tub stood against the wall, a skylight directly over it. The glass shower stall took up one corner of the room, its showerhead the size of a dinner plate.

The other rooms were bedrooms. Sylvie's was easy to identify with its Winnie the Pooh posters and smaller furnishings. The master bedroom at the end of the hall had a deck that opened out to the bay.

"I don't think I could ever leave this place if I lived here," Abby said after they had walked back downstairs and headed outside.

"Yeah, it gets a hold of you…" Marc left the sentence hanging as he locked the front door.

When he just stood there, silent, Abby placed a tentative hand on his shoulder. "Marc?"

"Sorry," he said, turning. "Old ghosts, y'know?"

She nodded.

"The truth is, Thérèse—that's my wife—she never cared for the place as much as I did. Always said it was too far off the beaten track."

Abby was silent, but she couldn't help thinking, *That's the best thing about it.*

Marc leaned against the porch railing, arms crossed, and looked out toward the bay. "My dad and I bought the place back when the money from fishing was good. It was in horrible shape— what you Americans call a real fixer-upper. But it came with twenty acres, plus access to the beach." He straightened, took Abby by the arm and led her down the steps and around the house.

"See?" he said.

They walked over to the cliff and Abby saw the wooden stairway that led down to a small cove.

"About four years ago, a mudslide blocked access to that cove from the rest of the shore-line," Marc said, "so it's almost like having a private beach." He looked back to the house. "My dad and I spent every weekend here after we bought it. I mean, this place needed a lot of work. We put in the skylights, redid the plumbing and wiring, replaced the windows, stripped every-thing down and shored up the foundation."

"You did a heck of a job," Abby said, with real feeling.

"Thanks," Marc said. "The shame of it is, after all that effort, my dad didn't get to see his grand-daughter living here. My dad died not long after we finished work on the house and then I went off to university. After Thérèse and I got married, we moved in, but that lasted just a year."

Marc kicked at a rock on the ground and Abby remained silent, waiting for him to continue.

"See, Thérèse was a graphic artist. A really good one. She could make an okay living here, but someone in Toronto saw her stuff and she got a really great job offer, too good to turn down. We'd just had Sylvie and decided to give the big city a try, just until Sylvie started school."

"What did you do in Toronto?" Abby asked.

Marc grinned. "At first, I did the house-husband thing and stayed home with Sylvie. And you know what? I loved it; we had a blast together. But, when she was old enough, we put her in day care and I got a job designing boats for a marine salvage company."

Abby just stared at Marc, thinking the guy had more layers than a Walla Walla sweet onion. She wondered if she would ever see them all.

Marc looked at his watch. "Hey, we'd better get a move on. Give me a moment to stow the table in back of the Jeep. I'll have it on board the *Percé* by Monday."

Abby nodded and they walked back to the Wagoneer. It was obvious Marc had traveled down memory lane far enough for one day. As they backed out of the driveway and turned around, Abby looked at the house. Isolated on that high bluff, it seemed lonely, ready to be loved again.

CHAPTER EIGHT

"Repeat second grade, *cognitive learning problems*," Françoise said, slamming her fist into a mass of bread dough. "Of all the stupid… I should call Beatrice Simard right now and tell her just what I think of her." She punched the dough several more times for emphasis, then turned from the counter to look at Marc, who was sitting at the kitchen table. "You're not seriously considering it, are you?" she asked, "You know that would devastate Sylvie."

"Of course not," Marc said. "But Madame Simard is. And if Sylvie does not show some improvement in her reading and writing by her next report card, that teacher is going to make some trouble."

Slam-punch, went Françoise's fists into the dough. "What kind of trouble can she make?" she asked.

Marc shrugged. "With the principal, I'd imagine. I mean, if Madame Simard told him

Sylvie was not able to keep up in school here, he might buy her argument that she belongs in second grade again and I'm running out of options."

Françoise put a towel over the bowl to cover the dough and joined her son at the table. "Did she really say Sylvie's drawings have nothing to do with learning?"

Marc nodded.

Françoise shook her head. "Why is a narrow-minded woman like that teaching young children?"

"I guess she figures she's doing her job," Marc said, standing. "Now I've got to convince Sylvie to try harder without scaring her."

"You're not going to tell her about repeating a year, are you?"

"No, no way," Marc said quickly. "That would terrify her. I mean, to you and me, being held back isn't such a huge deal, but to an eight-year-old it would seem like the end of the world. Is she outside with the dog?"

"Of course," his mother said. "She came through the front door, dropped her things and never stopped until she was out the back door and in the yard. Marc, hold on a minute." Françoise put her hand on her son's arm. "What exactly *are* you going to tell her?"

Marc blew out a breath. "I have no idea. I guess I'm hoping something comes to me between now and when I get out there."

"Before you do, can we talk a moment?"

"Sure, what's on your mind?"

"Sit back down," Françoise said.

She did not say anything right away. She'd been debating with herself all day the wisdom of approaching her son about what she knew was a sensitive area. But, after her talk with Abby that morning, she figured now was as good a time as any.

"Marc," she began finally. "You're a good son and a good father."

"Thanks," Marc said.

"And you were a very good husband." Françoise waited for his reaction.

"What are you trying to say?" he said evenly.

"Just hear me out and wipe that look off your face."

"What look?"

"That look that says you're going to listen to what I have to say only to humor me."

"Mom…" Marc sounded tired. "I've got a ton of work to do. Can you just come to the point? Please?"

"Fine," Françoise said. "The fact of the matter is, I'm worried about you."

"About me?" Marc looked surprised. "Why on earth—"

"I know how much you loved Thérèse, we all did," Françoise explained. "And we all miss her terribly. I guess I know better than anyone how hard it's been for you since the accident. But you can't keep going like this."

"Like what?"

"You said once it's like Sylvie is stuck in neutral with her learning?"

Marc nodded.

"It's the same with you. Your whole *life* has been in neutral since Thérèse died."

"Mom, that's ridiculous." Marc sounded defensive.

"Is it?" Françoise asked. "For the last three years I've watched you take care of Sylvie and no one will ever fault you on how you've done that. But as for taking care of yourself, well, you haven't. Marc, it's time for you to start living again."

"This is insane," Marc protested. "I'm fine. I'm working and keeping busy. What's the problem?"

"When's the last time you went out on a date?" Françoise asked.

"What the hell does that have to do with anything?"

"Everything, and don't swear at me, young man," Françoise said sternly, then softened her voice. "Did you ever stop to think for a moment that maybe if Sylvie saw you get on with your life, she'd be able to get on with hers?"

Françoise waited for her son's reaction, and it wasn't long in coming.

Marc stood up abruptly, pushing the chair back from the table. "That's enough. I don't know where you're trying to go with this, but I have things to do. If you'll excuse me?"

Françoise simply nodded as Marc stalked from the room. From experience she knew just how far she could push her son. She'd said her piece and planted the seed, a seed that had been growing in her own mind all day—Marc and Abby Miller were two souls who desperately needed each other.

GET ON WITH MY LIFE SO Sylvie could get on with hers? What was his mother thinking? Marc fumed. He stood just inside the back door and watched Sylvie romp with Figgy. Like it or not, he had to admit his mother was right about one thing—he did miss Thérèse.

Marc had loved Thérèse pretty much from the moment he first met her his freshman year in high school. They'd dated off and on until Thérèse graduated and went off to art school in Montreal. They'd managed to maintain their relationship long distance and were engaged by the time she'd come home to Tadoussac, graphic-arts degree in hand. Marc had been well aware of the sacrifice Thérèse had made when she agreed to remain in Tadoussac after they married. But at the time, he could not envision living anywhere else. He loved the bay, the fjord and the surrounding dark-green hills.

"This is your own heaven on earth, isn't it, *mon coeur?*" Thérèse had said to him teasingly on numerous occasions.

"If it is, you're the only angel I'll ever need," had been Marc's standard reply. But he'd known the only thing keeping Thérèse in Tadoussac was him. He could see she was content in the house on the hill, working over the Internet from her little office in the spare bedroom. Content, but not fulfilled. So it had seemed only fair when the opportunity came for her to work for a prestigious design firm in Toronto that it was his turn to make a compromise. He had closed up his beloved cliff-side house and driven off to the big city with his wife and infant daughter to follow Thérèse's dream.

Thérèse had blossomed in Toronto, and not just professionally. While Marc found living and working in Canada's largest metropolis too fast-paced, there was no denying it made his wife the happiest he had ever known her to be. And for

Marc, that was enough to make him happy. That and his little jewel Sylvie.

Sylvie. She was the reason Marc had not gone looking for female companionship. In the weeks and months following the death of his wife, little Sylvie had drifted between reality and fantasy. Marc recalled those dark days when his little girl happily carried on one-sided conversations with her mother, only to break down in near-hysterics later when she couldn't find her.

If time had not completely healed the wound caused by Thérèse's death, Marc was fairly certain it had at least put on a pretty strong Band-Aid. He shook his head. No, bringing a new person into their family would do nothing more than confuse and frighten Sylvie. Maybe there would be time for him to find love again in the distant future. But not now, not until he was one-hundred percent certain his daughter had recovered. That thought brought him back to the meeting with Madame Simard and the issue of Sylvie's schoolwork.

Looking out the screen door, he watched as Sylvie put Figgy through the teeter-totter routine for what Marc guessed must have been the twentieth time that day. The little dog showed no sign of tiring of the game, and Figgy trotted over to Sylvie's side for a job-well-done pat on the head.

Marc considered that a moment. "Maybe that's the bargaining chip I'm looking for," he muttered, and headed toward the yard.

"OKAY, FIGGY, up, up!"

Marc let the screen door shut behind him and watched a moment as Sylvie put Figgy through her paces once again.

"Good girl," Sylvie said, when the dog had successfully navigated the plank. Looking up, his daughter saw him and ran over. "Did you see, Dad? Did you see? Want me to do it again?"

"No, not right now, *ma fille*." Marc stopped Sylvie mid-stride on her way back to the teeter-totter. "Right now I want to talk to you, okay?"

His daughter sobered. "It's about Madame Simard, isn't it," she said glumly.

"Yes, Sylvie, it is. Let's sit on the porch a while and let Figgy have a rest for a bit." Taking his daughter's hand, he directed her to the old wooden church pew that sat in the yard by the side of the house.

"Now, Sylvie," he said after they had sat down. "The most important thing you need to know is you are not in trouble and no one is mad at you, okay?"

Sylvie looked up, eyes round, "Really? Honest?"

"Really and honestly," Marc said. "But we are worried about you and that's just as serious."

She twisted her hands in her lap. "So I am in trouble."

"No, but we do have to get some things worked out." Marc paused a moment. "Sylvie," he said slowly, "if I know one thing, it's this: when you put your mind to something, you are a very smart, bright and talented little girl."

"I am?" Sylvie looked a bit more cheerful.

Marc nodded. "No doubt about it. You draw better than most kids twice your age—heck, better than some adults. And what you've done in a day or two with Figgy, well, that's just amazing."

"I was just having fun," Sylvie said, but she was obviously delighted with her father's praise.

"Maybe," Marc said, "but you spent a good deal of time and energy on it, like you do your drawings. But now I need you to spend as much time and energy on your schoolwork, *ma fille*."

Sylvie's smile disappeared. "But, it's too hard. I can't do it. I don't get it."

A tear slipped from her eye and Marc struggled to maintain his resolve. Nothing had the ability to weaken him faster than his daughter's tears.

"I think you can get it," Marc said. "I think maybe you just don't want to."

"I do, I do!" Sylvie wailed. "I'm the only one in the class with baby books! I want to read the big-girl books, too!"

"I know you do, Sylvie," Marc assured her. "And you will. I promise. But you and I are going to have to make a deal here."

"What kind of deal?" Sylvie sounded suspicious.

"I know how much you enjoy playing with Abby's dog. So, here it is. You can play with her all you want, but—" his voice became stern as Sylvie gave a happy whoop "—but you have to spend *at least* as much time on your schoolwork as you do with Figgy."

"What do you mean?" Sylvie asked.

"If you want to play with Figgy for an hour, then that's how long you have to spend on schoolwork. If you want to spend more time with her, then more time at the books." Marc's voice was firm. "Can we agree on that?"

Sylvie didn't answer right away and Marc let her work the deal out in her own mind and in her own time. Finally, she looked up at him. "Okay, deal," she said quietly.

"And it starts today, right now," Marc said.

"Right *now?*" Sylvie protested.

"Right now. Your grandmother told me you've been out here since school got out, so how about you spend the hour before supper going over your homework." Marc watched Sylvie closely to see how she would react.

"Okay, dad. You win." Sylvie cast one last,

longing glance at Figgy, who was sitting in the yard staring at her. "I'll see you later, Figgy," she called.

Figgy cocked her head and wagged her tail.

As Sylvie opened the screen door, a thought struck Marc. "Sylvie?" he called.

"Yeah."

"I thought you told me this morning you were going to teach Figgy how to jump through a tire. That's why I pulled one up from the basement for you."

"Uh-huh," Sylvie nodded. "But she wasn't ready for that."

"Wasn't ready?" Marc repeated. "How could you tell?"

Sylvie shrugged. "I just could." Then the screen door slammed and she was gone, leaving Marc shaking his head.

CHAPTER NINE

ABBY HAD SEEN MARC ONLY for a brief moment over the weekend. He'd been on his way into his mother's house with a box full of Sylvie's things and she had been on her way out to get some groceries. They agreed to meet on Monday at 6 a.m. sharp aboard the *Percé*.

Come Monday, a steady breeze off the Saint Lawrence was dissipating the early morning fog. As Abby walked down the dock, the *Percé* loomed through the remaining mist like a phantom ship. Lights shone down from the bridge, and as Abby neared the boat, the heady aroma of strong coffee hit her.

"Hi there," Marc called from above. Looking up, Abby could make out his form against the gray sky.

"Good morning," she said, adjusting her folders and computer so she could climb aboard.

In an instant, Marc was down the ladder. "Here," he said, "I'll take those. Go on up. There's a fresh pot of coffee on the stove. Help yourself. Have you had breakfast?"

Abby shook her head. "No, I was too excited to think about eating and I forgot to grab something to bring here." She realized she hadn't thought about lunch or snacks, either.

"Don't worry," Marc said, as if reading her thoughts. "Food's included with the charter."

"No, I can't let you do that," Abby objected.

"You already arguing with the captain?" Marc asked her.

"Of course not but, look, it doesn't seem fair."

"It's fair. Won't be fancy and you may get sick and tired of my sandwiches, but it's fair. If it makes you feel better, you can buy me dinner a couple of times this summer. How's that?"

Abby had to laugh. "This deal just gets better and better."

"Okay, then." Marc grabbed her computer with one hand and the rung of the ladder with the other. "Let's get this show on the road."

On deck, Marc waited for Abby to climb aboard and then handed her back her computer and files. While she went below to stow the items, Marc began casting off the mooring lines. By the time she reappeared on the bridge, steaming cup of coffee in hand, the mist had started to clear and he was easing the throttle to gently guide the boat away from the dock.

Abby took a sip from the mug. "Wow," she said, her eyes wide.

"Was that a good *wow* or a bad *wow?*" Marc asked, never taking his own eyes from the depth gauge next to the wheel.

"A good wow, a very, very good wow." Abby took another sip. "This may just be the best cup of coffee I've ever had."

"Thanks," Marc said. "Most people tell me my coffee's too strong. Where do you want to start?"

Abby took another sip of the delicious coffee before answering. "According to my preliminary research and calculations, our best shot at finding the whales is at Baie Saint-Marguerite. When we get there, I'll show you the specific coordinates to set the gear."

Marc nodded and Abby watched out the windows as the boat cruised slowly past the western arm of the bay and entered the Saguenay. Right away, Abby could feel a difference in the roll of the boat and saw Marc push on the throttle.

"River current," he said. "Hey, looks like we're going to thread the needle."

"Excuse me?"

"Look." He pointed ahead.

Abby squinted, then she saw two shapes

moving toward the *Percé,* one from the port and the other from the starboard.

"What on earth?" She jumped at the sound of the air horns.

Marc laughed and pulled on his own horn, making a deafening sound.

"Morning ferries," he explained. "The horns mean there's enough room for safety and they're giving us right of way to pass between them."

"That's nice of them," Abby said.

"Yeah, I've known the captains for years." He gave his horn two more short bursts. Moments later, a similar response came from the two ferries, the age-old maritime sign of acknowledgment.

"You may as well get comfortable and enjoy the scenery," Marc said. "With this current, it's going to take at least an hour to get to your first site."

"Fine by me," Abby said. "This may be the only chance I have all summer to play tourist."

Marc made a slight adjustment to the throttle. "In that case, this may be *my* only chance to play tour guide. What do you know about the Tadoussac area?"

Abby thought a moment. "I know it's where the Saguenay River empties into the Saint Lawrence, and that the estuary is prime feeding and gathering grounds for several species of whales…" Her voice trailed off as she saw Marc shaking his head.

"No, no," he said. "I have no doubt you know just about everything there is to know about the ecology of this area. I meant about the *place* and its history."

"Oh." Abby winced. "It's embarrassing to admit, but I guess not much."

"Well, then, how about a quick history lesson to pass the time?"

"Okay," Abby said. "But can it wait while I go get a refill?" She held up her empty mug.

"Sure. And could you grab a mug for me and a couple of muffins, while you're at it?"

"Done and done," Abby said, exiting the wheelhouse. She returned five minutes later, a plate of muffins in one hand and two mugs of coffee clutched in the other.

"Thanks." Marc relieved her of one of the mugs. "You can set the plate on the chart table."

Abby did as he asked, helped herself to a muffin and then sat in the mate's seat next to the port-side window. The morning sun was a pale disk above the morning haze and the sides of the river were barely distinguishable from the mist swirling around. Abby shivered and wrapped her hands around the hot mug.

Marc glanced at her. "Yeah, it's kind of chilly now, but wait a few hours. It gets good and warm on the water once the sun gets higher."

"Okay, so tell me about Tadoussac," she said.

"Tadoussac exists and has existed for hundreds of years for one basic reason. Want to try and guess?"

Abby thought a moment and then made the obvious choice. "Fishing?"

Marc shook his head. "Try again."

She thought of the spruce-and-fir covered hills surrounding the town. "Lumber?"

"And it's another strike!" Marc said. "Want to go for three in a row?"

"No thanks, I concede the question."

"Tourism. For hundreds of years, that's what Tadoussac has been all about."

"You're kidding." Abby found it difficult to believe a town—even one as pretty as Tadoussac—had been a tourist destination for that long.

"In one form or another," Marc said. "The first one to drop in was Jacques Cartier in 1509."

"The French explorer?"

"Yeah, and mapmaker. It took a while, but by the early 1600s the local natives were hosting fur trappers and traders from the Hudson's Bay Company. In fact, there's a museum all about that not far from Mom's house, if you're interested.

Anyway, you weren't too far off on the lumber guess. The spot you've chosen for your first sampling site isn't far from what used to be a major lumber town along the Sainte-Marguerite River. Back in its day, there was a mill that ran 24-7 with hundreds of men working there."

"And now?" Abby asked.

"Now there's a few pieces of rusty machinery scattered around the woods. That's it. But a lot of people made a ton of money in the timber business and Tadoussac really came alive as a place for their families to spend holidays. It's thanks to the lumber trade that the Hôtel Tadoussac was first built in 1840. Not long after that, the word really got out and people from big cities like Montreal, Boston and even New York would come up on the steamers to get away from the heat and humidity of the cities."

"Summer people," Abby mused, recalling her conversation with Françoise.

"Yeah, well, it's really a full-time thing here now," Marc told her. "Just wait a couple of weeks. By July, you're lucky to get a seat in any of the restaurants in town."

"Must make it hard for the locals," Abby mused.

"Yes and no," Marc said. "More people means more money coming in and a better winter. So, we're willing to put up with no parking, traffic and crowds of people for four months." He looked down at the GPS unit mounted next to the wheel. "We're about fifteen minutes from your first site."

Abby quickly drained her coffee. "Great. I'm going to go get the sensors ready."

The clouds were breaking up and Abby could see patches of blue sky when she came back up on deck, a padded case in each hand. As she knelt down and flipped the catches open on the first case, Abby felt the boat slow, the pitch and roll of the deck increasing in direct proportion to the lack of forward momentum. An instant later, the boat came to a complete stop and Abby heard the motors soften to a steady idle. Marc appeared at the wheelhouse door.

"We're here," he called down to her.

Abby waved a response, then stood and looked around. Marc had brought them to a spot fifteen miles up the river and positioned the boat near the eastern shoreline. According to Abby's calculations, this was a prime spot for beluga.

This is it, she thought excitedly. *It all starts now.* She had spent most of Sunday calibrating her computer to match the frequencies of the acoustic monitoring equipment. Before the end of the day, she'd know if it had been worth the effort or a waste of time.

Offering up a silent prayer, she picked up one of the sensors, flicked a small switch, and snapped its cover closed. Walking to the side of the boat, she gently dropped it overboard.

"Tell me how this works again?"

She hadn't heard Marc walk up and Abby was certain she detected a heavy dose of skepticism in his voice.

"For all its sophistication, it's really pretty simple," she said, choosing to ignore his doubts. "What I just dropped in was a pop-up hydrophone. The working end is under the water and will pick up any sounds in the area, including the vocalization of the whales and all background noise."

"Background noise?" Marc asked.

"It's important to hear the whales and also what *they* hear," Abby explained.

As she talked, she went over to the cases and held one of the hydrophones up for Marc to examine.

Marc walked over, took it from her and inspected it. "Cute," he said, handing it back.

"Cute!" Abby felt affronted. "This is going to feed directly into this," she held up a small, square device. "It's a DAT—a digital audio tape recorder."

"And that's important because?"

"We're going to set these hydrophones in the river and let them record for twenty-four hours.

That's going to tell me how sound moves through this specific stretch of the Saguenay."

"That's it?" Marc asked.

"No, that's just the beginning." Abby didn't like the smirk she saw on Marc's face. "It's going to take repeated samplings like this to get a reliable sound map."

"And?"

"And then I compare that information to known gathering sites of beluga," she informed him.

"What, and then you give the whales a hearing test?"

This time Abby was certain she heard sarcasm in the question. "No, but it's going to tell me if the whales travel through areas of high noise concentrations and just what those noise levels are."

"What if they do?" Marc asked.

"Sound can have a tremendous impact on whale behavior. It's important to find out specifically what those effects are."

"Sure," Marc said. "In the meantime, should I tiptoe around the deck so I don't disturb any of them?"

Abby determined that by the end of the summer he would take her seriously. "Just keep the boat in one place long enough for me to set my instruments. How's that?"

Marc nodded. "I can do that. But I have to say,

I've never seen anyone go to all this trouble just to answer the age-old question."

"What question would that be?" she asked suspiciously as Marc walked back to the ladder leading to the wheelhouse.

"You know the one." He looked back at her over his shoulder. "If a scientist falls into the water and a whale isn't there to hear it, does she make a sound?"

IT WAS PAST NOON when Marc guided the *Percé* through the Saguenay-Saint Lawrence estuary. For the past five hours he'd crisscrossed the river and held the boat in place as Abby set her acoustic monitoring equipment. During that time he hadn't decided whether this was going to be the easiest or most difficult charter he'd ever taken on.

The work itself was non-taxing. To earn his money, all he had to do was steer the *Percé* in the direction Abby indicated, wait while she did her thing and then move on to the next spot. It was not exactly exciting work, but then it wasn't as unpredictable as day charters, either.

Movement on the deck below caught his eye. Abby had taken the empty cases below and had just returned above deck. As the sun had climbed in the sky, burning off the last of the mist, the temperatures, too, had risen. Both Marc and Abby had started the day in sweatshirts. Some hours earlier Marc had removed his and was now in a T-shirt. As he watched Abby on the sunny bow, she stripped off her long-sleeved shirt, revealing an aqua-green bikini top she had been wearing underneath.

Tossing the shirt to a nearby bench, Abby pulled off the band that had been holding her long hair in a ponytail. She glanced up and caught Marc staring at her.

He managed a halfhearted wave, cleared his throat and called down, "Did you want to make another run up and back today?"

Scooping up her shirt from the bench, Abby yelled back over the noise of the boat's engines, "Please, if there's time." Then she retreated into the shadows cast by the wheelhouse.

Marc stood a moment longer at the rail before whirling around and walking quickly back to the bridge. He took his position behind the wheel and, pushing the throttle, eased the boat around until they were cruising back up the river, the bow slicing through the water's slight chop.

He realized he was gripping the wheel tightly enough to turn his knuckles white. With a conscious effort, he loosened his hold and tried to banish the image of Abby from his mind.

No luck. The sight of her tanned body, taut midriff and hair flowing in the breeze was burned into his brain like a photograph, and Marc had a feeling it was going to stay there for a long time.

Concentrate, Doucette, he told himself. *She's out of your league. She's a research scientist and you're a charter captain; nothing more than a means to her end.*

SMOOTH, REALLY SMOOTH, Abby thought to herself in disgust. *Next time, why don't you plug in the radio and give him a show with music?*

She was standing under the narrow roof that extended from the wheelhouse above and, more importantly, hid her from Marc's view. The day had gotten decidedly warm and she hadn't thought twice about peeling off her shirt. She was wearing light nylon cargo pants—the kind with legs that zipped off, transforming them into shorts. She'd been about to unzip the legs when she looked up and saw Marc staring down at her. He must have thought she'd been performing a kind of shipboard striptease just for him.

She looked at the shirt in her hand and debated putting it back on. If she did, it might simply call more attention to herself. Besides, it was getting hotter outside on deck.

The heck with it, she thought. *It's going to be a long summer if I have to stay covered head to foot. He's just going to have to deal with it.*

CHAPTER TEN

ABBY WAS NOT HAVING a good day. In fact, she'd had several "not good" days in a row. Now, staring at her computer screen, headphones on and the remnants of the lunch Marc had provided spread on the small table next to her, she leaned back in her deck seat and threw her pen down in frustration.

"This doesn't make any sense," she said, and punched in the access codes for the tenth time. Nothing. No audio waves on the computer, no sound coming over the headphones. Silence, for the third day in a row. Abby felt like picking the laptop and chucking it over the side of the boat.

"We've been here awhile." Marc's shadow fell across her screen. "If we want to get to your other sites before dark, we'd better get a move on."

When she didn't answer right away, he walked around and stood in front of her. "Hey, did you hear me?"

"I heard you. Kind of hard not to, since it's the

only thing I have heard," she added with real disgust.

Marc stepped back and peered at the screen a moment. "What? The whales won't talk to you? Maybe if you asked them real nice and said please or…"

"Just take me back to the dock." Abby snapped the cover of the laptop shut. "I've had enough for one day."

"Quitting, huh?" Marc leaned back against the rail, arms crossed over his chest. "My my, and I thought all you scientists were so dedicated."

"I am not quitting," Abby said through clenched teeth. "I'm regrouping. That's what we do on studies like this. Things are always in a constant state of evaluation and modification."

"Right." Abby could hear the sarcasm dripping from his voice. "Just keep changing things around until you get the answers you want."

"Excuse me?" Abby said.

Marc shook his head. "Man, you science types are all alike."

"Meaning?"

"Meaning, you've been out here three days now playing with your audio whatsits and computers, then the moment you don't like the answers you get, you just change things around until you do. Typical."

It took a moment for Abby to formulate a response to Marc's outlandish accusations.

"Change our results?" she sputtered. "To get the answers we want? Are you kidding?"

"Don't look so offended," he said. "And don't worry, your secret's safe with me."

"Secret?" Abby said, "What secret?"

"That your results aren't panning out the way you wanted and you need a day or two to jig the project so you get what you want. No problem. I can use the time to…"

But Abby had stopped listening. She couldn't remember having been this angry in some time.

For three days now she'd been putting up with Marc's derisive comments about her research. She was fed up. Maybe he thought he was being funny. Perhaps she would have been more tolerant of his jibes if the project were going better.

Going better? *Be honest,* she told herself. *It's not going at all.*

Abby knew the beluga were out there in the fjord somewhere. Tourists spent millions of dollars annually to come see them, for heaven's sake! The region hadn't gained a reputation as a whale-watching mecca based on a lack of sightings. So what was she doing wrong?

What she had said to Marc was true—scientific

studies were rarely, if ever, glitch-free. She sighed, shielded her eyes and looked out over the water. Of course, she'd have been hard pressed to describe any problems with her parents' research projects. No, when it came to research, Norman and Lowell were known for generating ground-breaking data. The kind that got the couple written up in *Discover Magazine* or featured in a one-hour NOVA special. In fact, if they were here right now, Abby was quite certain the Saguenay River beluga would be putting on a full-scale production for her parents.

Maybe that's why she'd ducked her mother's call the previous evening and let the answering machine pick up.

We haven't heard from you in a while, Abby heard her mother say into the recording. *Your father and I are just wondering how everything is going up there. You must be very busy with the study and we can hardly wait to see your results. Oh, and before I forget to tell you, your father's been nominated for another Westinghouse Prize! Isn't that a hoot? Well, I told him, Norman—* Abby had reached over and hit the mute button at that point.

Deciding to ignore Marc for the moment, she turned back to her maps and charts. A moment later, a shadow fell over the papers and she heard

Marc chuckle. In her current state of mind, the sound grated on Abby like nails on a chalkboard.

"Step away from the charts," she said through clenched teeth.

"Oh, don't mind me." Marc spoke in an infuriatingly calm voice. "I wouldn't dare presume to comment on the all-powerful, state-of-the-art whale-location maps you have there. Not me. I'm just a guy who's spent his whole life on this river. What do I know?"

Abby whirled around. "And what's *that* supposed to mean?"

Marc shrugged. "Nothing. Or everything. I guess that would depend just how serious you are about this study of yours."

How serious she was? How dare he! Abby was ready to let him have it with both barrels, but something Marc had just said reminded her of a comment he'd made the first night they had supper at Pierrette's. She cast back in her memory. *Take some time to get to know the local people… You might even learn something.*

"Okay, you win," Abby conceded. "If you have any information that could help me, I'm willing to listen."

Marc cocked an eyebrow and looked at her.

When a few seconds passed without his saying anything, Abby nodded and gave a tight smile.

"Then again," she said, "I can't imagine anything making you happier than seeing my research go up in flames."

MARC DIDN'T ANSWER right away; he just stared off into the distance a moment.

"Yeah, I guess I deserved that." He looked back at her. "Can we send up the white flag? I've got enough problems without adding a pissed-off client to the list. I know I've been a jerk. Give me a chance. I might be able to help."

Problems? Abby thought. *She wondered what he meant by that.* But there was sincerity behind those blue eyes, and to be honest, things couldn't get much worse.

"I can't find the whales," she said simply. "I was sure I'd pick up vocalizations this afternoon. But not one of my spots has scored a hit."

"Where's the map and chart you were using to plot your sample sites?" Marc asked.

"Here." Abby retrieved the rolled-up papers.

"Let's take a look," Marc said.

Abby unfurled them on the table. "I don't know what you hope to find here," she said.

Marc looked closely at the chart. "The thing you have to keep in mind is that whales don't use maps. If I were you, I'd try this spot right here."

He pointed to a location several thousand feet from their current site.

"Why there?" Abby asked.

Marc shrugged. "Because I've been running trips along this river for years and we nearly always see whales there."

"Why are you just mentioning this now?" She couldn't keep the sound of accusation from her voice.

"Didn't think you'd listen," Marc told her. "You seemed awfully confident in your calculations. Hang on a second." He disappeared into the wheelhouse and returned a moment later with a battered leather case.

"My dad's old logs and charts," he explained. "Decades of whale sightings are listed in here."

Opening to the appropriate page, Marc bent over Abby's charts and began comparing coordinates. After a moment, he made a series of twelve dots, each representing what he felt were the most likely places to see whales. To her chagrin, she saw that none of them corresponded to her own projections.

"Dammit," she muttered.

"Mind a suggestion?" Marc offered.

"I'm all ears."

"We're not far from this point here." He pointed to the closest dot on the map. "Why don't we head over there and you can give it another try?"

Abby nodded, hope filling her. "Let's do it," she said. "You get the anchor up and I'll pull the hydrophone."

"Aye-aye, captain." Marc threw her a mock salute.

An hour later, Abby was whooping with joy.

Marc stood next to her as she watched the sound levels dance across the computer screen. "I take it your study is back on?"

"They're down there. The beluga are down there, right where you said they would be. I can hear them. They're vocalizing a mile a minute. This is going to work! Marc Doucette, you are a genius and lifesaver! How can I thank you?"

Then, almost giddy with delight, she kissed him full on the mouth.

"OH MY GOD, I'm so sorry." Abby pulled out of Marc's embrace and stepped back, her legs hitting the bench. She fought for balance, lost and sat down hard.

"I'm not." Marc grinned. "If I'd known I'd get that kind of response, I'd have dived down and gotten some whales for you personally!" He sat next to her and tried to put his arm around her shoulders.

"Marc, please, don't misunderstand me. You've probably saved my study from being over before it even began. And I'm grateful. But I just can't do this right now. I never should have kissed you like that. I'm so sorry."

Marc looked at her a moment, confused. He'd been more than just a little startled when Abby had kissed him so unexpectedly. But after that first instant, he'd tightened his arms around her, prepared to give back as good as he got. And, for a very long moment, it had been pure heaven. But when he pulled her even closer, she had stiffened and turned away.

Now he was cursing himself for misreading what he thought was a clear signal. *Fine. Two can play at this game.*

He released his hold on Abby. "No problem," he said mildly. "I'm just happy to help any way I can. That's what you pay me for, after all." With that, he turned from her and stalked back to the wheelhouse.

"Women!" he said as he flipped the switch and engaged the motor to reel in the anchor chain.

WHAT ON EARTH had made me kiss him? Abby thought grimly as she replaced the day's equipment in the cabin she had transformed into her onboard acoustic lab.

Sure, she'd been beyond grateful when she realized he had solved her problem with the missing beluga. But wouldn't a simple thank-you, followed-up perhaps by a hand-slapping high five, been a tad more appropriate?

Appropriate, maybe, but nowhere near as powerful or, she had to admit, as pleasant. When Marc was kissing her back, something had stirred in Abby's soul that she'd been certain was long buried and forgotten.

She was afraid to admit to the feeling, much less say it out loud, but there was no denying it. Physical contact with Marc had sent her emotions skyrocketing into areas she had no time to explore at this stage of her life.

CHAPTER ELEVEN

"GIVE ME A MINUTE to tie off these cables and I'll walk home with you," Marc called as Abby prepared to climb down the boat's ladder.

"Um, okay." Neither one had said anything about the kiss. In fact, they had shared barely a dozen words between them the entire cruise down the Saguenay into Tadoussac Bay. Abby had managed to keep herself to the main deck while Marc remained at the wheel. She had hoped to slip off the boat without talking to him, despite how rude she knew that would look.

"All set," he said, wiping his hands on the back seat of his jeans as he joined her at the rail. "I don't suppose I could talk you into joining me in a beer?"

"That's very nice of you," Abby said, thinking the last thing she needed was to spend any more time alone with Marc. "But I really want to start looking at the data we collected today, minimal as it is. How about a rain check?"

"Okay." Abby could have sworn she saw real

disappointment in his eyes. "In that case, maybe I'll hang on board for a bit. Make sure everything's gassed up and ready for the morning. You want to start at the same time?"

"Please," Abby said. "I was planning to do some background recordings in the bay tomorrow, but now I think I'll redo the river trip and hit those spots you identified."

On her way home, Abby walked past the driveway leading down to the marine center. She debated going to her lab, but decided to head straight to her apartment instead. What work she had to do was all on her laptop and she could do it just as well sitting on her couch as in her lab.

Unlatching the gate to the backyard, she automatically looked around for Figgy. She spotted the little dog immediately, sitting under a tree, but was surprised when she did not instantly bound over to greet her.

"Figgy?" Abby called out. "What're you doing?"

Abby walked over and saw that Figgy was sitting next to Sylvie. The girl had been hidden behind the tree and Abby could see she was crying. Figgy looked from Sylvie to Abby and the dog's expression seemed to say, *Do something!*

Abby hunkered down until she was eye level with the little girl. "Sylvie?" she said quietly, "What on earth is the matter?"

"N-nothing," Sylvie said, a sob catching in her voice.

"I think something is wrong. Your dad is down on the boat. He'll be here in an hour or so, but I could go get him now if you'd like."

At those words Sylvie's eyes flew wide open. "No!" she cried out, "You can't tell him where I am! Please?"

"Okay, I won't," Abby was mystified. She wasn't used to small children and had no idea what to do. "How about I go get your grandmother?"

"No, not Gran, either," Sylvie said. "Can't I just stay here with Figgy?" She hugged the dog around the neck.

"Of course you can," Abby said gently. "But wouldn't you rather come inside for something to drink and maybe a snack?"

Sylvie sniffed and wiped at her nose with the back of her hand. "Whatcha got?"

Abby made a quick, mental inventory of her kitchen. "I have some juice and milk, and I think there are some bananas and a bag of Oreo cookies."

"I like Oreos," Sylvie said, and Abby saw Figgy's ears prick up at the word "cookies."

"All right then, c'mon, you two." Abby stood up and put her hand out for Sylvie to take.

Inside, Abby poured two glasses of milk and set

the bag of cookies on the table in front of the couch. Sylvie sat down, picked up the glass in one hand, a cookie in the other and stared out the window. Taking her own glass, Abby took a seat next to her and waited, uncertain how to proceed.

"How was school today?" she asked, figuring that it was a safe subject. Sylvie's reaction told her she couldn't have been more wrong.

As Abby watched in horror, Sylvie burst into tears, dropped the cookie on the floor, put the glass back on the table and buried her face in her hand, shoulders heaving.

"Sylvie?" Abby said, worried. "I'm sorry, what did I say? Did something bad happen at school?"

Sylvie shook her head, still crying.

"Then what?"

With a mighty sniff, Sylvie pulled her hands from her face and turned to look at Abby. "They're going to make me stay back!" she wailed, new tears streaming from her eyes.

"Stay back? Sylvie, stay back where?" Abby asked.

"Dad and Gran and Madame Simard don't want me to be in third grade."

"Sylvie, what are you talking about?" Abby said. "Why on earth would your father or grandmother or your teacher not want you to go on to the third grade?"

"Because I'm stupid!" Sylvie cried. "Because I can't read or write good."

"What gave you that idea?" Abby knew Françoise and Marc would never refer to Sylvie as stupid.

"I heard Gran talking on the phone when I got home. She thought I was in my room. She said Madame Simard told Dad I have to do second grade all over again if I don't get good marks. I don't *want* to be with a bunch of babies! I want to stay with my friends!"

"Sylvie, Sylvie." Abby put an arm around the girl's shoulders. "I'm sure you're mistaken." As she tried to think of something to say to console the girl, Abby couldn't help but wonder if Sylvie was overreacting to the thought of repeating second grade. Was that really such a bad thing? Then she remembered her own childhood and the social minefield that was primary school. *Yeah, it is such a bad thing.* Kids could be cruel and quickly pounced on anyone perceived as different. From her own experience, Abby knew that students who were held back eventually blended with the new class and went on to academic success. But such hindsight was of little use to Sylvie, who was terrified of seeing her friends move on without her.

Abby realized Sylvie had said something.

"I'm sorry, Sylvie, what was that?"

"I said, it doesn't matter." She looked down at her lap. "I'm still dumb. And now everyone's going to know I'm dumb."

"You are not dumb!" Abby gave the little girl a hug. "Look at what you've taught Figgy. And that wonderful drawing you made for me. Plus, you speak two languages. I think you're pretty clever."

"Really?"

"Really," Abby said. "And repeating a grade has nothing to do with how smart a person is. It's more about how fast you learn. Some people just learn at different rates."

"That's what my dad says." Sylvie didn't sound convinced. "I just wish I could read and write good, but I just don't get how."

"What don't you get?" Abby asked, curious. She had begun reading and writing at a very early age and had often found solace between the covers of books.

Sylvie shrugged. "I look at the pictures and the writing, but when the teacher asks me to read out loud, I can't."

"But when you read to yourself, can you understand what you're reading?" Abby asked.

Sylvie nodded. "Sure. I can't read fast, but I can do it."

"But not out loud?"

"Uh-uh." Sylvie shook her head. "And Madame Simard makes us do all sorts of work in groups and stuff."

"What about writing?'

Sylvie shrugged. "It's hard and I hate it when I get stuff wrong."

"What happens when you get things wrong?"

"The teacher makes us go to the blackboard and do it over and over until it's right."

Abby flashed back to her own grade school days and the fear and humiliation that came with working out a math problem or writing sentences on the blackboard, back to the rest of the class, rows of students staring at her and the sounds of stifled giggles at the smallest of mistakes. If Sylvie's difficulties were rooted in a lack of confidence and self-esteem, it would be little wonder the girl chose to simply not do her work rather than risk public humiliation.

Abby patted the girl's head absently and handed her another cookie. Sitting back, she thought a moment. She hadn't just been trying to make Sylvie feel better when she said she was clever. The girl had a real intelligence, but obviously something had her good and spooked about reading or writing in front of anyone. How sad that this Madame Simard was basing her entire assessment of Sylvie on that reluctance. She heard Sylvie giggle and looked down to see Figgy, her head on Sylvie's lap, doing her best to beg a cookie.

"Figgy," Abby began with a warning tone, and then it hit her. She might have found a way to help Sylvie.

"Sylvie, can you do me a favor and wait right here for a half hour or so? Keep an eye on Figgy?" Abby could barely keep the excitement out of her voice.

"Sure, I guess so," Sylvie said. "Where are you going?"

"It's a surprise," Abby told her. "I'll be right back."

Rushing out the gate, she saw Françoise on her front porch. She quickly explained that Sylvie was in her apartment, helping her with something, before she took off toward the marine center at a fast walk.

"CAN I HELP YOU find something?" Marie asked Abby ten minutes later.

"No, I think I can manage." Abby scanned the shelves of the center's gift shop. "Ha! Here it is," she said in triumph, pulling a book from the children's shelf.

"That's a real favorite with the kids," Marie said. "I got one for my nephew last Christmas. He loved it."

"I'll take it," Abby said. "What do I owe you?"

Marie shook her head. "On the house. Call it a scholar's discount."

"Thank you!" Abby said with real feeling, pushing out the doors and heading back to her apartment.

She found Sylvie and Figgy right where she had left them, the now half-empty bag of Oreos on the table.

"I brought you a present, Sylvie," Abby said, holding up the shopping bag.

"Really? I love presents! What is it?" Sylvie's look of anticipation disappeared as Abby pulled the item from the bag. "Oh, a book," she said dully.

"Yes, a book." Abby sat down next to her. "And a very important book."

"What's so important about it?" Sylvie asked.

"Well, first of all it tells a very important story about a whale and his best friend a seal," Abby said. "And secondly, it's Figgy's favorite."

"Dogs can't read," Sylvie scoffed. "Even *I* know that!"

"Of course they can't. But some dogs, like Figgy, love being read *to*."

"They do not," Sylvie said. "Who ever heard of reading to a dog?"

Abby suspected that if Marc or Françoise had

been in earshot, they would have made Sylvie apologize for her rude tone, but Abby decided to let it slide.

"It's true," she said, silently praying that Figgy would cooperate.

Abby opened the book to the first page and moved it so it was positioned between Sylvie and her. Then she patted the cushion next to the girl and Figgy hopped up.

"Why don't you give it a try?" Abby suggested.

Sylvie shook her head. "Uh-uh, no way."

"Why not?"

Sylvie jabbed a finger at the first page. "It's too hard. That's a big-girl book."

Abby nodded. "I suppose it is, but I never got around to reading the whole thing to Figgy. Now, with all the work I have to do this summer, I doubt there's going to be any time. Can't you give it a try? I'd really appreciate it." Abby held her breath.

Sylvie looked down at the page, kicking her feet against the side of the couch. Then she glanced over at the dog. "Do you want me to read to you?" she asked.

Abby could have shouted for joy when Figgy flopped down and laid her head on Sylvie's lap.

"Okay," Sylvie said, pulling the book away from Abby. "But just Figgy."

"Oh, you want me to leave?"

Sylvie nodded.

"All right. I'll leave you two alone for a bit," Abby said. She made a show of walking out the door and shutting it firmly behind her. Waiting a moment, she cracked it back open and peeked inside.

"The…whale…" Sylvie read as Figgy remained, still as a statue, staring up at the little girl. Abby couldn't help but smile as she watched, then nearly screamed out loud when she felt a hand fall on to her shoulder. She whirled around and saw Marc looking at her, an expression of amusement on his handsome face.

"Dare I ask?" he said mildly.

She struggled to catch her breath. "Oh, Marc, yeah, I guess this looks kind of silly, me peeking in my own door like this."

"It's your apartment," he teased her. "I guess you can peek in all you want. Actually, I'm looking for Sylvie. My mom said she was with you?"

"She is." Abby held a finger to her lips, motioning for silence, and stepped away from the door. "Take a look for yourself."

WITH A CURIOUS GLANCE at Abby, Marc brushed past her. Cracking the door open three inches, he peered inside. He saw Sylvie right away, sitting on the couch, looking down at something she was holding on her lap. Abby's dog, Figgy, was curled up next to her.

Without moving from the spot, Marc turned his head and looked at Abby. "What's she doing in there?"

"Just look and listen," Abby said.

Marc turned back. Sylvie was obviously speaking, but what was she saying? It sounded like she was talking about whales. Marc opened the door a bit wider and stepped quietly into the apartment.

It took a moment for the scene on the couch to register with him, but when it did, it hit Marc like a thunderbolt.

Sylvie was sitting there, book opened on her lap, reading out loud.

Marc's jaw dropped and he spun around to look at Abby, who had quietly followed him inside. When he opened his mouth to speak, she gently tugged him back outside and shut the door behind them.

"How? What? I—" Marc knew he was stammering, but couldn't manage to form a coherent thought. His daughter was reading! And from the little bit he had heard, she was reading quite well. He took a deep, calming breath and looked at Abby. "You want to tell me just what I saw in there?" He jerked his thumb in the direction of the closed door.

"Call it a little creative crisis management."

"Come again?"

Marc listened intently as Abby recounted finding Sylvie, hiding and in tears, and their subsequent conversation.

"Dammit," Marc said. "I never wanted her to hear about the whole staying back a year thing. I knew it would upset her."

"I just wanted to do something." Abby hesitated. "I hope I didn't overstep."

"Overstep?" Marc repeated. "Hardly. Do you have any idea what you have done?"

Abby shook her head.

"Here, let's sit down a moment." Marc took Abby's arm and guided her to the bench on the porch. When they had both sat down, he stared out at the empty yard a moment.

"When Sylvie was born," Marc began, still looking straight ahead, "right away I could tell she was bright. I mean, I know all parents say that about their kids, but Sylvie, well, there was just something in her eyes, y'know? It's like she came into the world, and the moment she was born, looked around at all of us there in the birthing room and thought to herself, *bring it on*. From the minute we brought her home she was always taking everything in. When she started crawling, she explored everything, and when she started walking, look out! Her verbal skills were off the charts and she was doing really well socially in day care…" His voice drifted off.

"And?" Abby prompted gently.

Marc shifted on the bench, leaning forward and looking at the ground. "When Sylvie was five, her mother—Thérèse, my wife—was killed very suddenly in a car crash in Toronto."

"Oh, Marc, I'm so sorry," Abby said softly.

Marc shrugged. "Yeah, me too. It was a horrible time. Sylvie and I were just getting ready to go out when the cops arrived and told me. I guess I kind of freaked out—right in front of Sylvie. In front of my daughter!" He looked up and pounded his fist into his thigh.

"You were understandably upset!" Abby said. "I can't imagine what it would be like to hear something like that out of the blue."

"I was a selfish dope," Marc said. "Sylvie needed me. She was scared and kept asking for her mother. There were all these strangers in the house, lots of confusion, and I was too busted up during those first days to notice. I mean, I knew she was upset. But I just never figured how deep that could go in a five-year-old. Anyway, after the funeral, I wanted to get her back into preschool right off—y'know, try to get things back to normal as quickly as possible? Well, that was a bad move."

"Why? What happened?" Abby asked.

"I tried to drop Sylvie off and she went into hysterics. Wouldn't let go of me. So, I brought her home and tried again a few days later. Same thing. After a month of this, it was pretty obvious she wasn't about to let me leave her there. My mom had come to stay with us right after Thérèse died and she suggested we come back to Tadoussac for a while. It really seemed to do Sylvie a world of good. She always loved her grandmother. The next year, I enrolled her in school—first grade." Marc's laughter held no humor. "I have to admit I was scared there'd be a repeat of the day care hysterics the first day I took her to school. But she went, quiet as a lamb. And I guess that should have been some kind of clue."

"Of what?" Abby said.

"It was gone. Whatever it was that drove Sylvie to explore and learn was just gone. She does do her homework—just—and gets along fine with the other kids, but it's like her brain is stuck in gear and she can't or won't move forward."

"It must have been very hard for both of you," Abby said.

Marc nodded. "I'm at my wit's end. I met with her teacher and she's the one who said Sylvie would be better off in second grade again. And if Sylvie doesn't show any signs of improvement, that's the recommendation she's going to make."

"But she's in there now, reading to Figgy."

"Yeah, and it's a miracle," Marc said. "A flat-out miracle. Do you realize it's the first time I've heard her read with that kind of confidence? How'd you do it?"

Abby thought a moment. "I'm not sure I did anything. My roommate during my undergrad years was an education major and she went on to do research in literacy. A week or so before I left to come up here, my mom sent me a clipping from our hometown paper about my roommate winning this big award for her work using reading-therapy dogs to get kids to read."

"Reading-therapy dogs?" Marc repeated.

"Uh-huh." Abby nodded. "What my friend found was that children who do poorly in reading often just don't want to read in front of anyone. But dogs are different. They don't judge or make fun. It's a comfort level thing."

Marc leaned back. *A reading-therapy dog.* Now he'd heard everything.

"So what you're saying is that years of profes-sional teaching, counseling and support were a waste of time and all I should have done was go to the pound?"

Abby looked at him a moment. "Are you upset?"

Marc shook his head. "Upset? No. Frustrated? Yes."

"Why?"

"Why? Why do you think? It seems like everything I've done for Sylvie since Thérèse died has been a mistake. Sometimes I think I'm doing her more harm than good."

"That's just foolish!" Abby sounded impatient. "Marc, look at her. You said it yourself—she's bright and creative. That drawing she did of Figgy is fantastic. And from what you've told me, you've done everything in your power to help her."

"It just never seems enough," Marc said dully.

"It's enough," Abby insisted. "Anyone who's around the two of you for more than five minutes can tell she loves you very much and you love her."

"Thanks." Marc was grateful for the support.

"So why not give this a try?" Abby suggested. "She already plays with Figgy during the day, so why not let her read to her, too?"

"I guess it can't do any harm," Marc began, "at least until the next report card."

"When's that?" Abby said.

"The end of June." Could this be the answer he'd been looking for? Marc wondered. Was a silly little brown dog the key to unlock his daughter's wounded spirit? He shook his head. "A dog," he whispered, looking up at Abby. "You know, if this really works, I mean, if she really has some sort of breakthrough, there is no way I can ever repay you or thank you enough."

"Oh, yes you can," Abby said with a wide grin.

"Name it." Marc was prepared to agree to anything Abby suggested.

"You can let me be there when you tell that Madame Simard of yours just how Sylvie did it."

AFTER SUPPER that night, Marc joined Sylvie on the living-room couch and watched her a moment as she worked on a pencil drawing of the *Percé*.

"That's really good, *ma fille*," he said to her.

"Thanks, Dad." Sylvie looked up at him. "When it's done, will you hang it in the boat?"

"You bet. I'll put it right next to the wheel, so I can look at it every day." Marc dreaded what he was going to say next. "There's something we need to talk about so I need you to stop drawing for a bit."

"Okay." Sylvie put the pencil and pad of paper aside.

"This afternoon, Abby told me you were pretty upset about something you heard your grandmother say on the phone." Marc watched his daughter's eyes get big and round.

"I wasn't doing anything bad. I just wanted to get a drink of water, honest!" Sylvie's lower lip started to tremble.

"I know, *ma fille,* I know," Marc said soothingly. "And for now we are going to forget about that, because I owe you an apology."

"Really?" Sylvie looked surprised, struck by the novelty of a grown-up having to say they were sorry to a child. "Why?"

"Because I was not completely honest with you about what Madame Simard and I talked about," Marc explained. "I didn't want to upset you, but now I see that was wrong."

"You mean about staying behind?" Sylvie said in a very small voice.

"Yes," Marc said. "Sylvie, you have to understand that all of us—me, your grandmother and Madame Simard, we all want what's best for you."

"I know." Sylvie wouldn't look at Marc.

"And sometimes, well, sometimes grown-ups don't always agree on what's best," he said.

That made Sylvie glance up. "They don't?"

"Nope. In fact, as you get older, you're going

to find out that grown-ups actually disagree more than they agree."

"Really?"

"Really," Marc said. "Now, Madame Simard might think repeating second grade is what's best for you, but your grandmother and I don't necessarily agree."

"That's right, honey, we don't." Françoise walked into the living room and sat down in her favorite recliner.

"But, Sylvie," Marc chose his words carefully. "We want you to do well in school, and that might mean another year in grade two. And if that happens, it's not because you're dumb or in trouble. It's because that's the best way for you to learn, okay?"

His daughter gave a mighty sigh. "Will you still love me if I have to stay back in grade two?" she said in a small voice.

"Still love—? Of course we will!" Marc said.

"Sylvie, there's nothing you could do that would make us stop loving you," Françoise reassured her and Marc was glad to see his daughter looking slightly less downcast.

"Abby said she brought you a book today and that you're reading it to Figgy." Marc saw his mother sit up slightly. This was the first she had heard of it.

"Yeah, she did!" Sylvie said. "It was a present for me. She says Figgy likes to listen to stories, but she doesn't have time, so she asked me to read to her."

Feeling like he was about to step on to a newly frozen pond with no idea of the ice's thickness, Marc said, "How did you like it, reading to the dog, I mean?"

"It was fun! She didn't understand all the words, so I had to explain some of them to her." The pride in Sylvie's voice was unmistakable.

"Do you want to run and get the book and read to your gran and me?" Marc suggested.

"Do I have to?" Sylvie's enthusiasm of just a moment before evaporated.

"Don't you want to?" Marc gently prompted, but Sylvie only shrugged in response.

"Okay," he said. "It's getting late anyway and almost your bedtime. Why don't you go brush your teeth and put on your pajamas? I'll come tuck you in."

He watched as Sylvie hopped down from the couch, collected her drawings and went to give Françoise a kiss good night. "G'night, Gran," Sylvie said, scampering from the room. For a moment the two adults listened to her footsteps up the stairs and on the floor above.

"What's all this about reading dogs?" Françoise

asked when they heard the water running in the upstairs bathroom.

"Not reading dogs, reading *to* dogs," Marc explained.

"Fine, but what's it all about?" Françoise asked.

Marc shook his head. "Mom, I have to tell you, if I hadn't seen it for myself I never would've believed it." Marc told his mother about Abby finding Sylvie in the yard with Figgy, then convincing her to read aloud to the dog.

"Mom, you should have seen them. Sylvie was reading, actually *reading,* and I swear to God that dog was listening to every word she said."

"Remarkable," Françoise murmured. "Marc, I'm so sorry Sylvie heard me on the phone! I never should have said anything."

Marc held up his hand. "Don't worry about it, it's okay. I never should have tried to hide anything from Sylvie. Maybe hearing you was the best thing that could have happened."

"Maybe so," Françoise said. "Do you think there's anything to this reading-therapy dog business?"

Marc shrugged. "If you'd asked me that this morning I'd have said no. Now, I'm not so sure. Frankly, at this point I'm ready to give anything a try. And we both know Sylvie can read and write, it's just that she stopped doing both. Maybe that dog is the boost her confidence needs."

"I'm inclined to agree," Françoise said. "Oh, and before I forget, those people from Hull called. They will be here in two weeks."

Marc was surprised by the pang that once again went through his heart at the idea of strangers living in the house.

"She's really something, isn't she?" Françoise said.

"Who?" Marc asked.

"Abby, who else? Getting Sylvie to read with that little dog of hers. Quite a woman."

"You can say that again," Marc said. "Quite a woman."

CHAPTER TWELVE

"IS THAT WHAT I think it is?"

Abby looked up from her kneeling position on the cabin floor and saw Marc standing in the doorway. After a week of listening via the pop-ups, she was ready to move to the next phase of her research.

"That all depends," she said, shoving the long black case under the table and standing. "What do you think it is?"

Marc walked all the way into the cabin, stepping around several foam-padded cases, and set two mugs of steaming coffee on the table. He took the object from Abby's hands.

"I'm no expert on medieval weapons," he said. "But I'd lay good money what we have here is a good, old-fashioned crossbow."

"And you'd be right." Abby picked up one of the mugs and took a long sip. She was discovering many benefits to working on the *Percé,* and Marc's coffee was near the top of the list.

"Are we going hunting?" Marc asked, hefting the crossbow.

"In a manner of speaking." Abby reclaimed the crossbow. "Today I get to do my Captain Ahab act."

"Just call you Ishmael?" Marc said, playing along.

Abby laughed. "Sure, why not?"

"Well, they are white whales, after all," Marc said. "So what's the plan?"

Abby set the crossbow down on the table and pulled a case from a shelf on the wall. Opening it, she selected a square box with a suction cup on one end and antennae sticking out from the other. She handed it to Marc.

"Cute," he said, examining it and handing it back to Abby. "What's it for?"

Abby took the box from him and placed it back in the case. "It's an acoustic tag. It records ambient underwater sounds and can be tracked. These little babies," she patted the case, "are going to tell me how the beluga move through water and just what they hear along the way."

"And how do they do that?" Marc asked.

"First, you find some beluga for me," Abby said. "Then, I load one of the boxes onto the crossbow and fire it at the whale. If I do it right, the suction cup will adhere to the beluga and remain in place as it swims around for a week or so."

Marc frowned. "Seems kinda violent."

Abby shook her head. "This crossbow may look mean, but it's been designed specifically for this kind of job. It fires with just enough power to connect the box, but not enough to even be felt by the whales."

"Okay, then, let's go find us some whales."

To Abby's immense relief, she and Marc had actually been getting along. Of course, she thought, following Marc up to the deck, there had still been the occasional joke or comment about her work, but it almost seemed he was taking an active interest in the project.

"Go ahead, say it. You know you want to."

Abby looked over at Marc from her position perched at the end of the forward transom. "Say what?" she called back.

Marc grinned at her from the outside wheel as he gently guided the boat toward a small pod of beluga.

"You know," he said.

Catching on, Abby smiled back at him. "If you insist." She turned back to face the open water. In a moment, the gleaming white of a mature beluga broke the surface, its form a stark contrast to the sparkling blue of the fjord. Abby watched it for a moment and then shouted, "Thar she blows!"

Behind her, Marc laughed and steered the *Percé* on a parallel course to the pod.

"Okay," Abby yelled, motioning with her hand. "Not too close, this is good. Can you hold steady here?"

"You got it," Marc called, easing down the throttle.

Keeping a close watch on the largest of the five or so whales in the pod, Abby lifted the crossbow and sighted along its arm. Bracing her legs against the pitch and roll of the boat, she took aim at the beluga. "Easy, easy, that's it," she whispered. "Let him come to you." The whale breached directly in front of the boat and Abby let the projectile fly. Her timing was perfect and she allowed herself a cheer when she saw the suction cup with the electronic box attached hit the target just behind the whale's blowhole.

"Bull's-eye!" she heard Marc yell.

"One down," Abby said, reaching for another box and resetting the bow string of the crossbow. "On to the next pod!"

Four pods and three hours later, Abby abandoned her place at the transom. Setting the crossbow down on the deck outside the wheelhouse, she flexed her stiff fingers and went to stand next to Marc.

"Well, that has to be a first," he said.

"For what?" Abby asked, helping herself to a bottle of Gatorade from the cooler Marc kept in the wheelhouse.

"A sanctioned whale hunt."

Abby chuckled. "I'm not sure I'd call it a hunt. More of a catch and release."

"Now what?"

"Now I see if all that effort was worth it." She turned to descend to her onboard laboratory.

"You want me to hold steady here for a while?" Marc asked.

"Yeah," Abby said. "And can you cut the engines?"

"You got it."

As she made her way below, Abby heard the engines cycle down to a steady idle and then go silent. A moment later, she heard the metallic rattle of the anchor chain being dropped. "Let's see what we have here," she muttered, sitting at the small desk in the cabin and flipping open her laptop. Pulling on a set of headphones, Abby fiddled with the fine-tune control on the acoustic monitoring equipment while the laptop came to life.

"Okay, talk to me," she whispered.

First there was only silence in the headphones, then she heard a slight ping. After she boosted the power on the receiver, the next ping was more audible and she could hear a variety of others, their pitch varying slightly. At the same time, numbers popped up on the computer screen. A sigh of relief escaped her.

Scribbling some notes, she waited as the transmitting pings resolved themselves into separate and distinct tones, and then matched each with the on-screen coordinates. Four different pings and four separate coordinates meant all boxes were up and running. For the time being, anyway.

So intent was she on following the radio telemetry, Abby didn't hear Marc come into the cabin three hours later and she let out a small yelp of surprise when she felt him tap her on the shoulder.

"I didn't mean to startle you," Marc said, as Abby pulled the headphones down around her neck. "Sorry."

"That's okay. I guess I lost track of time."

"How's it going?" he asked.

"Pretty good," Abby said. "Take a look."

"Uh, okay, but what am I looking at?" Marc squinted at the computer screen and the jumble of numbers and lines radiating across it.

Abby pulled the headphones completely off and handed them to Marc. "Listen to this and I'll explain."

Marc held the headset up to one ear.

"Hear anything?" Abby twisted a dial on her machine.

"No, wait, yeah, kind of a steady rumble," Marc said.

"What you're hearing is what beluga number oh-five-two-seven-nine is hearing." Abby pointed to a blinking set of numbers on the screen. "Probably the engines of a passing boat."

"No kidding?" Marc said. "How do you know that?"

"Those boxes I attached to the whales? They also have radio tracking beacons built in so I can follow each of those whales and know where they are at any given time. The boxes also have receivers that pick up and digitally record everything the whale is hearing."

"Impressive." Marc handed the headset back. "But how do you know that's what the whale is hearing?"

"It's all about bioacoustics," Abby said.

"And what is that exactly?"

"In this case that box," Abby explained. "It's really a very sophisticated piece of technology that's been designed to replicate a whale's hearing according to the same frequency they vocalize." Abby turned back to her machine. "Of course, until we can actually give a whale a hearing test, it's still equal parts biology, technology and conjecture. But at least it gives us reliable readings of what sounds are reaching the whales."

Marc shook his head. "So, basically what you're doing down here is eavesdropping on the whales?"

"I guess that's one way to put it." Abby noticed that a slightly mocking tone had crept back into Marc's voice. "I'm not sure I'd put it that way, though."

"No, I don't suppose you would," Marc said. "I mean, I can't imagine anyone throwing away good money to listen in on underwater gossip."

Marc's sarcasm rankled Abby, but she refused to let him get a rise out of her. Not now, when her work appeared to be going so well.

"Don't you have a deck to swab or something?" she suggested.

"Fine, I can take a hint," Marc said. "I just came down to ask about the rest of the day."

Abby looked at her watch. It was close to one thirty, she saw. "I'd like to hang out here for a few hours and keep tracking the emitters. They'll continue to record on their own, but I want to keep an eye on them for now, just in case."

"Okay," Marc said, heading out of the cabin. "I'll be topside if you need me. There's salad and fruit in the fridge. Help yourself if you're hungry."

After he left, Abby put her headphones back on

and turned to the computer. Data was coming in a constant stream and she couldn't have been happier. It would require in-depth analysis, but the information would eventually yield a detailed acoustic map of the fjord and bay.

"Okay, whale number oh-six-six-five-two," Abby whispered, tapping on her keyboard. "Let's just listen in on your world."

THE DAY WAS SUNNY and conditions on the Saguenay were dead calm. Marc kept the *Percé* in excellent condition, so there was very little in the way of routine maintenance to keep him occupied while Abby fiddled with her whale-listening equipment down below. Since all he had to do for the foreseeable future was keep the boat steady and in place, it looked like he had some time to kill.

With little else to do, Marc decided to have lunch. He walked down to the galley and grabbed a sandwich and pop from the refrigerator. Back in the wheelhouse, he sat down and tried to focus on the view around the boat, but the image of Abby kept getting in the way. At last he gave up and allowed his thoughts to linger on the woman. True to his word, he'd been on his best behavior. The funny thing was, it hadn't been as hard as he'd thought it would be. While he wasn't sold on her research, he was starting to be intrigued.

Marc took a drink of soda and watched a trio of cormorants take off from the river, their water-logged bodies making the maneuver cumbersome. Okay, if he was going to be really honest, it was more than Abby's work that intrigued him. It was the whole package. He found himself looking for ways to surreptitiously watch her, and lately he'd been trying to draw her into conversation just to hear the sound of her voice or to make her laugh and flash that knockout grin.

A slight roll to starboard made Marc look up. The Saguenay cruise ship *Sainte Helene* was passing off to the side and he could see a dozen or so passengers lining the rails of the upper deck. Marc leaned forward and pulled the cord activating the *Percé*'s air horn. A moment later, the *Sainte Helene* responded with two quick blasts of her own.

Marc watched as the larger boat motored up and out of sight beyond a bend in the river. Stretching, he planted his feet back down on the floor and looked at his watch. Time to start thinking of heading in.

He was about to go see if Abby was ready to head back when she appeared at the top of the ladder.

"Had enough for the day?" Marc asked.

Abby nodded. "The equipment is still picking up plenty of sound. In fact, that must have been a pretty good-sized boat that went by."

"You just missed it. The *Sainte Helene*. She's one of the cruise ships that do tours up the fjord during the summer."

"How far up does she go?" Abby asked.

"All the way to Chicoutimi. It's a day trip." Marc keyed the ignition and the motors roared to life. Pushing the throttle, he brought the *Percé* around and increased the speed. The boat responded and cut through the small swells, sending up spray on either side.

"Oh, I almost forgot to tell you," Abby said. "I've got some good news."

"Oh?" Marc had to keep his eyes on the river in front.

"Yeah, I stopped by my office on my way in this morning and Pete said he'd have your first check ready for you at the end of day."

That was good news, indeed, Marc thought, thinking of his shrinking bank account. They made the rest of the trip back to the Tadoussac dock in a comfortable silence. The sun was just sinking behind the hills surrounding the town when Marc tied off the last of the mooring lines and met Abby on the deck.

"So," he said, suddenly not all that anxious to see her leave. "You had another good day?"

"A great day," Abby said. "Thanks for asking."

"Those sensor things working for you?"

"They are," she replied.

"That's good." Marc felt a bit foolish. "I mean, I've seen whales all my life, but until you came around, I guess I never gave much thought to *hearing* them."

"Really?" Abby arched an eyebrow. "Well, if you have a moment to spare, we can take care of that right now."

Trying his best to sound casual about the whole thing, Marc said, "Sure, I mean, why not? I'll try anything once."

LEADING THE WAY back to her onboard sound lab, Abby was a little surprised at Marc's newfound interest in whale communication. But it seemed sincere. At least for the moment.

Sitting at the small desk, she picked up a pair of headphones and handed them to Marc. "Here, put these on."

Marc took them and adjusted them over his ears. "Now what?" he said.

"Now *listen*." Abby adjusted several knobs on the audio monitor. A second later, waves of different colors—each indicating a different sound level—danced across the screen. She watched Marc carefully. His expression went from puzzled amusement to wide-eyed amazement.

"Those are whales?" he said softly.

"Yep."

"Wait a minute, what's that?" Marc asked.

Abby saw a wide red line cut across the screen. "That must be the big cruise ship you said passed by earlier."

Marc listened a moment longer and then removed the headset, handing it back to Abby.

"What did you think?" Abby asked.

"Well, not much of a beat, but they sure are noisy little cusses, aren't they?"

Abby rolled her eyes. She'd hoped he would have gotten more out of the experience. Still, at least he'd given it a go. *Baby steps,* she told herself, repacking the equipment.

"How's Sylvie doing?" Abby asked later as they were walking up the dock.

Marc shook his head. "Unbelievably well. She still doesn't want to read to me or my mom, but when it comes to that dog of yours, there's no stopping her. If she keeps up at this rate, I'm going to have to make a run to Baie-Sainte Catherine to get more books."

Abby laughed. "I think that sounds like a nice problem to have."

"You can say that again," Marc agreed, and slowed his step. "Seems like it's been a good week for both of us, all around."

Abby nodded. "It's going to take me all weekend just to sort through the data I've collected over the last five days."

Marc slowed his step a fraction more. "So, how about we go out and celebrate tonight?"

CHAPTER THIRTEEN

"MARC DOUCETTE," Abby said, trying to keep her tone light. "Are you asking me on a date?"

"A date? Let's see." Marc looked up at the sky. "Dinner, you and me, my treat. I guess it does sound that way. Sure, let's call it a date. You can even tell me more about those whales of yours."

Abby took a deep breath. "Marc, I'm not sure that's such a good idea."

"Dinner's not a good idea?"

"No, I mean, dinner's a great idea," Abby said hastily. "Just not the you and me part of it." She realized how bitchy that sounded, but couldn't help herself. Marc was looking at her, waiting for her to say more, but she just wasn't sure what to say.

"Is it really that scary?" Marc asked softly.

"To be honest, yeah, it is," Abby said.

"Can I ask why?"

"I'm not sure I can explain it to myself, much less to you," Abby confessed. "Let's just say I don't have the best track record when it comes to men and relationships."

"So you've given up on all of us?" Marc said.

"I wouldn't call it giving up," Abby objected. "It's more of a prolonged hiatus."

"How long?" Marc asked.

"Six years," she said.

"Six years!" Marc looked shocked. "Lady, that's more than a hiatus, that's a full bore retreat."

"Maybe so," Abby conceded. "But it was a strategic retreat. Or, at least it seemed so at the time."

"Yeah, but six years." Marc whistled softly. Then he looked at her hard. "He must have been some kind of jerk to break your heart like that."

Abby gave a small, humorless laugh. "Oh yes, he was some kind of jerk, all right." Without going into great detail, Abby quickly told Marc about that summer on Cape Cod with Nathan Herrington. "But how'd you know some guy had dumped me?"

"An educated guess," Marc gave a shrug. "When your own heart's been broken, it's pretty easy to spot another one. And listen, about dinner, no big thing, okay? Maybe another time."

Suddenly Abby felt very small and petty. As humiliating and devastating as it was at the time, her experience with Nate was nothing compared with the very real loss suffered by Marc. A loss that left him at once a widower and single father.

WHAT THE HELL had he been thinking, asking Abby out like that? She had taken the path leading to the marine center, leaving Marc to walk back to his mother's house on his own. And what on earth had made him think she'd have accepted. Then there was the inescapable fact he really did want to hear more about the whales. As much as he hated admitting it, listening to their sounds had hit Marc almost like a physical blow.

My God, he'd thought, standing in the small cabin, the odd vocalizations playing through the earphones. *These are actual whales and they're talking!* Then had come the deep rumble of the *Sainte Helene,* a noise so intrusive and out of sync with the whales, he'd actually wanted to wince. Was that really what a boat motor sounded like to the beluga? Did the *Percé* make that kind of underwater racket? He'd had a dozen or more questions he'd wanted to ask Abby, but his pride and the very real fact he might have to admit being wrong about some things had led him to make a lame joke, instead.

Abby didn't have to worry about a romantic date. Hadn't he told his mother a couple weeks back he wasn't interested in another relationship? He'd meant it, too. Nearing the house, he looked up, hearing a happy call from the front porch. Sylvie stood there waving at him.

Grinning, Marc waved back. Now there was the number-one lady in his life.

"HI, ABBY!"

Abby was shutting her apartment door to leave the next morning when she heard Sylvie call from across the yard.

"Good morning, Sylvie. How are you this morning?"

"Great." Sylvie hunkered down on her knees to scratch Figgy behind the ears. "Did you remember to bring us a book?"

"I sure did." Abby drew a book from her pack. "Here you go. It just came in yesterday."

Sylvie stood and skipped over to Abby, Figgy trotting alongside.

"It's all about a little girl, her brother and a baby whale who travel into space," Abby told her.

"Cool!" Book in hand, Sylvie turned back toward the house.

"Sylvie." Françoise was on the back porch. "What do you say to Abby?"

"Oh, oops. Sorry, Gran," Sylvie stopped and pirouetted around. "Thank you, Abby."

Abby grinned. "You are welcome, Sylvie."

"Can I play with Figgy for a few minutes?" Sylvie asked Françoise.

Françoise looked at her watch. "Okay, but just for ten minutes, then we have to get you to school."

Abby joined Françoise on the porch and the two women watched Sylvie run to a little chair Marc had placed under the large tree several days earlier. When Sylvie had asked to play with Figgy, Abby had thought the girl would run around the yard with the dog. Instead, Sylvie sat in the chair, opened the book Abby had just given her and waited patiently for Figgy to join her.

It wasn't a long wait. As soon as Figgy sat with her chin resting on Sylvie's leg, the girl began reading in a slow, strong voice.

"Every day," Françoise said.

"What do you mean?" Abby asked.

"Every day she's out here reading to your dog," Françoise said.

"When do the report cards come out?"

"Two weeks or thereabouts," Françoise said. "And unless I miss my guess, we're going to have something to celebrate. Something we all owe to you."

Abby was uncomfortable with the praise. "Sylvie's the one who deserves the credit," she said hastily, and then changed the subject. "Will

Marc be walking her to school?" She tried desperately to sound casual.

"No, he called earlier saying the *Percé* was acting up a bit. Nothing to worry about," Françoise added hastily, when Abby's eyes widened. "He said he'd have it fixed in no time, but would need an hour or so. He asked me to take Sylvie to school." Françoise settled back on the porch seat. "How are you and my son getting along?"

"Fine," Abby said, a bit quickly.

"Good."

Abby was beyond grateful when the older woman did not follow up with any more questions. She looked at her watch. "I'd better be going."

"Marc must have the boat fixed by now. He'd have called otherwise." She smiled at Abby. "Have a good day."

"You do the same." With a wave to Sylvie Abby walked out the back gate.

HAD ABBY TURNED AROUND, she would have seen Françoise staring after her, an appraising look in the older woman's eye.

Fine, Abby had said. *Now what could have she meant by that?* Françoise had tried to pose a similar question to her son the night before, but Marc had stubbornly refused to answer.

Françoise thought about the two of them—Marc and Abby. There was no denying both had been hurt when it came to matters of the heart. *They really are alike in that way,* Françoise found herself thinking. An image popped into her head of a science assignment Sylvie had come home with toward the end of last term. Each child in her class had been given two small rectangular magnets and were to find out all they could do with them. Sylvie, for once, had approached her homework with great enthusiasm. But what Françoise was remembering now was Sylvie's delight in using the magnet's reverse polarity to push the other magnet around the table.

"Look, Gran!" Sylvie had cried cheerfully. As Françoise watched, Sylvie used one magnet to chase the other away across the table. Then, by simply turning the one in her fingers around, its mate was pulled right back.

Marc and Abby are like those magnets, Françoise was thinking now. *All they need is someone to turn them around in the right direction.*

She tilted her head and regarded Sylvie. Françoise knew she'd need an accomplice to implement the scheme forming in her mind. But she would have to make certain Sylvie was supportive. Françoise would never do anything to cause her granddaughter more pain.

"Sylvie," Françoise called. "Could you come here, please?"

Sylvie patted the dog's head and said something to it before running over to her grandmother.

"What's up?" her granddaughter said, flopping down on the porch seat next to Françoise.

"Can I ask you a very important question?" Françoise began cautiously.

The little girl nodded. "I guess so," she said.

"What do you think of Abby?"

Sylvie's eyes immediately brightened. "I think she's cool!"

"Really?"

"Yeah," Sylvie asserted. "She's fun and doesn't treat me like a kid, and she's pretty, isn't she, Gran?"

"I'd have to agree on all counts," Françoise said.

"I just wish…"

"Wish what, little one?"

Sylvie kicked her feet back and forth. "I wish Dad liked her better."

"Oh?" Françoise struggled to keep her voice neutral.

"Yeah." Sylvie looked at her grandmother and then down at her feet. "We could all do fun things together. Like a real family."

Françoise was delighted to find an apparent ally in Sylvie, but her pleasure was bittersweet. How long had the little girl been yearning for "a real family" once again?

Swallowing the lump forming in her throat, Françoise hugged her granddaughter. "Sweetheart, how would you feel about helping your old grandmother with a bit of matchmaking?"

Sylvie looked up questioningly. "Match *making?* Why do we have to make matches? There's a whole box in the kitchen. Want me to get them?"

Françoise laughed and gave her granddaughter another hug. "No, Sylvie. This is a different kind of matchmaking. You run along and get your things. I'll explain it while we walk to school."

ABBY'S STEP WAS LIGHT as she walked down the street toward the docks. The project was going so well, each day bringing new discoveries.

She was rounding the curve in the street leading to the wharf when she heard a shout off to her right. Peter Bouchard came running across the marine center's parking lot toward her, a large envelope in his hands.

"Abby!" he was calling "Hold on a minute."

"Peter, is something wrong?" Abby said, concern in her voice.

The director stopped in front of her. "Let me catch my breath a moment. Here, this came for you first thing this morning by special courier." Holding up a hand, he gave her the large envelope.

"What is it?" she asked.

"Don't know," Peter said. "But a half hour after it was delivered we got a call from Woods Hole to confirm it had arrived."

"Woods Hole?" That was her funding sponsor. "Did they say anything else?"

Peter shook his head. "Nope. I tried to call you at your place, but no answer. I was just on my way up to try and find you." He nodded toward the envelope. "Well, are you going to open it?"

"I guess so." Abby tore off the top flap with shaking fingers.

Pulling out the single piece of paper, she began to read, and as she did, her frown turned to a smile of jubilation.

"Are you going to let me in on it, or is it a secret?"

For a moment, Abby had honestly forgotten Peter was there. Before answering him, she reread the letter, just to make sure she had not been hallucinating.

"Peter, it's amazing!" she said

"Good news, I take it?"

"The best," Abby confirmed. "It's from Dr.

Felix Bolton, the head of research projects at Woods Hole."

"I've heard of him," Peter said.

"He's a top-notch researcher," Abby told him, "and he's also the person who has final say on who gets funding and how much. According to this," she held up the letter, "he's read my preliminary reports and wants to come up in a month to see for himself what I'm doing. And if he likes what he sees, he's ready to offer me three more years of full funding on the spot."

"Abby, that's fantastic!" Peter gave her a bear hug. "Do you know how rare that is?"

"I do," Abby said. "Usually we have to beg on our knees for funding. A month… I can have so much to show him by then. I've got to get started!"

"No way." Peter took her by the hand and pulled her toward the center. "Good news has to be shared."

"Shared?" Abby repeated.

"Yes, shared," Peter said firmly. "And there's no time like the present. Most of the other researchers are in today and I know they're going to want to hear about this."

"Peter, that's more than kind of you to say, really," Abby said. "But Marc's waiting for me on the *Percé* and we're supposed to go up the fjord today…"

Peter shrugged. "So tell him there's been a change of plans. He works for you, right?"

"But I can't just leave him hanging. He's expecting me."

"Don't worry," Peter said. "I'll send Todd, one of the interns, over to explain."

"Okay," Abby relented. "I imagine he'll understand."

"What's to understand?" Peter said. "He's getting paid whether you go out or not."

"IT WAS TOUCH AND GO for a moment there, but I caught it early enough, so she won't be giving us any more trouble…" Marc stopped in midsentence when he turned around and saw a tall youth of about seventeen standing at the *Percé*'s rail. Where was Abby?

"Can I help you?" Marc said.

"Are you Marc Doucette?"

"I am," Marc said. "Who are you?"

"I'm Todd. They sent me over from the marine center, I've got a message about Dr. Abby Miller."

Marc's heart skipped a beat. "About Abby? Is she okay?"

Todd shrugged. "I guess."

"You guess?" Marc said impatiently. "What's the message?"

"I'm supposed to tell you that Dr. Miller doesn't need you today and she'll call you when she does," Todd said.

"That's it?" Marc was confused.

Todd nodded. "That's all I was told. You want me to take any message back for you?"

"No, I'm all set. Thanks."

"Okay, see ya." Todd swung back over the rail. Marc listened to him climb down the ladder and trot back up the dock.

She doesn't need you today and she'll call you when she does. What the heck did that mean? And what was so all fired important that she could not have come down and told him herself?

Marc reached for a rag and wiped his hands. He looked at his watch. If he hurried, he could still take Sylvie to school. Swinging down from the boat on to the dock, he quickstepped it up the road, but the sounds of loud laughter coming from behind the marine center stopped him.

Curious, Marc detoured and walked around the building. Off the side doors was a grassy area where the staff kept several picnic tables and chairs to use when on breaks. At the moment, each was full of people holding plastic cups raised as if in a toast. Marc recognized a few staff members, and standing at the head of one of the tables was Peter Bouchard, his own cup held aloft. His other arm was slung around Abby's shoulder, and she smiled as the crowd broke into a round of applause.

Marc didn't stick around to see what the gathering was all about. If Abby had wanted him around, she would have said so. "I guess I know for sure where I stand with her," he muttered, casting one last look at the group. Feeling like the one kid not picked for the kick-ball team at recess, he spun around and walked away as quickly as he could.

ABBY WAS MORE THAN A LITTLE embarrassed by all the attention and well wishes heaped on her. The funding hadn't even been approved yet. But her fellow researchers and the marine center staff were eager to celebrate.

When she was finally able to pull away for a moment, Abby caught Peter's eye and motioned to him.

"Are you going to ask me for a bigger office now?" he said in a teasing tone.

Abby smiled. "No, not unless I can have yours. Actually, I just wanted to make sure Marc got the message."

Peter looked blank. "What message?"

"About my not going out this morning," Abby said.

"Oh, of course. I sent Todd over to tell him." Peter pointed toward a tall youth standing in a small knot of teenage interns.

"Thanks." Abby walked over to the group. "Todd?"

"Yes?" the young man said.

"Peter told me you talked to Marc Doucette this morning?"

Todd nodded.

"I don't suppose he gave you any message for me, did he?"

"Nope," Todd said. "As a matter of fact, he really didn't say much at all."

"Are you sure?" Abby persisted.

"Yeah, I'm sure. Why?"

"No reason," Abby said quickly. "Thanks for going over there."

"No problem." Todd turned back to his friends.

Now why did the fact that Marc had not sent a reply via Todd bother her so much? Abby wondered.

"Anything wrong?" Chris had walked up behind her, a half-full bottle of sparkling cider in hand.

"No, nothing at all." Abby cast one last look in the direction of the marina and the *Percé*. "Everything's fine. Fill me up," she said, and held out her cup.

BY TEN O'CLOCK the doors of the building were unlocked to the public, marking the end to

Abby's party. As the tourists began streaming in, she made her way up to her private office and placed two long-distance phone calls.

"Woods Hole Institute of Oceanography," answered the voice on the other end of the first call.

"Dr. Felix Bolton, please," Abby said.

"One moment, I'll ring his office."

"Dr. Bolton's office," a woman's voice said after picking up on the third ring.

"Margot, hi, it's Abby. Is the Doc around?"

"Abby? Where are you? How are you?"

"I'm fine and I'm still up in Canada." Abby pictured Bolton's pleasant receptionist a thousand miles away, sitting at her neatly organized desk, the eye of calm in the midst of Bolton's research storms.

"It's so nice to hear your voice, dear," Margot said. "You hold on a minute, Felix just walked in. You take good care."

"You, too, Margot."

"Abby!" the deep baritone of Felix Bolton came over the line. "What a pleasant surprise."

"Surprise!" Abby said, grinning. "You had to know I'd be calling after getting that letter from you."

"Letter?" Felix said in a musing tone. "Hmm, can't say as I recall sending out any letters lately."

Abby laughed. "So I was right, it was a hallucination."

Now it was Felix's turn to chuckle. "Hardly, my dear. I can't begin to tell you how impressed we are down here by your work so far. Really top-notch stuff."

Abby was instantly humbled. Felix Bolton was not a man to hand out compliments lightly. "Thank you," was all she could manage.

"I should be the one thanking you," Felix said. "You're doing us all proud and we can't wait to come up and get a firsthand report."

"When are you planning on coming?" Abby asked.

"I want to bring the entire funding committee, so it's going to be a scheduling nightmare," Felix explained. "But at the moment we're looking at the last weekend in July or sometime in the first part of August. How does that sound? Can you have a formal presentation ready by then?"

"Sure," Abby said, "no problem."

"Liar." Abby could picture the grin on his face. "You know as well as I that there is nothing easy about preparing a formal dog and pony show for the bean counters."

"All right, you got me on that one," Abby confessed. "I can be ready."

They said their good-byes and Abby placed a second call, this time to her parents. When both were on separate extensions in the house, she told them the good news and listened for the next ten minutes as her mother and father talked over each other in their excitement.

When she was finally able to get a word in, Abby thanked her parents, told them how much she missed them and promised to call the following weekend. Hanging up the phone, she saw it was nearing lunchtime. She was too keyed up to do any work in the lab, so she decided to walk down to the *Percé* and share her good news with Marc.

ONE THING about having a boat, Marc thought, there was always something that needed doing. Since getting the brush-off from Abby that morning, he'd managed to keep himself busy breaking down the twin diesels to their seals, repacking the bearings and checking the various grease fittings. It was tedious work, but it kept him from thinking about Abby.

He was just replacing the final bearing and tapping the cover closed when he heard familiar footsteps on the deck overhead. Marc had removed his watch and hung it from a peg on the wall. Reaching for it, he saw it was close to noon. He looked down at his oil-caked hands, then shrugged. *To heck with it. She's hired a grease monkey; she might as well get the whole package.*

"Marc? Marc, are you down there?" Abby called from above.

"Yeah, I'm here. Hang on." He climbed up from the engine compartment, squinting into the bright daylight.

"Oh, there you are," Abby said, walking into the wheelhouse. "Wow, what oil vat did you fall into?"

Marc knew she was only teasing, but the knowledge did little to check his tongue.

"When you actually *work* for a living, you're bound to get a little dirty," he said coldly. "But I guess your pals over at the marine center are above this kind of thing. That's why you hire guys like me, right?"

The smile on Abby's face faltered.

"I'm not sure I follow," she said. "Did I do something wrong?"

"You? Do something wrong?" Marc was well aware of the sarcasm in his words. "Far be it from me to tell you where you should be—*or when*."

"Is this about this morning?" Abby said. "About my not going out on the water today?"

Marc shrugged.

"It is, isn't it?" Abby insisted. "Listen, I know I should have come down and told you myself, but I was just so excited and then Peter sort of got this impromptu party going for me and I guess I lost track of time. You can understand that, can't you?"

Another shrug from Marc.

"And it's not like I left you hanging." Abby was beginning to sound exasperated. "For heaven's sake, Marc, I sent a message down…"

"Yeah, that was mighty big of you."

"Is *that* what's bugging you?" Abby asked. "The fact that I didn't come down personally?"

Marc looked at her a moment and realized he was being a bit of a jerk. "Nah, forgot about it."

Abby looked uncertain. "Well, okay."

"Look, it's Friday and kind of late to go out today," Marc said.

"I figured as much," Abby said. "I can do some data analysis back in the lab. How about we get going around six on Monday?"

Marc nodded.

"See you then." Marc watched Abby climb down from the *Percé* and walk back up the dock.

When she had passed from sight, he blew out a breath and sat down on a hatch cover. Why had not getting asked to join in the celebration at the marine center bothered him so much? It's not like he was a huge fan of their work. "Be honest, Doucette," he muttered. The fact was, he'd been looking forward to seeing Abby and listening in on her research again.

It would no doubt surprise Abby—not to mention her buddies at the center—how much he loved the Saguenay River whales. He'd grown up watching them and, like most of the area's residents, felt somewhat protective toward them. He also believed the whales could do a lot for the local people, particularly as the star tourist attraction. There was no reason, as far as Marc was concerned, that the two species could not live together just fine.

It was obvious that Abby shared this deep feeling for the whales. His came from a life of observation, and hers from her research.

CHAPTER FOURTEEN

"OKAY, *MA FILLE*," Marc said the next morning, looking across the table at Sylvie. "What's it going to be?"

"I really get to choose?" Sylvie said, pushing aside her bowl of oatmeal.

Marc nodded. "But any choice you make hinges on your finishing breakfast."

Sylvie made a face at Marc—which he chose to ignore—then wrinkled her brow in concentration. Then her eyes brightened. "Can we go to the dunes?"

Marc nodded and was relieved she had chosen a destination so close to home. She could just as easily have said she wanted to drive the hundred miles to Lac Sainte-Jean rather than the five miles to the massive sand dunes east of Tadoussac.

"Can we take lunch and have a picnic?" Sylvie asked.

"If that's what you want to do, sure," Marc

looked at his watch. "It's eight-thirty now. Do you think you can be ready to go by ten?"

"You bet." Sylvie started scooping massive spoonfuls of oatmeal into her mouth.

"That means all of your chores done and your bed made."

Sylvie nodded.

"More coffee?" Françoise was holding the pot.

"Thanks," Marc said as his mother poured.

"Can I be excused?" Sylvie asked.

"Are you all done?" Marc said.

"Yep." Sylvie tipped the now-empty bowl for Marc to inspect.

"Off you go." He watched his daughter rush from the room.

"It's nice, the two of you spending the day together," Françoise said.

"I'm looking forward to it. I need the break. Besides, Sylvie deserves it. She's really kept to her end of the bargain about her studies."

"Nice day for an outing," Françoise observed. Marc recognized that tone. His mother was leading up to something.

"And?"

"Nothing." Françoise looked innocent. "I just said it's a nice day for an outing. I wonder…" She snapped her fingers. "Maybe Abby would like to join you two today."

Marc shook his head. "No way. Today's for me and Sylvie."

"Three's a crowd?"

He sighed. "That and, well, it's complicated."

"Tush!" Françoise snorted, getting up to refill her own mug. "Anytime young folks say that, I know it's nothing more complicated than plain stubbornness. And don't you grunt at me, young man," she added when Marc made a noise in the back of this throat.

"Mom, I'm sorry. But Abby made it pretty clear early on she's interested in a charter and nothing more. Okay?"

"And you're content to leave it at that?" Françoise asked.

"Yes, and I'd appreciate your dropping the subject."

"Consider it dropped," Françoise said. "You know me, never one to meddle where I'm not wanted."

"DAD! WATCH!" Sylvie yelled from atop the dune.

"I'm watching, *ma fille,*" Marc called out. His daughter leapt from the dune's crest and ran pell-mell down its side, her thin legs a blur and her feet kicking up clouds of sand. Three-quarters of the way to the bottom, she threw out her legs, landed on her rear-end and slid the remaining distance.

Laughing, Sylvie rolled to a stop and picked herself up.

"Gotcha!" Marc said, grabbing Sylvie from behind and swinging her up. She squealed in delight.

Setting her back down, he took a deep breath. "You're almost getting too big for that."

Marc loved spending time with his daughter. Sylvie possessed a keen interest in the world around her and watching her explorations gave Marc constant joy.

The two had spent the better part of the day on the beach across from the massive sand dunes—themselves a geological anomaly on the otherwise granite-bound North Shore. Much of that time Sylvie had spent dashing up and down the shoreline in search of whatever treasures the tide had brought in.

Periodically, she ran up to Marc, her hands full of objects for him to inspect and admire. Those she judged worthy, were passed over to him for safekeeping. By the time they spread their blanket on a flat rock to have lunch, his pockets were bulging with shells, special rocks, chunks of sea glass and odd-shaped pieces of metal.

"Dad?" Sylvie's voice brought Marc back to the present.

"Yeah?"

"Can I ask you something?"

"Of course, *ma fille*. What's up?"

"Are you okay?"

Marc looked hard at his daughter. "What makes you ask that?"

"I don't know." Sylvie scuffed her bare toes in the sand. "I can tell something's wrong. You don't laugh much. And you work all the time. Is it my fault?"

Marc could only stare at his daughter. "Oh Sylvie," he said. "I wish I had an easy answer for you, but I don't." He gazed out at the waves beyond. "But you have to understand, if I feel sad or unhappy, it has nothing to do with you, okay?"

Sylvie nodded.

"But when I feel happy—" he reached out and pulled his daughter into a hug "—that, my girl, is *entirely* because of you."

Sylvie let her father hug her a bit, then squirmed away. "I love you, Dad," she said simply.

"I love you, too, *ma fille*," Marc ruffled her hair. "How about we start picking up our stuff and think about heading home."

"Okay. Dad?"

"Yeah?"

"I really had fun today," Sylvie said.

"I did, too," Marc said, pleased at Sylvie's comment.

"Can we do it again tomorrow?"

"I don't know, *ma fille,* I've got some things I should get done."

"Please?" Sylvie begged. "I bet Gran would like to come on a picnic with us. Can we? Please?"

"What's this sudden interest in picnics?" Marc asked.

Sylvie shrugged. "They're just fun, that's all."

Marc tried to read her expression. "Are you sure that's it?"

"Sure."

"I don't know," he said slowly. "I just have the feeling I'm about to be hit up for something."

"That's silly!" Sylvie said. "C'mon, I'll race you to the car!"

As far as Abby was concerned, there was no better way to relax than a long walk in the woods with Figgy. This time they had trekked uphill and were being rewarded with an amazing view from the top. Unslinging her pack and pulling out a bottle of water, she gazed out at the panorama below.

"Are you thirsty?" she asked Figgy, who was sniffing at a bush near the wooden rails at the trail's edge. The little dog trotted over and waited patiently as Abby took a collapsible bowl from her pack, set it on the rocks and splashed a generous portion of water into it from her bottle.

"Drink up," she said and watched a moment as Figgy happily lapped up the water.

It was a picture-perfect day for a strenuous climb. The guidebooks had not lied. The nine-mile trek along the fjord trail in the Saguenay National Park was steep, but the strenuous workout had been just what Abby needed to clear her mind and avoid thoughts of Marc Doucette. And it had almost worked.

Abby knew she should be concentrating on the view of the fjord spread out below, but an image of Marc with his dancing eyes, crooked grin and hard body kept pushing its way to the forefront of her mind. More and more as the summer was wearing on, she found herself wondering what it would be like to accept a date with Marc, if the subject should ever be broached again. At the same time, she was annoyed with herself for wasting energy on such thoughts. She pulled an apple from her pack and started munching on it. She had to stay focused. Her research results were exceeding her expectations, and in a month or so, the people with the power to fund her work were coming to assess them.

But up on this mountain, with only a small dog

and her thoughts for company, Abby had to be honest with herself: she was attracted to Marc. Over the course of just a few weeks he'd become much more than a hired charter. But it was painfully obvious to Abby that his heart belonged to another, and Abby was smart enough to know better than to compete with an eight-year-old for attention.

Absently scratching Figgy's ears, Abby smiled at the thought of the little girl. Every day after school, according to Françoise, Sylvie came straight home and ran to the yard to get Figgy. Then, girl and dog would curl up on the grass, and Sylvie would read out loud as Figgy lay next to her, the dog's eyes never leaving her face.

"You've done a wonderful thing, you know that, don't you?" Abby said to Figgy, who thumped her tail in response. "Even if we adults can't seem to get it right, you've managed to do your part just fine."

"SHE'S BOUND AND DETERMINED we all go on a picnic tomorrow. Are you up for it?" Marc had found his mother sitting on the front porch in a rare moment of relaxation and enjoying the view of the bay beyond.

"A picnic, is it?" Françoise said, as Sylvie came up the steps, lugging the cooler that had contained that day's lunch. The girl slowed her progress a fraction as Françoise grinned at her.

"What was that?" Marc said quickly as Sylvie continued into the house.

"What was what?" Françoise asked.

"That look."

"What look?"

"Just now, between you and Sylvie. Don't try to tell me you two aren't up to something."

"I don't know what you're talking about," Françoise protested, standing. "But you're sounding paranoid. Now, if you'll excuse me, I have a picnic to plan."

"Oh no you don't." Marc followed his mother inside. "I smell a rat. You two are up to something."

"Paranoid," Françoise repeated. "Listen to yourself. Your daughter has a sweet idea for a family outing and you're suddenly suspicious."

Marc remained unconvinced, but he was prepared to let it go for now. He suspected he'd find out just what his daughter and mother were conspiring about soon enough.

WHEN MARC PULLED UP to the house the next morning, he saw Sylvie perched on the top step, arms wrapped around her knees, a picnic hamper and bulging paper bag at her feet. The moment she spotted Marc's Wagoneer, she hopped up and dashed inside. As Marc was getting out of the car, Sylvie reappeared, her grandmother in tow.

"Good morning, ladies," Marc said, walking to the porch and picking up the hamper and bag. "Looks like we have enough for an army here. Are you all set to go?"

"Well, now, something has come up," Françoise said.

Marc's brow furrowed. "Oh, what's wrong?"

"Nothing's wrong, exactly," Françoise explained. "It's just that I got a call last night and there's some sort of pastry emergency at the hotel. I'm afraid I need to be baking all day."

"On Sunday?" Marc said. "Can't they do without you one day?"

"I guess not."

Françoise seemed uncharacteristically blasé about spending an entire Sunday at the stove, Marc thought.

"Okay, then, I guess it's just you and me, *ma fille*," he said, looking at Sylvie, who had not budged from her grandmother's side. "Let's load up and…what?"

Sylvie was shaking her head. "Sorry, Dad. I promised Gran I'd help her today."

"You *what*?"

"Hey, look," Sylvie said, pointing. "There's Abby."

Marc turned in time to see Abby rounding the corner of the house. "Oh, good morning."

"Hello," she said, then turned toward the porch. "Françoise, Sylvie said you needed to see me this morning?"

"Did she?" Françoise said. "Well, I can't imagine it was for anything important. Say now, do you have any plans for the day?"

Marc was getting a very bad feeling.

"No, not really," Abby said.

"My, my, well, there you have it," Françoise sounded like the thought had just struck her. "You with no plans and Marc here with a delicious picnic lunch and no one to share it with. Abby, you can take our place. You kids run along now and have a good time."

Marc shot his mother a murderous look.

"Come along, Sylvie, we'd best get to work." Françoise smiled triumphantly and took the girl's hand, leading her into the house.

"Oh yeah," Sylvie said, a huge grin on her face, "we have all sorts of *baking* to do. Bye, Dad!"

Marc looked at Abby a long moment after Françoise and Sylvie had retreated into the house, then smiled in spite of himself. "You do realize we've been had, don't you?"

"Set up, is more like it," Abby said ruefully. "I knew those two were up to something."

"What do you want to do?" Abby asked. "I mean, it looks like they put a bit of effort into hatching this scheme."

"No doubt," Marc agreed. "Look the weather's great, there's a ton of food here. What if we actually go on this picnic?" He held his breath, half expecting a refusal. Instead, she nodded, a smile tugging at the corners of her mouth.

"Pretty sneaky, you have to admit," Abby said. "I never would have pegged either of them for this kind of plot."

"You haven't lived with them long enough." Marc picked up the hamper and bag and gestured toward his Jeep. "You know they're spying on us right now from behind the living-room drapes. Let's shock the hell out them and look happy about this."

"I'm game if you are," Abby said.

"Then hop on in." While Abby clambered inside, Marc dropped the tailgate and put the hamper and bag into the back. Deliberately avoiding looking at the front windows of the house, Marc got into the Wagoneer and drove off.

CHAPTER FIFTEEN

"ANYPLACE SPECIAL you have in mind?" Marc asked Abby as they turned onto Tadoussac's main street.

She shook her head. "Not really. How about you?"

"Up until a few minutes ago, I was under the impression my mom and Sylvie were calling the shots for the day."

Abby laughed. "And now you think they're not?"

"Hardly," Marc said, joining in her laughter.

Lord, Abby thought, *that's a nice sound.*

"Are you open to suggestions?" Marc said.

"Fire away."

"Baie Sainte-Marguerite is only a forty-five-minute drive from here. It takes about another half hour to walk in, but it's worth it, I can promise you that."

"Sainte-Marguerite it is, then," Abby said gaily. "Drive on." She glanced across at Marc, who kept his eyes on the road as he drove. A pair of sunglasses covered his eyes, but he was smiling and

Abby knew that meant his eyes were crinkling attractively at the corners.

She sighed and turned to look out the window at the passing scenery.

"Penny for your thoughts," Marc said.

Abby could have made a neutral reply, but maybe this was a time for honesty.

"The fact is, I've been bothered by something that happened and want to apologize."

"For what?" Marc said.

"That day on the boat, when I stuck around at the marine center and didn't come get you myself. That was rude. I'm really sorry."

Marc laughed. "Far be it from me to turn down an apology. But only if I can return the favor."

"Meaning?"

"I acted like a jerk," Marc said. " I never even asked what you were celebrating, and I'm sorry."

"Then I accept *your* apology," Abby said.

"So, what was happening at the center?" Marc asked.

Abby happily gave him the rundown on her letter and follow-up call to Felix. When she had finished, Marc let out a low whistle.

"I can see why you wanted to celebrate right away," he said.

"No, that was selfish," Abby began, but Marc interrupted her.

"Maybe it was, but we just agreed there was blame enough for both of us."

Abby nodded.

"As far as I'm concerned, it's all water under the bridge. Done and over. Deal?" He let go of the wheel with his right hand and held it out for Abby.

"Deal." She took his hand and gave it a hearty shake, but when she went to pull her hand away, Marc held it for a lingering few seconds.

"So tell me about the study?" Marc asked. "Why the excitement?"

"It's really quite mind-boggling," Abby said. "We always had a good idea that whales communicated using distinct vocalizations, but from what I've heard over the past weeks, it looks as if those vocalizations are changing, depending on the background noise."

"For instance?"

"For instance, in areas of high noise concentration, say with lots of Zodiac traffic, I've noticed the beluga are vocalizing with increased intensity and more repeated sounds," Abby explained.

"What does that tell you?"

"Initially, I'd just be guessing, but we do know that all communication boils down to one thing: *look at me.* That's why we talk, to get people's attention. Animals do the same thing when they vocalize; it's a way of attracting a mate, for one thing. We also know if creatures are having a hard time hearing each other, they use two strategies—they either talk louder or repeat themselves."

"And that's what your whales are doing?"

"Appears that way," Abby said. "But Marc, it really is too early to draw any meaningful conclusions from this."

"But it must mean something. Why else would your friends want to give you more money?"

"I hope you're right," Abby said with a smile.

Marc pulled off onto a narrow gravel road and, fifteen minutes later, they arrived at a wide parking lot in the middle of the woods. He pulled in and cut the engine.

"Okay, time to hoof it a bit," he said.

While he divided up the contents of the bag and hamper between their two backpacks, Abby peered through the trees, where she could just make out a one-story building.

"Interpretive center," Marc said, following her gaze.

"Is that water I hear?" she asked.

"Uh-huh. The river is just beyond those trees. We'll be following it all the way out to the bay. Ready?" He stood up and held out the two packs. "I think I got them pretty well evenly loaded, but you can have first pick."

Glancing up at the information kiosk at the

side of the parking lot, Abby saw the No Pets sign and was glad she'd left Figgy behind in the yard. She took the blue pack from him and slung it over her shoulders, tightening the straps and adjusting the padding.

"If these are equally weighted," she said, watching Marc put on his pack, "your mother fixed enough food for a week!"

He laughed. "That's her style. You should see it when she throws a dinner party." He looked across the lot and pointed. "The trailhead's over there. It's about a three-mile walk to the bay, but like I said, well worth it."

"Then lead on."

MARC HADN'T FIGURED his mother and Sylvie as matchmakers, despite what he might have said to Abby. But walking along the riverside path through the cool spruce forest, he had to wonder if the two of them weren't on to something. Just walking with Abby was giving him more pleasure than he would have thought. About a mile in, Abby let out a soft yelp when her foot caught a root. Only Marc's quick action checked her fall.

"Are you okay?" he asked, his voice deep with concern.

"I'm fine," she assured him. "You saved me from injuring anything other than my ego."

"Do you want to stop and rest a bit?"

Abby was indignant. "After walking only a mile, no way! I'm fine, really. From now on I'll pick up my feet higher."

"All right then, but be careful," Marc warned her. "These roots can turn this path into a twisted ankle just waiting to happen."

He'd caught her by the hand as Abby had begun to fall. Now, as they resumed their walk, it seemed the most natural thing in the world to keep his fingers entwined with hers. Abby made no move to pull her own hand away.

They walked along in a comfortable silence for some minutes until Marc halted and pointed off the trail to the right at some large, bulky objects hidden in the shadows.

Abby peered into the gloom. "What are those?"

"Remember when I told you this area was once a thriving mill town?"

She nodded.

"This is all that's left—just some rusty machinery, some old cables and a few stone outlines of building foundations." Marc led her over to a massive tube, about eight feet long with holes in each end.

"What did that do?" Abby asked.

"Some kind of steam-driven machine," Marc told her. Together they walked around the object, both marveling that a device, which at one time helped to feed a thriving economy, was now reduced to a rusting hulk.

"It's kind of a sad and lonely place," Abby said and Marc saw her shiver.

"Aw, I don't know." They headed back to the trail and resumed walking toward the beach. "I think it's testimony to all those who blazed a trail here."

Twenty minutes later they were walking along a wooden boardwalk, designed, Marc explained, to keep foot traffic off the fragile plants and ground cover. The boardwalk ended at the edge of a high cliff where a lookout offered views up and down the Saguenay River.

"You weren't kidding," Abby said, leaning on the wooden rail and gazing at the river below. "This was more than worth the walk."

"And check that out." Marc tapped her gently on the shoulder and pointed to a spot several hundred yards offshore. A pod of beluga broke the surface.

"Look at them," Abby said breathlessly. "One, two, three…is that a fourth right next to the first one?"

Marc shaded his eyes with his hand. "Could be. It's a bunch of them, that's for sure."

"Dammit! I don't even have my camera with

me." Abby turned to Marc. "Do you have a pen and paper? Anything I can write on. I need to get a better count of this pod and time the surfacings. Maybe if I get close enough I can hear some actual vocalizations and…"

"Whoa, slow down there, lady." Marc took her by the shoulders and looked directly at her. "Why don't you try to enjoy them by *not* being a scientist for once. Just someone who shares this planet with them."

"Are you kidding?" Abby said. "What's the point of that?"

Marc let out an exasperated sigh. "The point is, I think if you let yourself be a woman, an honest to goodness woman, instead of a scientist for just one day, you'd be happier, the whales would be happier, and I know for sure *I'd* be happier."

ABBY'S FIRST REACTION was to pull away from Marc. She felt stung by his remarks. But she stopped herself and considered his words. It had been a long time, years, in fact, since she had simply enjoyed watching whales just being whales. No sensing devices, no equipment of any kind. Maybe Marc was right and it was time to give her science side a mini-vacation. It was a glorious day and she was with a drop-dead gorgeous man. Why not let the woman in her take over? For a little while, anyway.

She smiled up at Marc. "You win. But can I at least use a pair of binoculars to watch them, or is that cheating?"

He laughed. "Be my guest. But I think we only have the one pair, so you're going to have to share."

"Shall we set up our lunch here?" They were standing in a covered viewing area.

"Nah," Marc said. "Look down there. The entire beach is empty. It will be just you, me and your friends out there."

"How's this?" Marc asked, indicating a flat patch of sandy gravel a hundred yards from the water. The spot, Abby noted, was slightly elevated, and every few minutes she spotted one or more of the beluga out in the fjord.

"Perfect," she said. "Here, let me give you a hand with that."

Marc had pulled an old checkered blanket out of his pack and was trying to shake it open against the breeze. "Thanks," he said as Abby grabbed two corners and helped ease it to the ground.

"Now, let's see what else Mom and Sylvie cooked up for us today," Marc said, pulling bags and plastic containers from the two packs.

CHAPTER SIXTEEN

"GOOD FOOD?" Marc asked.

Abby spooned the last of the potato salad onto her plate. "I'm afraid I'm going to get way too accustomed to this. It's wonderful."

"My mom loves to spoil people she likes with food. Judging by this feast, I'd say you're in good with her, no problem."

Marc reached for a deviled egg and looked up at Abby, who was seated cross-legged, leaning against a huge hunk of driftwood. He was lying on his side, his head propped up on one elbow. What he really wanted to do, he thought, was lay his head down in Abby's lap.

Instead, he sighed and rolled over onto his back, gazing up at the sky.

"Your mother really is quite the lady," Abby said.

"Yeah, tell me about it. I don't know how Sylvie and I would have managed without her."

"What was your father like?"

Marc rolled back onto his side. "What makes you ask?" he asked kindly.

Abby shrugged. "Curious, I guess. I mean, I see a lot of Françoise in you and a lot of both of you in Sylvie. I just wondered how your dad fits in. Listen, if that's too personal a question, I'm sorry…."

Marc held up a hand. "No, not at all. I guess I've gotten used to people not asking about Dad. I mean, most people around here know the story already."

"Is it hard to talk about?"

"Not really. It's been more than fifteen years since he died."

"How did he die?"

"Heart attack," Marc said flatly. "The guy wasn't sick a day in his life that I remember. But one morning, he gets up, goes to pour a cup of coffee, sits down on the front porch with his paper and wham! A minute later he's dead. The doc said his ticker stopped beating before he hit the ground."

"How old were you when it happened?" Abby asked.

"Just turned seventeen the week before." Marc remembered the day clearly. "He'd given me my first fishing boat for my birthday. We were supposed to take it out together the next day. But we never got the chance."

"It must have been very hard for you and your mother," Abby said softly.

"I won't lie, it was a rough go." Marc could feel the familiar anger rising. "Of course, it wasn't just us having it bad."

"What do you mean?" Abby asked.

"That spring Ottawa had cut the fishing quotas by two-thirds as a conservation measure. It killed the North Shore fleet. I think the morning my dad died, the reality of what those reduced quotas meant hit home for the first time and he just couldn't bear it."

"The day I met you and we went out to dinner, you said it was the scientists' fault the quotas were reduced," Abby said evenly.

"That was a bad generalization," Marc admitted. "Sure, the scientists are the ones the politicians listen to, but that's not their fault. It's easier for the suits in Ottawa to cozy up to a room full of academics than a rowdy bunch of North Shore fishermen. But here's the funny thing— both groups, fishermen and scientists, want the same thing."

"And what's that?" Abby asked.

"A healthy fish population," Marc said. "And a healthy waterway for them to live in."

"You really mean that, don't you?" Abby said.

Marc sat up. "You sound surprised."

"Maybe I am, just a little." Abby hesitated slightly. "Does that make you mad?"

"Nah." Marc shook his head. "Here's how I see it. We fishermen depended on the seaway for centuries. To a large extent, we still do. It feeds us, served as a major transportation route and we make our living from it. So, over the years, we got a pretty good handle on how to keep it healthy and productive, and that allowed *us* to stay healthy and productive. But not everyone looked at it that way. Did you know that the beluga you're studying are toxic?"

Abby nodded.

"That's thanks to years of chemical spills and pollution—none of it coming from the small fishermen, mind you. Most of it comes from illegal dumping and such. But the results are disastrous. The fish stocks were almost depleted. And who pays? Not the polluters, they're too removed from the fish and too busy paying off lobbyists. Nope, the public sees the fishermen killing the fish, so we must be the bad guys. Then the politicians just choose the science that gives them the answers they want for the easiest solutions."

"So what's your answer?" Abby asked.

"Like I told you that first night, let those of us who live on the water take care of it. There's a lot of knowledge you can get without electronic gizmos and gadgets."

"I'm not saying I completely agree with everything you're saying," Abby said. "But I can appreciate your point of view."

"Well, that's a step in the right direction." Marc looked past her. "Hey, you want to take another step?"

"Like what?"

"Take a look up there, just where the river starts to bend." Marc pointed. "How would you like to get really up close and personal with your beluga?"

ABBY TOOK THE HAND Marc extended to help her get up, then looked in the direction he had pointed. She saw a man surrounded by several brightly colored kayaks.

"Who is that?" Abby asked.

"Hard to say from this distance, but I guess it's either Bruno or Mathieu Dupuis. They run a kayak outfit up here." Marc released her hand. "C'mon, let's get our leftovers stowed and go over."

Shouldering the dramatically lighter packs, they headed toward the kayaks.

As they grew closer, Marc hailed the man. "Bruno! *Ça va?*"

"Marc!" Bruno called out. "*Oui, ça va?* And who is your pretty friend?"

Blushing slightly at the compliment, Abby

stood by while Marc introduced her to Bruno Dupuis, water guide and co-owner of *Bonne Mer* Sea Kayak Tours.

"I'm pleased to meet you," Abby said to Bruno. The man smiled widely and shook Abby's hand.

"Out enjoying the day?" Bruno asked.

"Oh yes," Abby said. "This is a beautiful place."

Marc pointed to the kayaks. "Say, Bruno. What would it take for us to rent one of these for the rest of the day?"

Bruno cocked an eyebrow at Marc. "Ah, *mon ami,* I think you have something special in mind for the end of your day with the lady, no?"

"You'll have to excuse Bruno," Marc told Abby, "the man's an incurable romantic."

"You could use a little romance yourself," Bruno said teasingly.

"The kayaks, Bruno?" Marc repeated.

Bruno waved his hand over the grouping. "Pick the one you want."

"That was too easy," Marc said. "What's the catch?"

"Catch?" Bruno said. "No catch."

Marc didn't believe him. "What's it going to cost me?"

"My friend, you think too much about the business. You are my friend who needs a kayak. I have some kayaks. All I would ask…"

"Ah ha!" Marc said. "I knew it, here it comes."

Bruno was looking at the packs Marc and Abby had dropped at their feet. "You say you've been on a picnic? Did Françoise prepare it?"

"She did." Marc sounded as if he knew what was coming next.

"And would those be leftovers in your bags?"

"They are."

"*Bon.*" Bruno rubbed his hands together. "I let you take one kayak, and you give me whatever you have in those bags. Deal?"

"My friend," Marc said solemnly, placing a hand on Bruno's shoulder. "You drive a hard bargain. But I think yes, we have a deal."

Abby had watched the entire exchange in silence, but now joined in the laughter.

"Will you be at the beach later today?" Marc asked Bruno.

"No," Bruno shook his head. "I'm guiding a trip. But Mathieu will be around."

"Okay, I'll ask my mom to run me back up here so I can bring the kayak back and get my truck," Marc said.

"You can leave the kayak down at the town dock," Bruno told him. "I needed to bring an extra one down anyway, so you're saving me the trouble."

"And I can bring you back here," Abby said.

"Then it looks like we're all set. Thanks, man." Marc clasped Bruno on the shoulder.

"Happy to help out." Bruno turned to his boats. "Here, you'll need these." The guide pulled three double-bladed paddles—one for each of them plus a spare—and two life jackets from beneath one of the crafts. "Have fun."

"We will," Abby said. "And thank you."

"It was very nice to meet you. Take care of my friend."

Abby laughed, "I'll try."

She and Marc watched as Bruno, lugging the two packs, walked off the beach and disappeared into the woods in the direction of the trail that headed back to the parking lot.

"So, how do we begin?" Abby asked, looking a bit askance at the kayak Marc had selected. It was twelve feet long with two cockpits. It was painted a brilliant shade of orange.

"First we get it down to the water," Marc said, hefting the back of the kayak. "Can you handle your end?"

"Of course."

Together they lifted the kayak and slowly walked it to the water's edge.

"Set it down easy," Marc instructed. When the craft was on the ground, he trotted back and snagged the two life vests and paddles. Returning, he tossed one of the vests to Abby and put the other one on himself.

"Ready for your first lesson?" he asked.

"I guess so," Abby said tentatively.

Marc handed her a paddle. "Hey, don't look so scared."

"You're not going to make me flip over in this thing, are you?" Abby asked.

"No, this is a sea kayak. You couldn't flip it if you tried. You're thinking of river kayaks. Big difference."

Abby felt slightly relieved.

"You'll be sitting in the front and that means you get to set the paddling pace," Marc said. "I'll be in the back steering."

"Okay. But I hope you're not expecting too much. I've never been in one of these before."

"Remind me again how a woman who grew up next to the sea has never been in a sea kayak?" Marc said, leaning on his paddle.

Abby shrugged. "We always had bigger boats. When I was on the Cape, few people had heard of sea kayaks, much less owned one. Of course, now they're the yuppie craft of choice."

"I know the type," Marc said. "The kind of folks who have the expensive mountain bikes that stay strapped to the roof of their Lexus SUVs and hardly get ridden."

"Exactly."

"For this trip back to town, the current's going to do most of the work for us," Marc said, "but, you will have to do some paddling. I want you to hold your paddle with both hands, straight out in front of you, like this."

As Abby watched, Marc held his paddle up and out until it was chest height and parallel to the ground.

"Like this?" she said, imitating him.

"Perfect. Now, place your hands so your elbows are at an eighty-degree angle. Good," he added when she had adjusted her grip. "Okay, for the moment, just watch me and see how I move the paddle. You want to put the blade in the water in front of you next to where your toes are in the kayak." As he spoke, Marc thrust the tip of his paddle outward. "The temptation is to pull in using just your arms. But you want to twist your whole torso, and let that motion pull the paddle in until it's even with your shoulder. When it is, lift it out of the water and let the opposite end drop in. See?"

Marc's movements were smooth and fluid.

He makes it look easy, Abby thought to herself.

"Now you give it a try," he said.

Abby did her best to imitate Marc's paddling technique, but she knew she was awkward.

"Not bad."

"Liar," Abby said, "but thanks."

"The best way to learn is by doing anyway." They headed over to the kayak. "Mind getting your feet a bit wet?" Marc asked.

"Not at all."

Marc pushed the kayak until it was floating in the water. "It's a pretty simple trick getting in," he said. "Just sit on that spot right behind the cockpit. Brace your hands to lift you up and over the back of the seat, then slide your legs in front of you."

Abby stepped into the chilly Saguenay water and swung one leg over the kayak. Lowering herself, she used her hands as Marc had instructed to inch her way forward until she was directly over the seat. Stretching her long legs out in front of her inside the kayak, she sat down and smiled up at Marc. "How'd I do?"

"Perfect. Just perfect. Feel around with your feet for the footrests. Got them?"

"No, wait, yeah, there they are," Abby said, her toes brushing against the metal blocks. "But I can barely reach them."

"Okay," Marc said hunkering down next to her. "I'm going to adjust them for you. Let me know when they're set so your knees are at a slight bend."

Marc reached into the kayak and Abby watched as he fumbled around a moment. Then he began sliding the footrests closer to her body.

"How's that feel?" he asked, his right forearm brushing lightly against her inner thigh. Abby gasped at the heat that streaked up her leg.

Marc pulled his arm out of the kayak, a pained look on his face.

Abby tried to salvage the moment with a laugh, but she couldn't get the sound past the dryness in her throat. Instead, she just nodded and pretended to be suddenly very interested in adjusting the strap on her life vest.

CHAPTER SEVENTEEN

IF ABBY WAS CONTENT to let the awkward moment go, then he would be, too. But his body was still humming with the heat of their contact. *Maybe I should just jump in the river,* he thought, settling into the rear seat and pushing off from the shore with his paddle. A cold dip might be just what the doctor ordered.

The combination of the steady breeze and flowing current soon carried the kayak to the middle of the Saguenay River. Abby, Marc saw, was doing a passable job paddling, but falling into the novice's trap of using her arms rather than the whole-body motion he had demonstrated on shore.

"Use your torso, remember?" he called out as he flipped the kayak's rudder from its position atop the back of the kayak into the water. Pushing at the foot pedals to control the rudder, he made some minor adjustments and sat back. "Let the current do most of the work," he said as Abby dug in for all she was worth with her paddle. "Just sit back and enjoy the ride."

Marc loved the *Percé,* but he'd forgotten the simple joy of being out on the water in a kayak. The small craft's low profile meant the passengers were almost level with the river, and it slipped silently through the waves, causing little or no disturbance.

This was obvious a moment later when Marc cried out, "Abby, off to your right. Look!"

He saw Abby's head turn and then heard her sharp intake of breath as three gleaming white beluga surfaced less than twenty feet from the kayak.

Marc allowed them to drift with the current, making only slight directional changes with the rudders, as the small pod moved closer to the kayak.

"Look," Abby said breathlessly. "The one in the middle, he's wearing one of the acoustic tags!"

Marc squinted, and sure enough, there was the round disc against the white skin of the whale.

"Maybe you should introduce yourself," Marc said. "I mean, you have been eavesdropping on them for weeks, now."

Before Abby could answer, the pod disappeared, surfacing minutes later off the left side of the kayak.

"They must have swam directly under us," Abby said, wonderment in her voice.

"They don't seem particularly bothered by us." Marc dipped his paddle to turn the kayak for a better look.

"Whales are curious by nature," Abby said. "That's one of the problems. Sometimes they're too curious for their own good and they get into trouble by getting too close to people."

"You have to admit, this is a pretty good way to observe them," Marc said, after they had watched the whales for several minutes.

"It's more than that." Abby sounded excited. "It may just be the missing piece of my research!"

BEING SO CLOSE to the whales was having a near-spiritual effect on Abby. The natural beauty of the fjord, the invigorating feel of the breeze against her face, the awesome presence of the whales and the complete silence of the surroundings. It was almost too much to take in. The only sounds were those of the water lapping against the low hull of the kayak and the blowing of the beluga.

So peaceful, Abby thought. *This must be what it's like all the time for the beluga when there are no tourists or researchers around.* "All the time," she whispered to herself. "All the time…"

Marc was saying something about this being a great way to observe whales, but she hardly heard him.

"This is it!" she cried out, her mind racing. "Oh, Marc, thank you! This is the piece of research that was missing!"

"Okay, I'll bite," Marc said from behind her. "What piece is this?"

She didn't answer right away. Was there still time to add this into her project presentation? Of course there was. The committee wasn't going to be here for another few weeks, at least.

"Hey, earth to Abby," Marc called up to her. "You still with me?"

Abby laughed gaily. "Of course!"

"Are you going to fill me in or just sit up there enjoying your brainstorm?"

"Oh, sorry. Marc, listen to this and tell me what you think." Abby knew she was talking fast, but in her excitement, the words just tumbled along. "All along I've been taking readings from your boat, right?"

"Yeah, I know. I was there, remember?"

"Right, sorry," she said, though she knew he was teasing. "But what if next summer, we use a kayak and a simple hydrophone and digital recorder. No background noise from a boat, and we could slip up on them so easily." In her excitement to share her idea, Abby had naturally used the word *we*. She caught herself and wondered if Marc had noticed, too. If he had, he wasn't saying.

"Will that make such a huge difference?" Marc asked.

"Oh yes," she said. "I mean, a kayak will still have an impact on their world, but nothing compared to a boat like the *Percé*. And then I can compare the vocalizations from this summer to ones I collect next year from the kayak." She leaned against the small backrest, inordinately pleased with herself.

What a perfect day this had turned into, Abby thought. From the reconciliation with Marc to the up close encounter with the whales to plan a whole new phase of her research.

All because Sylvie and Françoise had tricked them into going on a picnic together.

A FEW FEET behind Abby, Marc was thinking the same thing and wondering what he'd have to do to get Abby to look at him with the same joyous expression on her face that she had bestowed upon the whales. For now, though, he was just going to let himself enjoy the rest of their day together.

Reluctantly, they headed toward town once the pod moved on. Thanks to the current and conditions, it was an easy two-hour float down to the mouth of the Saguenay. Rounding the last bend in the river, Marc called out for Abby to stop paddling as they neared the ferry terminal on the

Tadoussac side of the estuary. Waving to the captain of the departing vessel, Marc held the kayak in place until the ferry was well away from the dock. The boat's captain gave two quick blasts of the air horn as a courtesy to Marc, indicating when it was safe for the kayak to continue.

"Okay, dig in," Marc said. Out of the corner of his eye he saw the ferry's sister ship departing the far shore and heading in their direction. Working together, he and Abby powered the kayak well past the dock with plenty of time to spare before the second ferry arrived. "Take a break," he said, slightly out of breath from the exertion.

"The water looks kind of rough ahead." Abby's voice was tinged with concern.

"Nothing to worry about," Marc reassured her. "It's just where the currents from the Saguenay meet the bay. It's always a bit choppy there. Nothing we can't handle."

"If you say so." Abby sounded unconvinced.

"I'm going to point the kayak toward the opposite side of the bay when we get past these rocks," he told her. "When I do, start paddling and we'll be over and through the rough water in no time."

"Promise?" Abby said.

"Promise." Marc spun the kayak into the current.

"Now!" he yelled.

Pulling together, they propelled the kayak up and down the whitecaps, the bow breaking through the waves and throwing up spray. In a few moments, they were free of the churning water and Marc called a halt.

"Let's just let it drift us across for a ways," he said.

"That was fun!" Abby called back to him.

"Told ya so."

The current had carried them halfway across Tadoussac Bay and Marc was just about to suggest they head toward the town beach when Abby screamed.

"Abby," he said in concern. "Are you okay?"

"We have to get to that beach, right away," she said, sounding frantic.

"We're heading to the beach, don't worry."

"No, no," she was shaking her head. "Not the one at town—there, over there." She pointed to a patch of beach on the far arm of the bay.

"Are you feeling sick?" he asked, thinking that was why she wanted to head to the closer point.

"Are you going to paddle or not?" Marc realized Abby was sobbing.

"Yeah, I'll paddle, but what the hell is going on?"

"I, I just hope I'm not seeing what I think I'm seeing. Hurry!" She dug in her own paddle.

"Abby, calm down!" Marc said firmly. Her voice was carrying all the hallmarks of hysteria and her paddling was erratic. "Time your strokes with your breath. That's it; slow, even power pulls."

Looking ahead, Marc tried to see what had agitated Abby, but could detect nothing out of the ordinary on the beach she had indicated. A handful of people were standing near a large rock, and there was the usual gaggle of seagulls.

Wait a minute, Marc thought. He'd gone by that beach hundreds of times over the years and he couldn't remember a rock. "What the heck?" he said. "Oh cripes, no way!"

Now he knew what had triggered Abby's outburst.

ABBY COULD SCARCELY SEE the shore through her tears. Her arms and shoulders were on fire from the exertion of paddling, and all of Marc's instructions about using her whole body had flown from her mind.

The kayak had no sooner scraped over the gravel of the shore than Abby was up and out and running down the beach shouting. Behind her, she was dimly aware of Marc pulling the craft out of the water, securing it on the shore and sprinting after her.

She came to a skidding stop and burst into fresh tears at the pitiful sight in front of her. It looked like the mature minke had been dead for several days before washing up on shore. The smell was almost overpowering.

"Holy cow, what a stench!" Marc said, reaching her side. "I can't remember the last time we had one of these wash ashore."

"Even one time is too many," Abby wiped her eyes. "Look at her, the poor thing."

"Her?" Marc said.

Abby nodded. "Statistically, odds are it's a female. No one knows why, but only females ever get found on land like this." She turned to look at him, "I need to call Peter right away and tell him about this."

"Right." Marc looked over at the small crowd of onlookers. "Hang on a moment."

As Abby watched, Marc walked over to a couple of teenagers who had been using a cell phone to photograph the dead whale. She saw him exchange a few word with them, and then the teen with the phone shrugged and handed it over.

"Here." Marc passed the phone to Abby.

"How did you manage that?" Abby asked.

"Just appealed to their better natures," Marc said. "And told them the marine center would buy them pizza."

"Thanks," she said dully. "Can you do me a favor and keep the people back?"

"Sure." He looked at her closely. "Are you okay?"

"No," Abby said. "Not really, but I can't just leave her here for the birds and tourists to pick over."

While Marc walked over to place himself between the small group of gawkers and the whale, Abby punched a series of numbers into the cell phone.

"Please be home," she whispered. To her immense relief, the phone was answered on the third ring.

"Hello?" a deep voice said.

"Peter, it's Abby." She struggled to hold back the tears.

"Abby? You sound like you're on Mars. This is a horrible connection. You're going to have to speak up."

Abby held the phone to her ear with one hand and swiped her running eyes with the other. "Sorry," she said. "But I don't think it's the connection." Before she could say more, her voice cracked.

"Abby? What's going on?" Concern was evident in Peter's voice. "Have you had an accident? Do you need me to come and get you?"

"Yes, I mean no, I haven't been in an accident." Abby fought to regain control. "But I do need you and the response team to meet me at the southeast point of the bay. We've found a dead minke."

She heard the director swear softly. "What's the state of decomp?"

"Fairly advanced," Abby said, the scientist in her taking over, much to her relief. "The carcass is intact, but she's been dead awhile. I'm guessing she's a mature adult, maybe ten meters."

"Any sign of what killed her?"

"Nothing obvious, but I really haven't gone in for a close look. I wanted to call you first."

"Okay," Peter said. "Can you stay on site until we get there?"

"Of course," she said and gave the director her location.

"Good, we'll be there as soon as we can," Peter said. The line went dead.

Abby shut the phone and turned back to the whale. Approaching it slowly, she breathed through her mouth to minimize the decaying carcass's stench. Marc, she saw, was doing an admirable job in keeping the onlookers at bay. He'd planted himself directly between them and the whale, feet apart, arms folded across his chest.

"Are they giving you any trouble?" she whispered after returning the phone to its owner.

"The tall dude in the Speedo tried. Said he wanted to make himself a whale's-tooth necklace.

I told him if he did, it would be a long time before he could get it over the body cast I'd put him in."

"Diplomatic," Abby said. "I'm going for a closer look. Peter and the response team should be here soon. Can you hold out until then?"

"No problem, do what you need to do. I'm not going anywhere." Marc scowled at a fat couple inching their way closer to the body.

"I don't suppose there's a way you could make them leave without resorting to physical violence, is there?" Abby said.

Marc turned and looked at her. "You want the site cleared?"

Abby nodded.

"You got it." Marc stepped forward. Immediately, the dozen or so spectators moved away from him.

"Folks, can I have your attention, please," he said in a commanding voice. "The show's pretty much over here. I don't see a boat nearby, so I'm guessing you all walked over from town. The tide's going to be up soon and that's going to cut off the trail back. I suggest you start walking back."

None of them made a move.

"*Now,*" Marc said, staring them down. "And I want to remind you, Canadian law provides stiff penalties for harassing expired marine wildlife."

That got them moving. Abby watched them

file past, muttering unhappily, a few taking some final snapshots.

Abby waited until the group was out of earshot. "Harassing expired marine wildlife? That's a new one on me."

Marc shrugged. "Well, if it's not a law, it should be. Now what?"

"We wait," Abby said, walking closer to the whale. Only DNA testing could determine if it was a female. Walking around to look at the whale's back, Abby caught her breath.

"What is it?" Marc asked, joining her.

"Look." Her tears started anew as she pointed to a series of deep, parallel cuts along the whale's back. "Propeller gashes." She turned to look at him. "You see? This is what happens when whales and boats get too close together. The whales *always* lose. The poor, poor thing."

"Hey," Marc said softly, putting an arm gently around her shoulders and pulling her close. "You don't know if that's what killed her. I mean, she could have lived a long, happy life and died of old age, right?"

"It's just such an undignified ending for a majestic creature," she said sadly.

CHAPTER EIGHTEEN

THEY WERE STILL STANDING like that, looking at the dead whale, when the sound of two Zodiacs coming up quickly made them turn around. As the craft ran ashore, Abby pulled herself from Marc's grasp and rushed over. She got to the first boat just as Peter was stepping out.

"I see you managed to get everyone away from here," he said to her, and then spotted Marc standing to one side, hands stuffed into his pockets. "*Almost* everyone."

"Marc's been very helpful." Abby led the director over to the carcass while a dozen researchers and interns began unloading gear onto the beach.

"I'll just bet," Peter said. "Phew! She has been here awhile, hasn't she?" He squatted down next to her for a close inspection. "Right, we'll collect some tissue samples, measure and weigh her as best we can. Then all that's left to do is the rendering and disposal."

"Rendering?" Marc said.

Neither Abby nor Peter had seen Marc walk over to join them.

"Oh, hello, Doucette," Peter said coolly. "What are you doing here?"

Abby immediately sensed the tension between the two men and stepped in, lightly touching Peter on the arm.

"Marc was with me when we found the whale," she said softly. "He's the one that kept people from doing any further damage. I couldn't have done it alone."

"Is that so?" Peter said, never taking his eyes off Marc. "I guess thanks are in order. But you can go ahead and shove off now. We'll take over from here."

Abby saw Marc's jaw clench and she felt a jab of embarrassment at her director's rudeness.

"Marc's my ride home," Abby said. "I need him to stay around."

"We can get you back to the docks," Peter told her. "There really shouldn't be any extraneous people hanging around here."

Several staff members had begun to drift over, lugging heavy equipment. Two others were stringing a roll of yellow cautionary tape to create a large perimeter around the dead whale.

Marc looked at Abby and then back at Peter. Abby held her breath.

"Yeah, well, I need to go check on my daughter," Marc said finally. "It's going to take awhile to paddle back alone." He looked at Abby. "You going to be okay?"

"I'm fine." He started to walk back to the kayak. "Marc, wait a minute," she called.

"Yeah?" He slid her paddle in the front cockpit and bent down to grab his own.

"Marc, do you really have to leave?"

"You heard your boss, you don't need me here anymore." He sounded bitter.

"Forget what Peter said. It's not about *needing* you here, I *want* you here."

Under almost any other situation, Abby's words would have been music to Marc's ears. But as much as he would have liked to remain at her side, he knew this was not the time or the place and said as much to her.

"They need you here." Marc nodded his head toward the group of scientists and interns buzzing around the whale.

Abby bit her lip. "I *would* like to hang around," she said slowly. "There's a lot to do and I'd like to help as much as I can. They're going to pull some samples and then clean what's left of the body off the bones."

"What for?" Marc asked.

"The bones will be brought back to the lab,

where they'll be boiled, cleaned and reassembled into a complete skeleton. She'll serve as an educational model."

"And the rest of her?" Marc asked.

"Hauled far out into the seaway and dumped," Abby said sounding bitter. "Are you sure you can't stay?"

Marc shook his head. "I really do need to go check on Sylvie. She'll be wondering where we are. And you said yourself, there's a ton of work to be done here. I'd just be in the way."

"You wouldn't be in my way," Abby said, "but I understand." She hesitated a moment. "This is probably a wildly inappropriate time to say this, but thank you for a really nice day."

Marc reached out and ran his forefinger along her jawline. "Take care of things here. We can talk about today later." He looked once more at the scene on the beach before shoving the kayak back into the water and settling into the rear cockpit. Back-paddling the craft from the shore, he watched as Abby slowly returned to the group of scientists.

Turning the kayak toward the town beach, he began paddling with strong, even strokes. Marc was a powerful paddler, but there was nothing easy about operating a double kayak solo. This was not the way he'd envisioned ending the day.

After he'd dragged the kayak up on the beach, Marc began to secure it to the wooden railing with the other *Bon Mer* craft when he heard a familiar voice calling from the boardwalk above.

"Hi, Dad!" Sylvie said. "Where's Abby?"

"Hello, *ma fille*," Marc waved and spotted his mother standing behind her. "I'll be right up."

He finished tying the kayak off and trotted up the paved ramp to the street above.

"You didn't leave her alongside the river, did you?" Françoise asked.

Marc frowned. "Leave who?"

"Abby."

He laughed and shook his head. "No, but I did leave her out on the far point." Before his mother could ask any more questions, he shot her a warning look and then looked down at Sylvie.

"*Ma fille,* could you do me a favor and run and grab my fleece jacket from the hall closet? We'll watch you cross the road, okay?"

"Sure, Dad," Sylvie said. "But I want to hear about the picnic."

"I'll tell you all about it, I promise." Marc watched her closely as his daughter scampered across the street and up the front steps of his mother's house.

Quickly, before Sylvie could return with the jacket, Marc gave his mother a rundown of the day's events, starting with the time they'd spent at Sainte-Marguerite Bay and ending with the discovery of the whale.

"So, I figured I'd get out of her way and let her do her job," Marc finished. "What I really need now is a ride back to my Jeep."

"I want to go, too!" Sylvie arrived at his side slightly out of breath. She handed him the jacket.

"We'll all go," Françoise said. "And maybe stop for ice cream on the way home."

Sylvie clapped her hands. "Oh boy. But shouldn't we wait for Abby?"

"Abby had to go to work for a bit," Marc said. "But you'll see her tomorrow."

"Did you and Abby have fun?" Sylvie asked.

"As a matter of fact, yes. And I guess I have the two of you to thank for that. By the way, did you get your baking emergency taken care of?"

Françoise looked flustered. "About that…"

Marc laughed. "Never mind, you never could tell a lie, Mom." He turned to his daughter. "Why don't you tell me all about the book you're reading to Figgy on the way to Sainte-Marguerite?"

Sylvie kept up a constant stream of chatter from Tadoussac to the lot where Marc's Jeep was parked. Along the way, he heard about the new book she had just finished reading, the new trick she was teaching Figgy and how Suzelle Beaupré had been caught holding hands with Martin Cyr in the grade two cloakroom, and now the whole school knew they had cooties and no one would sit with them at lunch.

It was dark by the time Marc pulled up to his mother's house. Sylvie was dozing in the passenger's seat. There were no lights on in Abby's apartment, so he guessed she was still out with the crew and the dead whale.

MARC HADN'T REALIZED how tired he was until he slumped down yawning on the small couch in the boat's galley area. Sylvie had barely been able to keep her eyes open during supper and had gone to bed with little argument. Marc bid his mother good night soon after and was looking forward to a hot shower and crawling into his own bed when he heard footsteps on the deck.

"Marc?" Abby called from the darkness beyond the hatch. "Are you in there?"

She sounded as tired as Marc felt. He walked to the bottom of the stairway and looked up to see her silhouetted against the deck lights.

"Come on in," he said, inordinately pleased she'd stopped by. "Sit down and relax a bit."

"Thanks." Abby made her way down the stairway. "I'm almost afraid to sit anywhere, I'm such a mess."

Marc regarded her with an appraising eye. Her hair was a riot of windblown tangles and her clothes and skin were coated with dirt, sand and what Marc could only surmise was whale slime. There were dark bags under her red-rimmed eyes and the not-so-subtle aroma of dead whale was wafting from her in waves. She was completely lovely.

"It's a boat," Marc said. "You can't do any damage. Here." He took her hand and lead her to the couch. "Sit down before you fall down."

Abby sank to the cushioned seat, put her head back against the bulkhead wall and blew out a breath.

"Tough time?" Marc said sympathetically.

"The worst." Abby didn't even open her eyes. "After you left I helped pull some tissue and blood samples from the whale. Then we all took turns carving the flesh from the bones."

"Sounds like a nasty job." Marc sat down on the padded bench across from her, the galley table between them.

"Oh, it gets worse," Abby said. "Remember how I told you all beached minkies have been females?"

Marc nodded. "Yeah, but you said you wouldn't know for certain until you got the DNA results back."

"Right." A small tear slid from her eye. "Well, we found out pretty quick she was a female. There was a fetus in her womb."

With that, she crossed her arms on the table in front of her, lowered her head and started to cry softly.

"Abby, Abby," he murmured, reaching out and taking one of her hands in his own. "I'm so sorry." He couldn't think of anything else to say, so he just let her cry it out.

After a few minutes, her head came up and she sniffed loudly, wiping her eyes with her free hand. "I thought I was all cried out hours ago," she said, a rueful grin on her face.

"No explanations needed," Marc told her. "What can I do?"

She shook her head. "Just being here and letting me come by and sit with you is enough, believe me. But I'd better get home and see about Figgy."

"Don't worry about it," Marc said before she could get up. "Sylvie and I fed her supper hours ago and I let her out for a last run around the yard before I came back here. She's fine."

"Thanks," Abby said.

"Now, what about you?"

"What about me?"

"Can I fix you something to eat, maybe a drink?"

Abby shook her head. "I don't think I could eat anything."

"How about a nice cup of herbal tea?"

"That sounds wonderful, if it's no trouble."

"No trouble at all." Marc released the grip on her hand and stood up. "Give me a minute. You just stay put."

"Aye-Aye, Captain," Abby said with a small trace of humor.

Marc went to the stove and struck a match to the burner. He put the teapot over the blue flame and collected cups, saucers and spoons from a cupboard overhead. From a second cupboard, he pulled down several boxes of tea bags.

""What'll it be?" he asked, looking over the selection without turning around. "There's peppermint, chamomile, lemon and ginger-honey."

When Abby didn't answer, he glanced over his shoulder. "Abby?"

While he had been fussing at the stove, his guest had turned so her back was against the boat's hull and her long legs were stretched out in front of her on the couch. Abby's arms were folded loosely across her chest, her eyes were closed and she was sound asleep.

CHAPTER NINETEEN

ABBY WAS HAVING the oddest dream. In it, she was on a raft in the open ocean. As her dream-raft bobbed up and down among the swells, she looked over and saw a baby whale sitting next to her, drinking a cup of coffee. The baby whale was trying to say something to her, but Abby couldn't hear it because every time the whale opened its mouth, a foghorn blasted, drowning out its voice.

Suddenly, a large wave struck the raft, throwing Abby to the side just as the foghorn sounded again. With a start, she opened her eyes. Right away she could tell she was not in her own bed, though the room looked vaguely familiar. Sniffing the air, she could smell coffee. The room was, in fact, moving ever so gently, so just in case she looked on both sides of the bed. No baby whale. That was something of a relief.

Where am I? Abby thought. Then, as she came fully awake, it hit her. She was in the third and unused cabin on the *Percé*. She must have spent the night. Abby felt her stomach lurch in time with the bobbing of the boat as she slowly lifted the covers, almost afraid to look. Thankfully, her clothes were still on. She must have slept in them. "But how did I get here?" she asked herself.

With a groan, she swung her legs over the edge of the bed, sitting so her feet were on the floor. Between the kayak trip down the fjord and the effort of rendering the dead whale, every muscle in her body was sore.

At the memory of the dead whale and her baby, Abby's shoulders sagged. The image of the mother whale, reduced to a rotting carcass, was one she knew would be with her for a very long time. She didn't need Freud to tell her what had triggered the earlier dream. What Abby did need and want, however, was breakfast and a hot cup of coffee.

"And a shower," she said, standing and getting a good whiff of herself. The scent of dead whale was not one that improved with age, she thought with disgust.

Opening the cabin door, she could hear activity in the galley. The closer she got to it, the stronger the smell of coffee.

"Well, good morning," Marc said from his seat at the small table. "I was getting ready to send a search team after you."

"Good morning, yourself," Abby said through a yawn, helping herself to a cup of coffee from the pot on the stove and joining Marc at the table.

"Sleep well?" he asked.

"Must have," Abby said. "Since I sure don't remember much after getting here last night."

"Yeah, you were pretty wiped out."

"What time is it, anyway?" Abby said, savoring Marc's deliciously strong brew.

Marc looked at the clock mounted on the wall above Abby's head. "Just past ten-thirty," he said.

"*Ten-thirty!*" Abby exclaimed. "In the *morning?*"

Marc nodded. "You didn't leave a wake-up call. Is there someplace you needed to be this morning?"

"No, that's not it. It's just that I can't remember the last time I slept this late."

"You needed it," Marc said.

She had to ask. "While we're on the subject, how exactly did I get into bed last night?"

"I carried you and pulled the covers up over you."

Abby felt herself blush. "That was very gallant of you."

"If you recall, the first time we met I told you I have a real soft spot for damsels in distress," Marc teased.

"I remember," Abby said. "Oh no!"

"What's wrong?" Marc asked.

"Figgy, she needs to be fed and let out and…"

Marc held up his hand. "Done and done. I called my mom and she and Sylvie took care of her."

"Thank you, *again*." Abby sagged in her seat.

"Now, don't take this the wrong way," Marc said, "but you're more than welcome to avail yourself to the shower in my head."

"Oh, Marc, I'm sorry." Abby felt mortified. "I'm surprised you haven't pulled on a gas mask."

"Nah, I've been around a lot worse, believe me. One summer I worked shoveling fish-gut fertilizer. I'd say right now you're nowhere near that bad. A close second maybe."

"Ha ha, very funny." Abby wrinkled her nose at him. "Seriously, Marc, I'm afraid you'll have to burn those sheets I slept in."

"Nothing some bleach can't take care of."

She sighed. "A hot shower does sound wonderful. But there's just one problem. I don't have a change of clothes."

"Look in the closet in the hallway," Marc said. "There's a clean jumpsuit. It may be a little big on you, but you can wear it until you get back to your place."

Abby stood. "I won't be long."

"Take your time," Marc said. "I don't think we're going anywhere today."

"Why not?"

"Look out the window."

Abby did, and saw the steady rain pelting the portholes.

"All reports say this is going to hang on through the end of the week," Marc said. "I hope you have some indoor work to keep you occupied."

Indoor work, Abby thought a short time later, sudsing her hair with Marc's shampoo. The rainy weather couldn't have come at a better time. Last night, before leaving the center, she'd checked her e-mail and seen one marked Urgent from Felix. The funding committee, all eight members, had been able to coordinate a trip sooner than expected and would be in Tadoussac the following Wednesday. Could she have a presentation ready for them?

"You bet I can," Abby said, scrubbing at her scalp. "And it's going to knock your socks off."

MARC HEARD the water running in his shower and marveled at having a woman on his boat for reasons other than a charter. Getting up to pour another cup of coffee, he found himself wondering if his relationship with Abby would ever progress beyond employer and client. All day yesterday there had been subtle indications that it might, but the discovery of the dead whale and the arrival of Peter and his crew had put an end to exploring that possibility, at least for the moment.

Still, he had been the one she had come to last night. Carrying her sleeping form into the spare room, removing her shoes and pulling the blankets up over her had brought out a very protective feeling in Marc. He had to admit he was falling for her. But *was that such a bad thing?* he wondered. Sylvie and his mother didn't think so, and that meant a lot. He was especially concerned about his daughter. She'd been through so much already with the loss of her mother, and Marc would never consider seriously pursuing a woman Sylvie didn't like.

The shower stopped and minutes later Abby reappeared in the galley. The baggy blue jumpsuit he kept on board in case he needed some dry clothes in an emergency somehow made her look even sexier.

Damn, he thought, *does this woman ever look bad?*

"Better," Marc said.

Abby twirled around. "Oh yeah, this outfit is really me—the fashion statement I've been searching for my whole life."

"Hungry?" Marc said, consciously restraining himself from crossing the small room and taking her in his arms.

"Famished. Is there any more of that coffee?"

"Just brewed a fresh pot," Marc said. "Have a seat and I'll get some chow going."

Abby refilled her mug and sat at the table, looking at the pieces of paper spread on its surface. "What are all these?"

"Weather reports and charts," Marc said. "This rain isn't going to amount to a major storm but it does look like it's going to hang around for several days. I wasn't kidding about finding something to do that's indoors."

"No problem." Abby told Marc about Felix's message and the upcoming visit.

Marc whistled softly as he worked to make Abby breakfast. "Middle of next week, you say?"

"Yeah," Abby said.

"Kind of short notice."

"Not really. I mean, it would be if they were looking for a formal presentation of research results."

"And they're not?" Marc set a plate heaped with food in front of her before sitting down.

Abby stared at two fried eggs, strips of bacon, hash browns and biscuits that Marc seemed to have conjured from thin air. "Dear Lord, you don't expect me to eat all of this, do you?"

"Just give it your best shot," Marc said. "So what are those Woods Hole folks looking for?"

"Oh, well, projections mostly. I'm just getting into my research, so they're not expecting any hard results yet. But what they do want to see is where my research is heading and what promise it has for future findings."

"Do you know where it's heading?" Marc asked.

"Pretty much, yeah," Abby said. "And what makes it even more exciting is the whole idea of doing studies from a kayak next summer. I bet they're going to love that. This is delicious, by the way," she added.

"Thanks," Marc said.

"Plus, I've been sending regular reports down to Woods Hole. They must like what they've seen so far, or they wouldn't be coming all the way up here. Still, I'm not taking anything for granted. If the weather's going to be as bad as you say, looks like I'll be in my office for the week, chained to my computer."

"Yeah, guess it's a few days of routine maintenance for me," Marc said. "The people renting the house called about a couple of windows that're sticking, so I'll have to go up there, too."

Marc shuffled the papers in front of him for a moment, considering his next words carefully.

"Abby, you know, Friday's the full moon and I was wondering...I mean, I know you're going to be strapped getting ready for your presentation, but how would you feel about a night cruise up the fjord? I mean, if the weather clears." Marc held his breath, waiting for her response.

Abby looked at him. "A cruise?"

"Yeah, take the *Percé* up the Saguenay a ways. It's really something to see the river under a full moon. We can even have supper on the boat. How about it?"

"I think that sounds great," Abby said. "I'd love to go." She pushed the empty plate away and sat back. "Marc, that was a terrific breakfast. And it should hold me over for the rest of the day!"

"Glad you weren't really hungry," he said mildly, arching his brow at the cleaned plate.

"Okay, so I have a good appetite, sue me." Laughing, Abby stood up to leave. "But if we want to go cruising Friday, I'd better get started on that presentation."

CHAPTER TWENTY

ABBY LISTENED TO THE RAIN pattering against her office window for the fourth day in a row and mentally congratulated Marc's weather forecasters for a correct prediction. All week long on her short walk to and from her office she had passed Gore-Tex-clad tourists hurrying in the rain, their feet splashing through the rivulets of water running down the streets. The *Percé* wasn't the only boat to remain at dock, Abby had noticed. The larger tour boats and the fleet of Zodiacs had kept close to their moorings.

Abby had spent the week seated at her lab table, headphones on, listening to the hours of whale vocalizations and background sounds she had recorded. For a change of scenery, she would retreat to her third-floor office to work on the outline of next year's study. It had come together even better than she'd expected. The funding committee was bound to see the study's potential, wasn't it?

Abby sighed and looked out the window, its panes streaked with rainwater. Oversight committees were funny animals, she knew from experience. So much depended on their own scientific backgrounds and bias. She hated having her future in the hands of a committee, but that was all part of the research game and she'd known it going in. Their approval meant at least three-and-a-half more years in Tadoussac. The thought of all that time to study the whales excited her tremendously.

But to be honest, that wasn't the only thing about remaining in Tadoussac that excited her.

Marc. Countless times that week, she'd felt her thoughts drift to him. Even now, as she was wrapping up this all-important presentation, his laugh, his smile, the sound of his voice kept pushing their way into her thoughts.

If I didn't know myself better, I'd think I was falling for him, Abby thought. But that was just plain silly, wasn't it? He was attractive, that was for sure. And despite their rocky start, they were getting along well. She found herself looking forward to seeing him, talking to him and listening to his thoughts on her work. But beyond that?

Sylvie and Françoise had been none-too-subtle in their efforts to bring the two of them together. Abby felt a strong affection for the little girl and older woman. Who wouldn't be enamored with Sylvie? And Françoise was one of the kindest souls she had ever met. Being a part of their lives had been a rare treat for Abby. She wouldn't want to jeopardize that by risking a relationship with Marc. No. It just couldn't happen.

The sound of a motor outside made her look up and she gasped in pleasure. A bright arc of sun was streaming through a hole in the clouds and, for the first time since Monday morning, no rain was falling. Acting on a whim, Abby picked the cradle of her desk phone up and punched in Marc's cell number. She did it quickly before she lost her nerve.

He answered after five rings.

"Hello?"

"Am I getting you away from something?" Abby asked.

"Abby." She desperately wanted to believe he was as happy to hear from her as he sounded. "What's up?"

"Where are you?" she asked.

"On the *Percé* belowdecks, why?"

"Look out the porthole and tell me if you see what I see," she instructed.

"Okay, hang on." A second later, he was back. "Looks like the storm broke. Right on schedule."

"It sure does," Abby said. "Were you serious about that moonlit cruise tomorrow night?"

"I was and still am," Marc said. "Are you going to have time?"

"Definitely." Abby flipped through the pages of the report in front of her. "All I need to do is collate the graphs and charts into the text, make a dozen or so copies and then bind them."

"I thought the center had minions for that kind of work," Marc said in a teasing tone.

"They do, but I've never been assigned one. However, I think I can figure out the complexities of the copy machine here."

"If you can't, I think there's an old hand-operated mimeograph machine in the attic over at the school you could probably use," Marc deadpanned.

"Gee, thanks. What time do we shove off tomorrow?"

"How does seven o'clock sound? We can take our time heading to Sainte-Marguerite and then have a nice, leisurely supper and watch the moon come up."

"Sounds heavenly," Abby said. "I'll see you then."

"I'll be waiting."

"A DATE IS IT?" Françoise said the next morning after Marc told her about the moonlit cruise. "And to think you did this all by yourself with no help from me or Sylvie."

"What did Dad do by himself?" Sylvie said, coming into the kitchen.

Marc shot his mother a look and turned to his daughter. "Nothing, *ma fille,* I'm just taking Abby for a boat ride tonight."

"Really? Can I go, too?" Sylvie slid onto her seat and poured herself a bowl of cereal.

"Uh, Sylvie, it's not really a kid's kind of trip," Marc began, not wanting his daughter to think she was being deliberately excluded.

"Oh, I get it. It's a date. About time." Sylvie started to pour milk into her bowl.

Marc was shocked. "What do you know about it? And that's enough milk."

Sylvie looked at him and rolled her eyes. "Geez, Dad, I'm not stupid. You get all mushy with Abby."

Marc's jaw dropped. "I do not!"

"It's okay," Sylvie consoled him. "Abby gets mushy, too. Only it's girl mush."

Marc looked at his mother, hoping for some assistance, and saw to his horror that Françoise was having a very difficult time holding back laughter.

"Thanks a lot," he muttered.

Françoise feigned innocence. "What did I do?"

"You have to take her flowers," Sylvie said through a mouthful of corn flakes.

"Don't talk with your mouth full," Marc chided gently. "And what do you mean about flowers?"

"C'mon, Dad, when you go on a date, you have to take flowers. Everybody knows that," Sylvie said.

"Who said anything about going on a date?" Marc said to the room at large. "Abby and I are going on a boat ride."

"And having supper under the full moon," Françoise added.

"Yep," Sylvie said. "A date. Better bring the flowers, Dad."

"And it wouldn't kill you to shave and put on something other than a T-shirt and cutoffs," Françoise said.

"Michele Raymond's big sister goes out on dates and the guy brings flowers *and* picks her up at her house."

"Enough with the flowers," Marc said. "And I'm not picking Abby up. She's meeting me down at the boat, and do you know why?"

Françoise and Sylvie shook their heads.

"Because this is *not* a date," Marc said through clenched teeth. "It's just two people having dinner together on a boat at night."

This time Françoise made no effort to hide her laughter. "Oh no, that's not a date."

"Don't worry, Dad," Sylvie said, getting up to take her empty bowl to the sink. "I'll pick some flowers for you."

MARC LOVED his mother and his daughter more than life itself. But there were times when they could drive him to distraction.

"A date," he said. "Since when does a man and a woman having dinner on a boat constitute a date?" Marc stopped coiling the rope he'd just untangled and sat down hard on one of the *Percé*'s hatch covers. "Since about always, you stupid sap," he answered himself.

He had spent the better part of the day cleaning up the boat and airing out the galley and cabins, which had begun to smell a bit musty after four days of solid rain. When he was certain everything looked shipshape, he'd started on dinner. Not wanting to be cooking that night, he'd prepared a variety of salads—shrimp, chicken, mixed greens and fruit. He planned to serve them with a generous cheese platter and selection of fresh bread supplied by his mother. To top off the meal he'd baked a batch of fudge brownies earlier that day and planned to reheat them in the microwave and serve them with vanilla ice cream topped with his own homemade chocolate sauce and bourbon-infused whipped cream.

He looked at his watch and saw he had just enough time to take his mother's advice of a shave and change of clothing before Abby arrived. That meant braving the scrutiny of

Françoise and Sylvie since all of his good clothes were stored up at his mother's house.

"Okay, okay," he said to the seagull perched on the far rail. "I give up. It's a date."

"I DON'T LIKE IT," Sylvie said, sitting on the edge of her grandmother's bed and watching her father adjust a necktie in the dresser mirror.

"Don't like what?" Marc said, fiddling with the collar on his button-down white shirt.

"That tie," Sylvie wrinkled her nose. "It makes you look *old*."

"Old?" Marc repeated, looking at his daughter and lifting an eyebrow.

"Yeah, old and *boring*." Sylvie jumped off the bed and came to stand next to him.

Marc regarded himself in the mirror. Suit pants, white shirt and jacket. Should he lose the tie?

"Well, we can't have that, can we?" Loosening the knot, he pulled the tie off.

"Better," Sylvie said, looking up at him.

Marc looked at the girl a moment and then crouched down to her eye level. "Sylvie," he said. "What do you think of Abby?"

"I think she's neat!" Sylvie said with obvious enthusiasm.

"You do?"

"Sure."

"So, you don't mind my going out with her?" Marc said casually.

Sylvie frowned. "Why would I mind?"

"It's been just you and me for several years now, *ma fille,* I want to make sure you're okay with it."

Sylvie's smile returned. "You bet I am. I don't like it when you're sad."

"What do you mean?" Marc asked.

Sylvie looked down. "When Mom died, you were sad. Me, too. I just want us to be *not* sad."

Marc felt a lump rise in his throat, followed by a rush of love for his daughter. He gathered her up in his arms. "Me, too, *ma fille,* me too," he whispered into her hair, wondering if Dr. Abby Miller was the answer for both of them.

MARC WALKED down the stairs and met his mother's appraising eye.

"Okay, you might as well weigh in, too," he said. "I've already passed the upstairs' inspection—barely. And thanks for pressing this shirt."

"You're welcome," Françoise said. "And I think you look fine. But don't you think you should wear a tie?"

Marc sighed, amazed as always how comments from his mother could instantly reduce him to a twelve-year-old. "Sorry, Mom. You've been over-ruled by a higher authority."

Françoise nodded. "Then I think you look perfect for your lady friend."

WHEN SEVEN O'CLOCK had come and gone, Marc began to get nervous. Over the course of the charter, Abby had been extremely punctual. Had something happened? Was she standing him up? He had just decided to wait another ten minutes before calling her, when he heard footsteps coming down the dock.

"Thank goodness," he said to himself and went to the rail to meet her.

"Abby? Is that you?"

"Of course it's me. Were you expecting someone else?"

"No, no, of course not," Marc stammered, trying his best not to stare at her. Abby was simply stunning in a soft green dress, her shoulders bare. "Lady, you look beautiful."

"You don't look so bad yourself, but I'm going to need some help getting up the ladder tonight. These shoes are definitely not made for walking!"

Laughing a bit self-consciously, she held her hands up for Marc to grab from above. "I never could climb well in heels," she said, once she was safely on deck.

"YOU LOOK BEAUTIFUL," Marc repeated, in a tone that let Abby know she was forgiven for being late. It had been worth the extra time she had taken with her hair, actually setting it so it fell in gentle layers to frame her face.

But her hair was not the only reason she'd been delayed leaving her apartment. Just as she was on her way out the door, her phone had rung. Thinking it was Marc with a last-minute change, she had been surprised to hear the voice of her mentor and research director, Felix Bolton.

"Abby, I've got great news for you," Felix had said without preamble. "We almost lost the funding committee thanks to a rash of scheduling changes, but we do have one day available to meet with you."

"That's good, Felix," Abby said, reaching for the desk calendar she kept by the phone. "I take it next Wednesday is out. What's the new date?"

"Tomorrow."

"Tomorrow? Felix, you're kidding, right?"

"No, it's then or probably never. Or at least not until next summer. And I don't need to tell you, it's far better to catch this group while they feel like they've still got loads of money to shower on you."

"Felix, I totally agree, but tomorrow?" Abby couldn't believe this was happening.

"Has to be," Felix said. "By some modern

miracle, we all managed to get on the same flight to Québec City; a terribly early flight, mind you. From there we've rented a van and will drive to Tadoussac."

"What time do you think you'll arrive?" Abby asked.

"We land in Québec at five, so I imagine we'll be in Tadoussac by eight-thirty. But let's play it safe and plan on hearing from you at nine."

"Nine it is," Abby said.

"You will be ready, won't you?"

"Of course, not a problem," Abby said, trying to inject as much confidence as possible into her voice.

"That's my girl," Felix said. "See you tomorrow and make sure you get a good night's rest."

Now Abby was wondering how to break the news to Marc.

"Well, I was supposed to meet my charter here," she said to him in a teasing voice. "A Marc Doucette, but you don't look anything like him."

"Ha!" Marc turned around for her to admire him. "The boy cleans up nicely, doesn't he? It's been awhile since I've had this suit on, but at least it still fits."

I'll say, Abby thought, doing her best not to stare at the Adonis-like figure Marc cut. She was also feeling guilty that the whole thing may have been for nothing.

"May I escort you below so we can get under-way?" Marc said.

"Marc, hold on a second, there's something I have to tell you." Quickly, she summarized the conversation with Felix and the tight timetable.

"I see." Marc sounded glum. "It's kind of hard to play the night before the big game. Okay, if you want to take a rain check, I understand. I mean, there will be other full moons, right?"

Now Abby felt even worse. Marc was being sweet and charming after all the effort he'd un-doubtedly gone to so she could have a special evening. She thought it over and came to a decision.

"Hang on a second. My report is done and it won't take long to make copies. I can go in early to do that. Can you have us back here at a decent hour?"

"You mean you still want to go?" Marc sounded doubtful.

"Yes, yes I do. Heck, if we don't, it's two hours of hair setting shot to hell."

Marc laughed and shook his head. "Then allow me," he said, offering her his arm.

"Thank you." Abby followed him through the hatch. "But Marc, we really do need to be back here early."

"I'll get you back in plenty of time, trust me," Marc said, ushering her into the galley.

Abby gasped in delight. Marc had placed a lovely white cloth over the table and heaped it with platters of raw vegetables, crackers and several kinds of dip. A chandelier of candles hung above the table, casting a flickering light, and soft music was piped in over the boat's sound system.

"Oh, these are for you." Marc handed Abby a bouquet of freshly picked summer wildflowers—compliments of Sylvie, she was sure. She put them to her nose and breathed deeply.

"Thank you," she said, touched by the gesture. "Can I put them in water?"

"Uh, sure, hang on." Marc opened a cupboard and rummaged around. "Here, I'm afraid it's the best I can do." He handed her a quart-sized mason jar.

Abby looked at it and then at Marc, and they broke into laughter.

"Now that's what I call class with a capital *K*," Abby said, going to the sink and filling the jar with water. She arranged the flowers and set them on the table.

"There you go," Marc said. "I'm sure I read somewhere there isn't a table anywhere that can't be dressed up by flowers in a canning jar."

"So true," Abby agreed.

CHAPTER TWENTY-ONE

MAGICAL. That was the only word Abby could think of to describe it. The *Percé* was anchored in a small, sheltered cove several miles upriver from Baie Sainte-Marguerite where the river took a slight bend. From their vantage point on the gently bobbing deck, they had an unobstructed view for miles up the fjord. The full moon had risen between the sheer cliffs on either side and was now casting a brilliant silver light and sparkling reflection on the river below.

Abby tightened her shawl against the slight chill in the air and picked up her glass of wine.

"Are you getting too cold out here?" Marc asked.

"I'm fine," Abby said. "I wouldn't want to waste a night like this inside."

They were sitting opposite each other on the small table Marc had set on the boat's forward deck, the remnants of their supper spread out on it.

"Did you get enough to eat?" Marc asked, reaching over and refilling Abby's wine glass.

"Plenty," Abby said. "As usual, it was fantastic."

"So, no regrets on playing hooky tonight?"

Abby smiled. "None at all."

"Are you nervous at all about tomorrow?"

"A little," Abby confessed. "I mean, it's only my future we're talking about, right?"

Marc laughed softly. "Well, from what I've seen over the last several weeks, I don't see how those guys can't give you more money."

Abby was surprised and flattered by the comment. "Thanks," she said. "Too bad you're not on the committee."

"No, I mean it." Marc filled his own glass from the pitcher of lemon water on the table. "I have been watching you and I have to say I've learned a few things."

"Oh?" Abby was curious. "Like what?"

Marc twirled his glass by the stem a moment before answering. "Okay," he said, leaning forward. "Now, I'm never going to be convinced we should shut down all boat activity around here. But I now see there have to be controls over how many and how we operate. I guess it's hard for those of us who've lived so long *on* the water to appreciate how we affect the critters *under* the water."

Abby was stunned by Marc's statement, a major endorsement of her work from a man she had initially considered an adversary. Maybe it was time for some honesty of her own?

"Marc, that means a lot to me," she said. "And I guess I've got a pretty good idea now of the importance of not overregulating people and places. It's all about balance, after all."

"I'll drink to that." Marc raised his glass to hers. "So, you want to give me a rundown of your presentation, like a dress rehearsal?"

Abby shook her head. "Don't take this the wrong way, but I'm pretty superstitious about things when it comes to my presentations. I've read it to myself about a dozen times, but the first time I do it out loud, it has to be in front of the committee." She laughed self-consciously. "Silly, huh?"

"Hey, you're talking to a man of the sea. I can bury you in superstition." He stood and walked to the rail behind her. "It really doesn't get much prettier than this, does it?"

Abby joined him, leaning her elbows on the rail and breathing in the night air. "It's the closest to paradise I've ever been," she said dreamily. "I think I could stay here forever."

"I don't know about forever," Marc moved closer to her, taking her left hand in his right, "but I bet we have enough food and supplies on board to hold out for a few days, anyway."

"You don't think somebody would send out a search party before then?" Abby asked in a teasing tone.

"Probably, but I know a few places to hide along the river," Marc said, taking her gently by the shoulders and turning her so they were facing each other.

Abby looked up at him and felt her breath quicken. A slight shiver ran through her that had nothing to do with the falling temperatures. Just as she was certain Marc was going to kiss her, a small popping sound came from somewhere inside the boat and every light went out, plunging them into darkness.

MARC HAD BEEN DETERMINED to take things slow and easy that night. At the same time, if he got the right signals from Abby, he was not about to let any opportunity slip by. Standing at the rail, gazing at the moon, she looked more desirable than any woman had a right to look. And when she didn't resist as he pulled her gently toward him, his heart soared in anticipation. Then things when south in a hurry.

"What th—" Marc straightened up and looked over his shoulder at the dark interior of the boat. "Did you hear that?"

"Hear what?" Abby looked a bit dazed.

"I'm not sure," Marc said. "Stay put, I don't want you tripping over anything in the dark. I'm going to check things out."

Leaving her at the rail, Marc found his way into the galley and snagged the flashlight he kept strapped to the wall. Clicking it on, he opened the hatch to the engine room and climbed down the stairs. His first stop was the electrical panel. Shining his light on the rows of breaker switches, he could detect nothing amiss. Next, he examined the main breaker and then gave it a quick flip on and off. A moment later, the lights came back on and he could again hear the music he'd had playing up in the galley.

"That was odd." He'd have to give the electrical system a thorough going-over the next day.

Back up on deck, Abby had left the railing and was clearing dishes from the table. Marc sighed. The brief power failure may have been a minor glitch, but it had sure killed the evening's mood.

"All fixed," he said, stepping outside and taking the pile of plates from Abby.

"That was quick." She followed him back inside.

"Yeah, these old boats can act kind of quirky sometimes."

"Marc, it's been a truly wonderful evening, but

I think we should start back, it's getting kind of late."

Marc nodded. "Yeah, I guess you're right. All good things have to come to an end, right?"

"Well, maybe only a temporary end," Abby said, kissing him lightly on the cheek. "I'm going to bring in the rest of the dinner dishes."

"Thanks." All the way to the wheelhouse, Marc knew he was grinning, but he couldn't help it.

Marc was so caught up in thinking ahead to his next date with Abby that it took a few moments to register that the *Percé* was not responding as it should. Frowning, he checked to make sure the key was in the "on" position and hit the ignition switch again. The engine sputtered but refused to catch.

Peering hard at the gauges, he confirmed there was plenty of fuel and the electrical was reading in the safe zone, despite the earlier mishap.

"Come on, baby, work with me," he whispered, hitting the switch again. The engine refused to turn over.

"No, no, no," Marc said. "This can't be happening."

Abby came up behind him. "What can't be happening? Why aren't we moving?"

"Abby, you're not going to believe this, but we seem to be having some sort of engine trouble."

"I don't understand," Abby said, frowning. "She was working just fine when we came up the river a few hours ago."

"I know. I'm sure it's nothing. Just give me a few minutes to check it out, I'll be right back."

Marc hurried back to the engine room and did a quick systems check. In the end, he could find no reason for the boat's refusal to crank over. He knew Abby was nervous about getting back in time to be rested for the big presentation, so he decided to make that his top priority.

"Any luck?" she asked when he came back into the wheelhouse.

Marc shook his head. "This may take some time to diagnose and fix. But don't worry, I'm going to call a taxi for you."

Abby looked surprised. "A taxi? Out here?"

"There's bound to be somebody up at the marina. I'll get them to send a boat up for you. You'll be home in a jiffy, don't worry." Marc reached for the radio mic and thumbed the receiver on.

"*Percé* calling Tadoussac Marina, come in, please," he said into the mouthpiece.

There was no response. Taking the radio away from his mouth, he reached up to adjust the frequency and felt his stomach drop.

"Oh crap," he said.

"Now what?" Abby sounded slightly alarmed.

"Abby, you're not going to believe this," Marc began.

"Believe *what?*" she said.

"We may want to go out and buy lottery tickets. Somehow we've lost both running power *and* the radio in one night."

ABBY STARED AT HIM a moment. "Marc Doucette, if this is some kind of bad joke you're playing on me the night before my presentation, you can stop it right now. It's not funny."

"No joke," Marc said. "We are, as they say, dead in the water."

"How can that be?" Abby was aware her voice was rising. "How can you just stand there and tell me the boat won't run and the radio's not working. That just doesn't happen!"

Marc shrugged. "Like I said, we should buy lotto tickets. The odds of this kind of massive malfunction are astronomical. Maybe it had something to do with the electrical…"

"I don't really care what it had to do with," Abby said with impatience. "What I want to know is how are we going to get back to town?"

Marc blew out a breath and shrugged. "It's going to mean a long night of troubleshooting down below. To be honest, the *Percé*'s been running so well all summer, I'm not even sure where to start."

"Fine," Abby said. "I guess it's up to me to get us home."

"Come again?" Marc said.

"I've got my cell phone in my purse. What's the number of the marina?" she said, retrieving her purse from the table on which she had set it several hours earlier and pulling the small phone out.

Marc shook his head. "Don't bother," he said.

"What's the number?" Abby repeated in a measured tone.

"Have it your way," Marc said, "but I'm telling you, it won't do any good." As he rattled off the digits, Abby punched the keys on her cell phone.

"Hmm," she said, squinting at the screen.

"Problems?" Marc said in a tone Abby found mocking.

"No reception," she muttered. "I'm going outside."

Once outside, she hit Redial, but her luck was no better. The only response from the phone was the Out of Reception Area message flashing on the screen. After ten minutes of walking up and down the deck and holding the phone at different angles, she conceded defeat. Snapping the device closed in disgust, she walked back into the cabin and was annoyed to see Marc had made no move to work on the engine problems.

"You're still here?" she said.

"Just waiting to see if the rescue party was on the way," Marc said.

"Very funny," Abby said. "Look, Marc, I don't want to be a pain about this, but when do you think we might be underway?"

Marc shrugged. "Could be an hour, could be six. You never know with old boats like this…"

Abby was shaking her head. She had an uncomfortable feeling Marc did not appreciate the seriousness of the situation. "Not good enough," she said. "Marc, this is bad, really bad. I've got that committee coming tomorrow and I have to be back in time."

"I understand," Marc said. "But you know, some people might go so far as to say this is kind of romantic."

Didn't he get it? "You're not serious," Abby said.

"Sure, you, me, the full moon."

"Marc, I can't be distracted by you and full moons right now!" Abby said, a bit more harshly than she had intended. "All I care about is getting back to Tadoussac as soon as possible so I can get ready for tomorrow. I can't think of anything else until then. Certainly not *romance*." She instantly regretted her words when she saw the hurt look flash through Marc's eyes.

"Right," Marc said, walking toward the hatchway leading to the engine room. "If you'll excuse me, I have a boat to fix." He hesitated a moment, looking at her. "Maybe I'm not the right guy, but y'know something?"

"What?" Abby said.

"You really should start giving some thought about finding happiness outside a laboratory. Before it's too late."

Then he brushed past her and was gone.

CHAPTER TWENTY-TWO

MARC SAT BACK against the engine room's inner hull, threw the wrench across the floor and swore mightily. His dress shirt was streaked with oil and grease, his good pants were torn in several places, sweat was pouring down his face and his knuckles all were either scraped or bleeding freely.

He'd been at it five hours straight. He'd taken apart and checked every piece on both of the boat's diesel engines and could find nothing wrong. Nothing! The fuel lines were clear and he'd replaced the filters only two weeks ago.

It sure looked like the *Percé* was trying to scuttle whatever chances he might have had with Abby. *Okay,* he thought, flexing his fingers, *I guess I shouldn't have been so unsympathetic earlier.* But did she honestly think he didn't care she might miss her big meeting? The truth was, he felt horrible about the whole thing, and making light of it was the only way he knew to deal with it.

Marc had no idea where Abby had been while he was below deck. He'd hadn't heard any splashes, so he figured she hadn't jumped overboard to swim back. *All I care about is getting back to Tadoussac,* she had said. And it sounded like she meant it. Fine, as far as he was concerned, as soon as the boat was running and they'd gotten back, his job was finished. The day before he'd run into the mechanic at the local boatyard who'd told him the marine center's boat was due out of dry dock within the week. Marc was tired of hitting his head against the wall when it came to Abby. Every time he thought he had made headway with her, something had come along to ruin it. He was forced to acknowledge, when it came to him or her research, he'd always take a backseat. He sighed and slowly stood. Too bad. He'd really thought they'd had a shot at something good together.

Tools were spread out on the narrow floor and he kicked a hammer on his way out of the engine room. *Might as well go try the radio again,* he thought.

Abby, it turned out, was almost right where he had left her. Sitting in the captain's chair in the wheelhouse, arms folded across her chest, feet tapping impatiently on the floor.

"Have you been sitting here the whole time?" Marc asked when he walked in.

"Oh no," she said sarcastically. "I've been out building a raft so I could float back down to Tadoussac. Yes, I've been here the whole time."

"Sorry I asked." Marc brushed past her to the radio. The past several hours of waiting had obviously not done much to improve her mood. He flicked the switch, twirled the knobs and listened. Nothing. There was definitely juice getting to it since the dials were backlit, but nothing was going out or coming in over the wires. Sticking his head out the hatch, he could make out the antennae far above. Still in place.

"Might as well check it out," he muttered.

Clambering up the narrow ladder to the top of the mast, he closely inspected the antennae in the watery light of dawn. All looked well and the wires leading down to the radio were tight and free of breaks or knicks.

Climbing back down the mast, Marc reentered the wheelhouse and considered his options. Eventually, a boat would come by, so all they had to do was sit tight and wait and then hitch a ride back home. That, however, did not solve the more immediate problem of getting Abby back in time for her presentation. He looked at his watch. It was just approaching 6:00 a.m. Even if they were able to get underway that moment, they'd be cutting it awfully close.

"I'm going to make some coffee," he said.

"Coffee?" Abby was incredulous. "How can you even be thinking of that when we're just, just *floating* here?"

"Because I'm tired, hungry and fresh out of ideas," Marc said. "I'm hoping the coffee will help me think."

He stalked out of the wheelhouse and cursed as a large drop of water fell from the overhang and landed on the back of his neck. He stopped.

Water drops. Rain. All this week it had rained nonstop. It couldn't be as simple as that, could it?

Changing direction, Marc ran back down to the engine room. He went straight to the fuel-water separator near the motor. How could he have missed it? Turning the spigot, he filled the plastic cup he kept on hand for just that purpose. Amber liquid splashed into the jar. He let it get three-quarters full before turning the tap off. When he held the cup up to the light, his suspicions were confirmed. Water in the fuel.

Marc smiled in weary relief to have the problem solved at last. Water in the fuel line was a boatman's nemesis, but simple to fix.

Taking two new filters from a box, he quickly spun off the old ones and installed the new ones. Normally, the filters were good for much longer than two weeks, so he'd had no reason to immediately suspect them as the problem. The heavy rainfall must have allowed water into the engines and the gas lines. No boat on the planet would start with water in the fuel.

Back in the wheelhouse, he twisted the key, flipped the ignition switch and sent up a silent prayer.

The *Percé's* twin engines ground several seconds, missed, coughed and caught with a solid roar.

"It's about time," Abby said flatly.

"We can make it," Marc said. "It's going to be close, but I'll push her for all she's worth."

"You do that."

Marc decided to ignore her, concentrating instead on getting them both back to Tadoussac in one piece.

Now, THE *PERCÉ* fairly leapt from the water as Marc ran her at full throttle. Abby looked at her watch. It was going to be close. Even assuming they did make it back to the docks by nine, her report was on her desk where she'd left it the day before. One thing at a time, she told herself. Get to the marine center and then figure out a way to quickly make the needed copies.

When the boat rounded the last bend in the fjord and the ferry terminal came into sight, Abby returned to the wheelhouse to collect her shawl.

She and Marc had not spoken a word to each other during the dash down the Saguenay. Now, as he guided the boat around the last point into the bay and up to the docks, she went and stood at the railing, ready to climb off the moment the boat stopped.

To her surprise, Abby spotted Peter waiting at the dock.

"Everyone is here and waiting for you," the director said, helping her down the ladder. Behind her, she heard the *Percé*'s engines idle a moment before cutting out entirely. Without a backward glance to the boat or to Marc, Abby allowed Peter to take her arm and propel her toward the inter-pretive center.

"How long have they been waiting?" Abby asked anxiously as they hurried along.

"About half an hour," Peter said. "Don't worry," he added when Abby groaned out loud, "I've been keeping them entertained. But I could tell they were getting restless. That's why I was so glad when Doucette radioed you were fifteen minutes away. Where the heck have you been anyway?"

"Out," Abby said curtly. "You said Marc radioed in?"

"Yeah, about twenty minutes ago. Told me where your report was and what needed to be done to get it ready. Now, I'm not one to criticize, but you really should have taken care of doing all that yourself."

Abby halted, putting a hand on Peter's arm to stop him, too.

"What did Marc do?" she asked.

"Hey, no time to dawdle, keep moving." They turned down the driveway leading to the building. "He said you needed a dozen copies of your report and the group of charts and photos had to be inserted inside. You weren't here, so we collated as best we could on our own."

"I'm sure it will be fine," Abby said distractedly.

"Okay, showtime," Peter said, pushing open the center's doors and ushering her inside. "And I must say, you certainly dressed to kill."

Abby had forgotten she was still wearing her outfit from the night before. Of course, there had been no possibility of going home to change into something more suitable.

The heck with it, she thought, walking toward the conference-room doors and the committee waiting within. They were here to pronounce judgment on her work, not her choice of dress.

"Dr. Bolton." She nodded at her mentor, who was seated at the large conference table, flanked by several distinguished-looking people she recognized from Woods Hole. Each had a bound copy of her report in front of them. "Ladies and gentlemen, thank you so much for coming. If you'll pick up the headphones in front of you, we can all listen to what the beluga have been telling me."

MARC HADN'T EXPECTED Abby to thank him for getting her back to the dock with only minutes to spare, but he had thought she'd at least have the courtesy to say good-bye. But by the time he'd cut the engines and gone on deck, he could see her hurrying up the wharf with Peter Bouchard.

Shaking his head with real regret at what might have been, he went back inside to change out of his ruined dress clothes and clean up the mess he'd left in the engine room.

Once he had replaced the faulty filters, it had been an easy guess as to what was wrong with the radio. The same water that had worked its way into the fuel lines had likewise infiltrated the wires running from the antennae to the radio. Like the filters, it was a quick fix, but maddening until he'd figured it out. None of it was his fault, but he still felt responsible. That's why, once the radio was up and running again, he'd hailed the marine center and spoken to Peter Bouchard directly. Without going into details, Marc had told him Abby was unavoidably delayed and needed his help.

Now he could only hope that Peter had come through for Abby and that the committee had hung around long enough for it to do some good.

MARC HAD JUST CLIMBED DOWN the ladder from the boat and was wondering if he had the energy to head over to his mother's when he spotted a lone figure ambling down the dock toward him. A minute later he recognized the marine center's director.

Great, Marc thought, *this looks like the perfect end to a perfect morning.*

He stepped into the middle of the dock and watched Peter as he strode up. "Hello, Pete," he said evenly.

"Marc," Peter said. "How are you?"

"Fine. Can I help you with something?"

Either Peter was not picking up on Marc's hostility or he was choosing to ignore it. "I just came from Abby's presentation," he said.

"Did you, now?"

"Yeah, I have to say, she made a hell of an impression on that group from Woods Hole. On me, too, for that matter."

"That's great," Marc said. "But I can't imagine you walked over here just to tell me that."

Peter shook his head and looked out across the bay. "No, no I didn't. I wanted to tell you what else impressed me today."

"Yeah?" Marc couldn't imagine what the director was leading up to.

"Yes," Peter said. "You impressed me."

"Me?" Marc was stunned. "I don't understand."

"First of all, your alert to us to get Abby's documentation ready saved the day. Then, on top of that, to hear her tell it, her studies wouldn't have gone half as well if not for your help. I have to say, I had no idea you were such a supporter of our work here."

Marc was speechless.

"Ah hell, I had no idea about a lot of things," Peter said. "Listen, you and I go back a long ways. What happened with those college students, well, it shouldn't have gone down the way it did. I was wrong. Wrong about you and about them."

If the director had suddenly sprouted a pair of wings and begun flying around the bay, Marc couldn't have been more surprised.

"I owe you an apology. I just hope it's not too late." Peter hesitated a moment, then stuck out his hand.

Marc looked at the offered hand and then directly into Peter's eyes. There was no doubt the man was sincere. Marc knew they would never be best friends or even buddies meeting over a tall pint, but he also knew he no longer had an enemy.

Marc grasped Peter's hand firmly. "It's not too late; not too late at all."

"Good," Peter said, with a smile. "Now, if you'll excuse me, I have some VIPs from the States to squire around."

"Good luck." Peter had barely taken a half-dozen steps before Marc called out, "Hey, Pete, hang on a minute."

"Yes?" Peter stopped and turned around.

"That committee, the ones from Woods Hole, did they tell Abby anything about her funding?"

Pete nodded. "You bet they did. They offered her another three years, right there on the spot. Funny thing though, she didn't look as happy about it as I'd have thought she would."

CHAPTER TWENTY-THREE

MARC WAS STILL CONTEMPLATING Peter's apology and the news about Abby's project when he spotted Sylvie running down the dock, his mother walking quickly behind.

"Hello, *ma fille,*" Marc scooped his daughter into a hug. "Hi, Mom," he said as Françoise reached them. "What brings my two favorite women down here?"

"Dad, let me go!" Sylvie said, wriggling out of Marc's embrace. Standing on the dock, she planted her hands on her hips and glared up at him. "You have to stop her! Go now! Don't let her go away and take Figgy!"

"Who's going where?" Marc said with a sinking feeling in the pit of his stomach.

"You have to hurry." Sylvie grabbed his hand and started to tug on it. "C'mon!"

"Sylvie," Françoise said. "Hush and calm down. Let me talk to your father, please."

Sylvie did as she was told, but impatiently hopped from one foot to another.

"What's this all about?" Marc said.

"I'll tell you in a moment, but first I want you to look at this." Françoise handed him a folded piece of paper. "I didn't have a chance to check the mail yesterday."

"What is it?" Marc asked, taking it from her and unfolding it.

"Just read it," Françoise said.

Marc gave her one last glance and then looked down at the paper. It was Sylvie's report card. Raising an eyebrow, he again looked at his mother.

"Read," she repeated.

At first, Marc's brain was unable to accept what he was seeing in black and white. "Is this for real?"

"As real as it gets," Françoise said with a huge grin.

For what felt like the first time in months, a massive weight lifted from Marc's shoulders. He reached out and pulled his daughter to him. "Sylvie, I'm so proud of you," he said with real feeling.

"Yeah, yeah, fine," Sylvie's voice was muffled against his chest. "But what about Abby and Figgy?"

"What about Abby and Figgy?" Marc said.

"I don't want them to go!" Sylvie cried. "Do something!"

"Sylvie," Françoise said. "Could you give your father and me a few moments alone?"

"Go up into the galley, *ma fille,*" Marc said. "Grab a can of soda from the fridge."

"Really? Can I?" Sodas were a rare treat in the Doucette household.

Marc nodded and Sylvie instantly scampered up the ladder and over the rail.

"Now, what's going on?" he asked when he was certain his daughter was out of earshot.

"You know perfectly well who's to credit for that report card," Françoise said.

"Yeah, yeah I do."

"And?"

"And, what?"

"Saints preserve me, I've raised a fool for a son!" Françoise sounded exasperated.

"Come again?"

"Marc, I loved Thérèse as much as you did, you know that. I saw what the loss of her did to you and to Sylvie. It broke all of our hearts. But you survived, and that little girl is a testament to how well you love and are loved."

"What are you getting at, Mom?"

"This. For three years I've watched the two of you go it alone. Oh, I know you have me around," she said when Marc tried to interrupt her, "but we both know that's not the same thing as a soul mate."

"No, I guess it's not."

"Then this summer, Abby Miller and that silly dog came along and suddenly I saw a new spark of life in my son and my granddaughter. Don't try to tell me you didn't feel it, too."

"Of course I felt it," Marc said more roughly than he intended. "But some things just aren't meant to be."

"Hogwash! If two people were more meant to be together, to be a family, then I'd like to see them!"

Marc sighed. "Mom, I just don't think Abby feels the same way about it."

"Of course she does!" Françoise said. "But you're going to have to move right quick if you want to do something about it."

"Why?"

"That's what Sylvie was talking about. Right after Abby got back this morning, she came to tell me she wanted out of her lease and that she was going to look for an apartment in Baie-Sainte Catherine."

"What?" Marc said, alarmed.

"Yes. So now I want to know, my boy, what are you going to do about it?"

What, indeed, Marc thought. Emotions were

swirling around in him, but one kept trying to rise to the surface: love. He was in love with Abby Miller.

"I love her," he said softly, unaware he had spoken aloud.

"Well, bang the drums and sound the trumpets," Françoise said. "It's about time you admitted it!"

"I need to tell her. And thank her for what she's done for Sylvie. I'll do it tonight…" Françoise shook her head.

"You'll do it now, right this minute. When we left the house, Abby was packing her car."

"Okay, keep an eye on Sylvie, will you?" Marc turned to run back to his mother's house.

"No, not that way, you'll never catch her," Françoise said. "Look!"

Marc turned to see Abby's car heading toward the ferry. He swore under his breath.

"Now what?" he said.

"You'd best hurry," his mother urged him.

"What's the use? I'll never catch her before she boards."

"Then catch her *on*board," Françoise said.

"What?"

Françoise sighed. "You have a boat? Go after her!"

Marc's mind was racing as he considered his mother's suggestion.

"Just get a move on!" Françoise said.

There was no time to waste. "Grab the stern line when I cast off," Marc ordered his mother. "And wish me luck!"

He climbed the ladder and swung onto the deck. Taking the line, he tossed it down to Françoise, who gave him a thumbs-up when she caught it. Marc ran to the wheelhouse and turned the engines over. With complete disregard for harbor protocol, he backed away from the dock and, as soon as he saw the waters in front were clear of any craft, he pushed the throttle to the stops. The *Percé* jumped in response.

I can just make it, he was thinking as the boat rounded the point and he caught sight of the ferry pushing away from the Tadoussac dock.

"Where are we going?" a voice behind him said.

Sylvie! He had completely forgotten she was aboard. His hands hard on the wheel, he turned and looked at his daughter. What the heck, she was part of this, too.

"We're going after Abby and Figgy," he called above the roar of the engines and Sylvie's subsequent cheer. "Hang on!"

ABBY HAD NEVER believed in playing the shoulda-coulda-woulda game. But standing on the deck of the ferry that was about to take her away from Tadoussac, she found herself surrounded by images of what could have been, if only…

If only she had given Marc more of a chance.

If only she'd been more honest with herself and with him about her true feelings.

Not that any of it mattered now. In the wake of their most recent altercation, the news of her continued funding was bittersweet, at best. The moment Felix had told her, Abby had wanted to run to the *Percé* and share the news with Marc. But an instant later she knew it would have been impossible. How on earth could she have expected him to care about her work after the callous way she had treated him. And after he had come through in the end, calling Peter and salvaging her presentation.

How could she even think of remaining in Tadoussac? No, it would be far better for her to make new living arrangements in another town. Peter had said the marine center's boat would be ready for use in a few weeks and she planned on moving her project to it. After ruining any chance she had with Marc, she didn't see how she could work with him or live in a place where she'd see him everyday.

She felt the ferry's engines throttle up and the craft slowly began to ease from the dock, battling the strong Saguenay currents as it moved into the river. From her vantage point, she watched the village she had grown to love over the course of the previous weeks grow smaller and smaller. She'd still be working in Tadoussac, of course, but Abby knew it would not be the same. Not without Marc. A tear escaped her eye. She dropped her hand and scratched Figgy behind the ears.

The strong breeze coming off the river blew hair into Abby's eyes. Turning her collar up against the slight chill, she debated taking Figgy and going back to her car to get out of the wind. Unlike the larger St. Lawrence ferries, the Saguanay River craft was a open-air vessel that allowed passengers to stay in their vehicles or walk the decks with their pets.

Abby was fighting a losing battle trying to keep her hair in its ponytail when a movement around the far point had caught the dog's attention.

As she looked out across the water, Abby was dimly aware of an elderly couple that had come and stood at the railing several feet away, and she could hear them chatting about the area's natural beauty. Abruptly, their tone changed.

"Will you look at that!" the woman exclaimed. "I think that boat is trying to catch us. You don't suppose they're pirates, do you?"

Her husband laughed. "I doubt it. But if you want them to be pirates, pirates they are!"

It was the kind of banter that came from a long relationship, Abby knew. But when she looked at the boat racing toward them, mild interest changed to shock. It was no pirate boat. It was the *Percé*.

Moving along the rails to gain a better vantage point, Figgy at her heels, Abby leaned over to see Marc at the wheel. "What's he doing?" she wondered.

Abby felt the ferry give a slight lurch as the engines slowed, allowing the vessel to hold its place against the current. Two long blows from the horn rang out and were immediately answered by two blasts from the *Percé*.

By now a small crowd had joined Abby at the rail, all curious about the arrival of the smaller boat. After a moment, a uniformed Quèbec Maritime deck worker elbowed his way through the group to Abby.

"Dr. Miller?" he asked.

"That's me," Abby said.

"I'm Tony. We seem to have a situation here and need your help."

"Me? What sort of situation?"

"The captain of that boat out there is refusing to let us pass until you join him onboard," Tony said with a grin.

A happy tingle began in Abby's toes and in no time had raced up her spine and throughout her whole body.

"He wants me with him?"

Tony nodded. "Yep, but you'd better move it. We all like Marc a lot, but not even the skip can keep this ferry on hold for much longer."

"I understand, but how?"

"Just watch this," Tony said. He spoke a few words into the radio clipped to his shirt, and immediately the *Percé* closed the remaining gap between the two vessels and eased alongside.

"This is insane!" Abby said. "I can't just jump overboard! What about Figgy? What about my car?"

"We can lower your dog," Tony said. "And transferring you is no problem. But make up your mind quick, okay?"

"My dear, we'll take care of your car and leave it in the parking lot on the other side."

Abby turned to her left and saw the elderly woman standing inches away.

"You'd do that?" Abby said.

She and her husband nodded. "But only if you go to meet whoever is on that boat," the woman said. "You don't want to cheat an old lady out of a happy ending, now, do you?"

Abby laughed in pure delight. "No, no I don't, and thank you!" She gave the woman her car keys and pointed out her car, followed by a quick hug.

"I'm ready," she said to Tony. "How do we do this?"

"Follow me."

Together Abby and the man walked to the midpoint of the railing, where she could see the ferry was actually touching the *Percé*. Working fast and with an economy of movement, Tony unfastened a rescue sling from the side of the boat and swung it free. One end was attached to a winch controlled by a lever.

"Okay, four-legged passengers first," he said, lifting Figgy into the sling.

"It's okay, girl," Abby said. "Just stay."

She could tell by the look in Figgy's eyes that this new game was anything but okay. Still, the little dog didn't move a hair as the sling was gently swung away from the ferry's hull and down to the *Percé*'s decks, where an overjoyed Sylvie helped her out.

"You're next," Tony said, as soon as the sling was winched back. "Ready?"

"More than you can ever know," Abby said, kissing him on the cheek.

"Hang on," he told her. To the cheers of the ferry passengers—none of whom seemed angered in the least by the temporary halting of their crossing—Tony helped Abby fit herself into the sling and she was soon suspended directly over the *Percé*'s deck and slowly lowered into Marc's waiting arms.

He quickly pulled her from the sling and signaled for it to be hauled back to the ferry. With a loud horn blast, the ferry set off once again for the opposite shore.

"How did you get here?" Abby asked, still in Marc's arms.

"I'm not sure I even know," Marc said, looking into her eyes. "But I do know I came very close to losing something that was right in front of me." He regarded her a long, silent moment. "We're a lot different, Abby. I know that, now. But maybe that's a good thing when it comes to being in love."

"What? What did you just say?" Abby could scarcely believe what he was saying.

"In love. That's right. Abby Miller, I'm head-over-heels crazy in love with you!" Marc sealed his declaration with a kiss so reflective of that love, it took Abby's breath away.

"Me, too! Me, too!" Sylvie cried, hopping around them and laughing.

"Yes, you, too," Abby said, pulling the little girl into the embrace. "Both of you, all three of us, for that matter."

Marc pulled back a fraction and handed Abby a piece of paper.

"What's this?" she asked.

"Take a look," he said, a huge grin on his face.

Abby scanned the document. She felt her eyes burn with happy tears.

"Oh Sylvie, all *B*'s and one *C!* Good for you!"

Tilting her head up and looking deeply in Marc's eyes, she said, "I do love you, Marc Doucette. You and Sylvie."

Marc's grin widened. "I understand you dropped your lease with my mom."

"Do you think she'll let me back in?" Abby said, returning his smile.

"I imagine she can be talked into it, but…"

"But what?"

"Well, that place is going to get pretty small before three years are out," Marc said.

"And I suppose you have a better idea?" Abby asked.

"Well, I do know of this great spot up on the hill with a terrific view that's going to be available at the end of the summer. Reasonable rates, too."

"Really," Abby said, teasingly. "I don't know. I mean, I'd kind of just rattle around in a big house like that all by myself."

"I don't think that's going to be a problem," Marc said. "The place comes fully stocked with two people, and I know for a fact that one of them loves dogs."

Abby felt tears of pure joy. Burying her face in Marc's chest, she reveled in the wonderful sensation of his strong arms holding her there and the simple delight of Sylvie's small arms around their waists. While Figgy barked happily nearby, Abby finally and fully opened her mind and her heart to the infinite possibilities of life and love with the Doucette family.

Tightening her own grip on Marc, she allowed her right hand to drop away to stroke Sylvie's hair. The kindly woman on the ferry had been wrong about one thing. This was not a happy ending. Rather, a wondrous new beginning.

* * * * *

Turn the page for a special preview of the final two titles in the Raintree trilogy, Raintree: Haunted *by national bestselling author Linda Winstead Jones and* Raintree: Sanctuary *by New York Times bestselling author Beverly Barton.*

Look for Raintree: Haunted
in April 2008
and
Raintree: Sanctuary
in May 2008
only from Mills & Boon® Intrigue.

Raintree: Haunted

by

Linda Winstead Jones

Monday Morning, 3:37 a.m.

When Gideon's phone rang in the middle of the night, it meant someone was dead. "Raintree," he answered, his voice rumbling with the edges of sleep.

"Sorry to wake you."

Surprised to hear his brother Dante's voice, Gideon came instantly awake. "What's wrong?"

"There's a fire at the casino. Could be worse," Dante added before Gideon could ask, "but it's bad enough. I didn't want you to see it on the morning news without some warning. Call Mercy in a couple of hours and tell her I'm all right. I'd call her myself, but I'm going to have my hands full for the next few days."

Gideon sat up, wide awake. "If you need me, I'm there."

"No, thanks. You've got no business getting on an airplane this week, and everything here is fine. I just wanted to call you before I got so tied up in red tape I couldn't get to a phone."

Gideon ran his fingers through his hair. Outside his window, the waves of the Atlantic crashed and rolled. He offered again to go to Reno and help. He could drive, if necessary. But once again Dante told him everything was fine, and they ended the call. Gideon reset his alarm for five-thirty. He would call Mercy before she started her day. The fire must have been a bad one for Dante to be so certain it would make the national news.

Alarm reset, Gideon fell back onto the bed. Maybe he'd sleep, maybe not. He listened to the ocean waves and let his mind wander. With the solstice coming in less than a week, his normal electric abnormalities were really out of whack. The surges usually spiraled out of control only when a ghost was nearby, but for the past few days—and for the week to come—it didn't take the addition of an electrically charged spirit to make appliances and electronics—or planes—in his path go haywire. There was nothing he could do but be cautious. Maybe he should take a few days off, stay away from the station altogether and lie low. He closed his eyes and fell back asleep.

She appeared without warning, floating over the end of the bed and smiling down at him, as she always did. Tonight she wore a plain white dress that touched her bare ankles, and her long dark hair was unbound. Emma, as she said she would one day be called, always came to him in the form of a child. She was very much unlike the ghosts who haunted him. This child came only in dreams and was untainted by the pain of life's hardships. She carried with her no need for justice, no heartbreak, no gnawing deed left undone. Instead, she brought with her light and love, and a sense of peace. And she insisted on calling him Daddy.

"Good morning, Daddy."

Gideon sighed and sat up. He'd first seen this particular spirit three months ago, but lately her visits had become more and more frequent. More and more real. Who knew. Maybe he had been her father in another life, but he wasn't going to be anyone's daddy in this one.

"Good morning, Emma."

The spirit of the little girl drifted down to stand on the foot of the bed. "I'm so excited." She laughed, and the sound was oddly familiar. Gideon liked that laugh. It made his heart do strange things. He convinced himself that the sense of warm familiarity meant nothing. Nothing at all.

"Why are you excited?"

"I'm coming to you soon, Daddy."

He closed his eyes and sighed. "Emma, honey, I've told you a hundred times, I'm not going to have kids in this lifetime, so you can stop calling me Daddy."

She just laughed again. "Don't be silly, Daddy. You always have me."

The spirit who had told him that her name would be Emma in this lifetime did have the Raintree eyes, his own dark brown hair and a touch of honey in her skin. But he knew better than to trust what he saw. After all, she only showed up in dreams. He was going to have to stop eating nachos before going to bed.

"I hate to tell you this, sweetheart, but in order to make a baby there has to be a mommy as well as a daddy. I'm not getting married and I'm not having kids, so you'll just have to choose someone else to be your daddy this time around."

Emma was not at all perturbed. "You're always so stubborn. I am coming to you, Daddy, I am. I'm coming to you in a moonbeam."

Gideon had tried romantic relationships before, and they never worked. He had to hide so much of himself from the women in his life; it would never do to have someone that close. And a family? Forget it. He already had to answer to the new chief, the rest of his family and a never-ending stream of ghosts. He wasn't about to put himself in a position where he would be obligated to answer to anyone else. Women came and went, but he made sure none ever got too close or stayed too long.

It was Dante's job to reproduce, not his. Gideon glanced toward the dresser, where the latest fertility charm sat ready to be packaged up and mailed. Once Dante had kids of his own, Gideon would no longer be next in line for the position of Dranir, head of the Raintree family. He couldn't think of anything worse than being Dranir, except maybe getting married and having kids of his own.

Big brother had his hands full at the moment, though, so maybe he would hold off a few days before mailing that charm. Maybe.

"Be careful," Emma said as she floated a bit closer. "She's very bad, Daddy. Very bad. You have to be careful."

"Don't call me Daddy," Gideon said. As an afterthought he added, "Who's very bad?"

"You'll know soon. Take care of my moonbeam, Daddy."

"On a moonbeam," he said softly. "What a load of…"

"It's just begun," Emma said, her voice and her body fading away.

* * * * *

*Turn the page
for your first look at*
RAINTREE: SANCTUARY
by New York Times *bestselling author*
Beverly Barton

Raintree: Sanctuary

by

Beverly Barton

Mercy Raintree sat on the firm, grassy ground, her eyes closed, her hands resting in her lap. Whenever she was troubled, she came to Amadahy Pointe to meditate, to collect her thoughts and renew her strength. The sunshine covered her like an invisible robe, wrapping her in light and warmth. The spring breeze caressed her tenderly, like a lover's soft touch. With her eyes closed and her soul open to the positive energy she drew from this holy place, this sanctuary within a sanctuary, she focused on what was most important to her.

Family.

Mercy sensed impending danger. But from

whom or from what, she did not know. Although her greatest talents lay in being an empath and a healer, she possessed latent precognitive powers, less erratic than her cousin Echo's, but not as strong. She had also been cursed with the ability to sense the emotional and physical condition of others from a distance. *Clairempathy*. As a child, she'd found her various empathic talents maddening, but gradually, year by year, she had learned to control them. And now, despite both Dante and Gideon blocking her from intercepting their thoughts and emotions, she could still manage to pick up something on the outer fringes of each brother's individual consciousness.

Dante and Gideon were in trouble. But she did not know why. Perhaps it was nothing more than stress from their chosen professions. Or it could even be problems in their personal lives.

If her brothers thought she could help them, they would ask her to intervene. That knowledge reassured her that their problems were within the realm of human reality and not of a supernatural nature. Her brothers were, as they had pointed out to her on numerous occasions, grown men, perfectly capable of taking care of themselves without the assistance of their baby sister.

Past experience had taught her that when their souls needed replenishing, their spirits nurtured, her brothers came home, here to the Raintree land, deep in the North Carolina mountains. The homeplace was protected by a powerful magic that had been established by their ancestors two centuries ago after The Battle. Within the boundaries of these secure acres, no living creature could intrude without alerting the resident guardian. Mercy Raintree was that guardian, protector of the homeplace, as her great-aunt Gillian had been until her death at a hundred and nineteen, and like Gillian's mother, Vesta, the first keeper of the Sanctuary in the early eighteen hundreds.

Taking a deep, cleansing breath, Mercy opened her eyes and looked at the valley below, spread out before her like a banquet feast. Late springtime in the mountains. An endless blue sky that went on forever. Towering green trees, the ancient, the old and the young growing together, reaching heavenward. Verdant life, thick and rich and sweet to the senses. A multitude of wildflowers blooming in abundance, their perfume tantalizing, their colors pleasing to the eye.

Mercy wasn't sure exactly what was wrong with her, but she felt a nagging sense of unease that had nothing to do with her brothers or with anyone in the Raintree tribe. No, the restlessness was within her, a yearning she was forced to control because of who she was, because of her duty to her family and to her people. Whenever these strange emotions unsettled her, she climbed the mountain to this sacred peak and meditated until the uncertainty subsided. But today, for some unknown reason, the anxiety clung to her.

Was it a warning?

Seven years ago, she had allowed that hunger inside her to lead her into dangerous territory, into a world she had been ill prepared for, into a relationship that had altered her life. She would not— could not—succumb to fear. And except for brief visits to Dante and Gideon, she would not leave the safety of the Raintree Sanctuary. Not ever again.

* * * *

Jordan King seems too good to be true for Kate Brogan, and it turns out she's right – although Jordan is determined to prove her wrong. Can Kate resist Mr Irresistible?

Turn the page to read a sneak preview of Karina Bliss's Mr Irresistible. *Available in April 2008!*

CHAPTER ONE

SCANDAL.

The fashionable Auckland restaurant reeked of it, along with Chanel, the fruitiness of Chianti and mouthwatering stone-grilled meats so calorie-loaded Kate Brogan tried not to inhale too deeply. She was saving herself for the tiramisu.

Glancing at her watch, she saw that Lucy was late, as usual. Kate drained her water glass and caught the eye of the waiter hovering on the edge of the terraced courtyard, ostensibly enjoying the sunshine between duties, but plainly checking out his female patrons.

"Signorina?" Despite the fact that his taste clearly ran to full-breasted blondes, he was all politeness.

Kate smiled, her amusement growing as she watched him up her babe rating. "Antipasto for two and the dessert menu, please." Lucy might have the afternoon to play, but Kate had a deadline to meet.

While she waited, she scanned the place for diversion. This overpriced restaurant, its patrons a self-conscious mix of chic wives and corporate raiders, had always been a good hunting ground for her weekly newspaper column.

Across the courtyard a jacaranda daubed the diners in patches of sunshine and shade, while bright-eyed sparrows perched in its branches, quicker than the waiters to clear an empty table.

To her left an overripe politician devoured a much younger woman with his eyes, while his fat, moist hands stroked her upturned palms. Recognizing Kate, he froze.

She raised her glass to him, and Diggory scowled. Eighteen months earlier he'd lost his ministerial portfolio after investigations proved his taxpayer-funded business trips had doubled as dalliances with his personal assistant. Investigations sparked by one of Kate's newspaper columns, "More Bang(ing) for Your Tax Buck?"

To her surprise, he got up and came over. "You're back."

"And nothing's changed," she said dryly. "You can't be faithful to your mistress, let alone your wife."

"Margo left me," he retorted. "I can date whom I like. Since you've been overseas, I presume you missed my good news." He smiled, revealing smoker's teeth. "I was reelected last week." Kate sat back, stunned, and his smirk broadened. "Don't you want to congratulate me?"

"How did you rig that?"

Diggory's expression hardened but his tone remained pleasant. "A little breast-beating…public involvement with good causes…. People love a reformed sinner. I won by a landslide. What does that tell you?"

Her tone was equally pleasant. "That cockroaches have more lives than cats."

Diggory stopped smiling. "Now who's being a poor loser?" He leaned so close, she could smell the garlic on his breath. "It tells you, missy, that you don't get the last word."

"Your wife left you, didn't she?"

For a moment Kate saw violence in his eyes, then Diggory shrugged and stepped back. "I recommend the humble pie."

He left and, under the table, Kate unclenched her fists. Her hands trembled slightly and she frowned, not wanting to give him another victory. He'd still be sitting on the backbenches for the rest of his parliamentary career. But she drummed her fingers on her knees in frustration.

As she brooded, her gaze fell on a mismatched couple across the courtyard. The woman, whose iron-gray hair was cropped short, addressed her younger male companion in a manner as crisp as the white blouse under her navy power suit.

Jordan King. His size, looks and silky blond hair, which fell extravagantly past his very broad shoulders, would have distinguished him in any crowd. But in this conservative stronghold he looked like a peacock among pigeons. Sprawling on a chair that seemed too small to hold him, in his well-worn suede jacket and faded denim shirt, conspicuously in need of an iron.

His powerful fingers toyed with the delicate filigree ironwork of an adjacent chair, the softness of his hair at odds with his profile—all strong lines and clean angles. Despite the fair hair, his skin was tanned the translucent brown of wild honey.

By rights Jordan King should be gay.

The tabloids made it very plain he was not. He was also the only person in the history of Kate's influential column to turn down a personal profile. She could have accepted it if the tourism entrepreneur's refusal hadn't been so blunt. When she'd pressed, he'd said; "I wouldn't be comfortable doing the touchy-feely stuff."

Then he'd added insult to injury by asking her for a date.

"I wouldn't be comfortable doing the touchy-feely stuff," she'd retorted.

He'd laughed. "This is exactly why I don't give interviews…my comments are always taken out of context."

Six months later a bouquet of roses had arrived with Jordan's number and a note: "If you change your mind." As if.

Still, there was a slight smile on her lips when Jordan turned his head and recognized her. He smiled, too, eyes the blue of arctic ice sweeping over her, insolent in their frank appraisal. Kate frowned and crossed her arms, before realizing that only accentuated her cleavage under the open-necked green shirt.

His gaze lifted to meet hers and his message was direct, sexy and very explicit.

Hot color flooded her cheeks. He thought she'd been trying to pick him up, and his answer was definitely *yes*. She straightened and shot back a glacial look.

He shrugged, utterly arrogant, and turned back to his companion. The woman shook her head, said something.

Jordan responded with a wolfish grin, then glanced again at Kate, mouthing, *"Coward."* Adjusting his chair, he turned away and casually resumed his conversation.

Her mouth fell open. Picking up a linen napkin, she crumpled it tightly. No one should be so…so *raw.* There was no other word for it. He was blatant in his looks, in his invitation and in his dismissal.

"Get a haircut," she growled, and felt much better.

Tray in hand, her waiter approached, swerving sharply to avoid a collision with the slim brunette in a scarlet dress who was also intent on reaching the table.

Lucy sank into the chair opposite Kate. "Sorry I'm late." She peeled tendrils of long dark hair back from her overheated face. "She ordered for me, didn't she?" At the waiter's nod, she turned to Kate. "I was stuck in another postproduction meeting." A researcher for television news, Lucy often fed Kate leads the state broadcaster turned down as too hot.

"Don't worry, I filled in the time people watching." The waiter started unloading the tray and Kate reached for a sun-dried tomato. "Jordan King caught me staring and thought I was trying to pick him up."

"He's here? You're kidding me." Lucy swung around in her chair, then turned back, incredulous. "If I'd done what he's done, I'd go bush for a few weeks—or wherever he hides out when he's not empire building."

Obviously intrigued, the waiter busied himself with removing the extra cutlery.

"What did I miss?" Kate offered Lucy the focaccia, then took a slice herself. Jordan King built Triton Holdings from a small river-rafting company started with two university friends into a huge tourism conglomerate. Kate's boyfriend, Peter Walker, was contracted to develop accountancy software for Triton, but rarely mentioned King.

Lucy's silver bracelets jingled as she leaned forward, and Kate looked pointedly at the waiter, who had dropped any pretense of table clearing. He left reluctantly.

"He was caught in bed with a married woman…by her husband," Lucy said in a hushed voice. "Six months later, the couple is in the middle of a divorce and hubby has gone to the media, giving all the salacious details. He's bent on revenge, I'm guessing because he lost out on full custody."

The bread stuck in Kate's throat. She washed it down with a sip of water, aware of a strange disappointment. She didn't like King, after all. "Those poor kids," she said.

The two friends ate in a thoughtful silence.

"Wait a minute." Kate paused with an olive halfway to her mouth. "Isn't Jordan involved in setting up a holiday camp for children from broken homes?"

"Yes, that's what burns me up about it—the hypocrisy." Lucy brightened as she looked at Kate. "What a perfect topic for your column."

Kate ate the olive. "No," she said firmly. "I'm writing light and frivolous this week. No more crusades." And she avoided the subject of infidelity, because she didn't trust herself to be dispassionate about it.

"Oh, my God." Lucy clapped a hand over her mouth. "I just remembered we're here to celebrate your new independence. How was Australia? Did your baby sister settle in okay? More importantly, how do *you* feel?"

"Courtney loves the Townsville campus, and we found her some great roommates." Kate passed Lucy a dessert menu, and to her relief, her friend opened it. "And when I flew home on Sunday a postcard was waiting from Danny." She grinned. "I suspect my new sister-in-law is behind that thoughtfulness. They're having a wonderful honeymoon and—"

"I said how do *you* feel?" Lucy shut the menu.

Kate opened hers. "Great, absolutely fantastic."

Lucy reached across the table for her hand. "Sweetie, you've played mum to your brother and sister for years. Of course you're missing them."

To Kate's horror, she felt the prickle of tears. "I need to visit the bathroom. Order me the tiramisu, will you?"

In the ladies' room, she locked the cubicle door, leaned against it and cried— short, sharp sobs she tried to smother with toilet tissue. She was twenty-eight years old, for the first time in her life she had no dependents, and she hated it.

Hated not making dinner for three, hated not buying washing powder in bulk, hated finding the apartment still tidy when she came home from work. Last night, when she'd got stuck on the cryptic cross- word, she'd called out the clue… before remembering they'd gone.

She'd expected to be dancing for joy. Instead, she felt like she was missing her limbs.

Wiping her eyes with the damp tissue, Kate glanced at her watch. Ten minutes. She was taking too long. Blowing her nose, she washed her face at the basin and checked her appearance critically in the gilt-framed mirror.

Low heels, nondescript black pants, tailored shirt and a man's watch. Clean and tidy. Early responsibility had given her a pragmatic approach to clothes, though she always wore labels. They lasted longer.

She touched up her nude lipstick and dragged a comb through her short wavy hair, frowning at how red it looked under the lights. She was a brunette, damn it.

A button had popped open on her shirt; Kate did up two for good measure. Satisfied, she stepped into the corridor.

A door had been left open to the tiny utility courtyard, where crates of empty wine bottles were stacked alongside big bins. Leaves flew in on a gust of wind, and Kate went to close it. A shadow stretched across the doorway and she stopped.

Jordan King came into view, a cell phone pressed to his ear. "I'm sure if I lie low, stick with 'no comment,' it'll blow over…. Yes, Christian, I know how to lie low. Where am I?" He grinned. "Meg and I are having a quiet bite at Amici's." Jordan laughed and held the phone away for a moment. "Okay, okay, I'll make more of an effort. But no denials. I'm not compounding my error of screwing a married woman by lying about it."

Kate had heard enough. Returning to the table, she found Lucy stealing a spoonful of her dessert. Her friend's eyes widened when she saw Kate's expression. "It was only a mouthful," she said feebly.

"It's yours. I've lost my appetite."

"Listen, I was thinking…this is your opportunity to break out and have some fun." Lucy frowned at Kate's buttoned-up shirt. "I've got the afternoon off, you work flexible hours. Let's go buy you some sexy clothes."

Marking King's return to his table, Kate shook her head. "I've got a column to write." Women everywhere stopped talking to watch him. All Kate saw was a lowlife.

"Tonight then?"

She dragged her attention back to Lucy. "Pete's taking me out."

Lucy wrinkled her nose. "That wet blanket. Trade him in for a real man before he bores you to death."

Involuntarily, Kate's gaze returned to Jordan. Diggory walked past with his date, and for a moment the prince and the frog were both in view. She narrowed her eyes and pulled a notebook and pen out of her bag.

"In medieval times you could pay to have your sins forgiven," she wrote, holding up a finger at Lucy, who rolled her eyes and went back to eating Kate's tiramisu. "The practice was called indulgences—

possibly because you got to keep indulging your bad habits.

"These days the morally bankrupt buy a new image by making a hefty donation of time or money to charity."

She stopped and chewed on her pen, then scrawled the headline. "Do You Want Absolution with That?"

Celebrate 100 years of pure reading pleasure with Mills & Boon®

To mark our centenary, each month we're publishing a special 100th Birthday Edition. These celebratory editions are packed with extra features and include a FREE bonus story.

Now that's worth celebrating!

4th January 2008

The Vanishing Viscountess by Diane Gaston
With FREE story The Mysterious Miss M
This award-winning tale of the Regency Underworld launched Diane Gaston's writing career.

1st February 2008

Cattle Rancher, Secret Son by Margaret Way
With FREE story His Heiress Wife
Margaret Way excels at rugged Outback heroes…

15th February 2008

Raintree: Inferno by Linda Howard
With FREE story Loving Evangeline
A double dose of Linda Howard's heady mix of passion and adventure.

Don't miss out! From February you'll have the chance to enter our fabulous monthly prize draw. See special 100th Birthday Editions for details.

www.millsandboon.co.uk

M/

FREE!
2 Books
and a surprise gift!

We would like to take this opportunity to thank you for reading this Mills & Boon® book by offering you the chance to take TWO more specially selected titles from the Superromance series absolutely FREE! We're also making this offer to introduce you to the benefits of the Mills & Boon® Reader Service™—

- ★ **FREE home delivery**
- ★ **FREE gifts and competitions**
- ★ **FREE monthly Newsletter**
- ★ **Exclusive Reader Service offers**
- ★ **Books available before they're in the shops**

Accepting these FREE books and gift places you under no obligation to buy, you may cancel at any time, even after receiving your free shipment. Simply complete your details below and return the entire page to the address below. You don't even need a stamp!

YES! Please send me 2 free Superromance books and a surprise gift. I understand that unless you hear from me, I will receive 4 superb new titles every month for just £3.69 each, postage and packing free. I am under no obligation to purchase any books and may cancel my subscription at any time. The free books and gift will be mine to keep in any case.

U8ZEF

Ms/Mrs/Miss/Mr ....Initials....................................
BLOCK CAPITALS PLEASE

Surname ....

Address ....

....

....Postcode ....

Send this whole page to:
UK: FREEPOST CN81, Croydon, CR9 3WZ